THE
YEAR
OF
STARTING
OVER

BOOKS BY KAREN KING

Snowy Nights at the Lonely Hearts Hotel

Karen King

THE
YEAR
OF
STARTING
OVER

bookouture

Published by Bookouture in 2019

An imprint of StoryFire Ltd.

Carmelite House
50 Victoria Embankment
London EC4Y 0DZ

www.bookouture.com

ISBN: 978-1-78681-810-2
eBook ISBN: 978-1-78681-809-6

For my amazing mum, Doris Hemming. You're an inspiration xx

Chapter One

February

Crash!

Holly groaned as she looked at the illuminated red numbers on the bedside clock: two thirty. Scott was finally home. He'd obviously gone on to a club with his mates and was now drunk. Again. She'd asked him not to be late back as she was on the early shift at Sunshine Lodge tomorrow, but he'd protested that it was Friday night and he'd been working hard all week, adding, 'I need to chill out, babe. It's not my fault you have to work tomorrow.' It was a fair point, which made her feel guilty – as it was meant to do. Scott worked long hours as assistant manager of a games shop and often had to work weekends himself so couldn't always have a Friday night out.

But when *he* had to work weekends, she didn't come crashing in and wake him up in the early hours of the morning, did she? She swatted down her irritation, reminding herself that was because she didn't like going clubbing. She preferred to spend her days and evenings off work either making cushions and throws to brighten up their flat or creating designs for the mugs, clocks and phone covers she sold on Dandibug, an online arts and crafts marketplace, hoping that one day she could turn it into a full-time business. Anyway, if she did come in late, she doubted if Scott would notice: he slept like a log and snored like a mechanical saw.

Holly turned over and tried to go back to sleep. Her friend Susie was always telling her, 'You're too much of a pushover, Holly. You should stand up to Scott.' Susie didn't understand that Holly hated conflict of any kind. She didn't want to argue. She wanted to live in a nice, peaceful home like Pops and Nanna had. She missed them so much. Holly's parents had split up when she was a baby; she'd never known her dad, and her mum was out at work all day, so she spent a lot of time with her grandparents.

Pops and Nanna had adored Holly, and each other, and their love had shone out like a beacon of happiness. They'd been together since they were fourteen, got married at twenty-one and lived happily ever after. Nanna died two years ago, and Pops had missed her so much that when he too had gone peacefully in his sleep a few weeks ago, the knowledge that he was now with Nanna helped Holly and her mother cope with the grief of losing him. Nanna and Pops had both lived until their early nineties so had a good few innings, as Pops would have said.

Ever since she was little, Holly had dreamt of being happily married, just like Nanna and Pops, but all the guys she'd dated seemed to want a good time with no long-term commitment. She was hoping Scott was different; she loved him so much and he said he loved her too, but they'd been living together for over a year now and he hadn't shown any sign of proposing yet.

Holly groaned as she heard the cooker fan go on and Scott whistling loudly out of tune. *He's having a bloody fry-up!* There was no way she could go back to sleep until he'd finished cooking. Knowing Scott, he'd fall asleep on the sofa and forget about the frying pan then the flat would go up in flames and they'd both be burnt alive. She heard about that kind of thing happening all the time, and even though they had a smoke alarm and a fire extinguisher, it didn't stop Holly worrying. She listened until the fan went off and she heard Scott going into the lounge. Now she could go back to sleep. She closed her eyes then jolted awake again as the sound of screaming filled the flat. It took her a few seconds to realise Scott was watching a horror film.

Great. Fan-bloody-tastic! She reached out for the other pillow and stuck it over her head. The trouble with this flat was every noise carried. And Scott made a lot of noise. *Please don't let him be disturbing the neighbours,* she thought. They'd already had a couple of complaining letters shoved under their door.

Somehow, Holly managed to drift back off to sleep and was woken by the alarm four hours later to find Scott's half of the bed unslept in and the TV in the lounge still blaring. Exhausted, she stumbled out of bed and into the bathroom. She was going to need a very strong cup of coffee before she went to work today.

Holly showered, dressed, put on her make-up and walked into the lounge to find Scott still fast asleep on the sofa. She paused to look at him. Even with his mouth open, his top button undone, his clothes askew he looked incredibly sexy. That was the trouble: Scott was so handsome – and he knew it. He only had to gaze at her with those deep blue eyes and smile, and her heart crumbled. She loved him so much.

But right now she was angry with him too. And she damn well wasn't going to tiptoe around him. He had all day to sleep while she had to work. She stomped past him and into the kitchen, banging cupboards, doors and utensils about as she made a cup of coffee and bowl of muesli, but Scott didn't even stir. Holly resisted the urge to pour a glass of water over his head. Instead she just wrote a note – 'Gone to work. See you tonight.' – and went out, feeling a bit out of sorts that she hadn't even got a goodbye kiss off him. If she hadn't been so angry, she'd have kissed him on the forehead and whispered goodbye. Well, he'd better be sober and guilty enough to cook a slap-up 'I'm sorry' meal for her when she came home that evening.

Chapter Two

Holly made her way to the car park at the back of the block of flats and pressed the remote button to open the doors of her yellow Mini. Pops had bought the car for her when she finally passed her driving test – it had taken five attempts and a bottle of Rescue Remedy. The boot was already packed with the books and other odds and ends she'd collected yesterday from Pops's little bungalow. She'd had the day off work so she and her mum had finally plucked up the courage to go and empty the bungalow, ready for it to be sold. There was already a buyer waiting. They'd both been really sad as they'd gone through Pops's and Nanna's things – Pops had refused to let any of Nanna's stuff go when she had died – and they had ended up crying in each other's arms.

'You'll probably have your share of the money in two or three months,' Mum had told Holly as she dried her eyes. 'We'll all get just over £30,000. Have you decided what you want to do with it yet?'

Holly had shaken her head. She was used to being skint and still couldn't believe that Pops had left her a share of the money from the sale of his bungalow – along with Mum, Uncle Tim and the Royal British Legion. Thirty thousand pounds was an amazing amount of money and she wanted to spend it wisely. 'Nanna and I want you to use it to make your dreams come true, Holly,' Pops had written in the letter he'd left her. 'You've looked after me and your Nanna for years. Now it's time to think of yourself a bit.' Holly's eyes had filled with tears when she'd read it. She'd loved spending time with Pops and Nanna; they had always looked after her when she was younger so she thought it was her turn to look after them as they got older. It was her love for them that had urged her to get a job in Sunshine Lodge Care Home when she left art college, so she could earn a living looking after other old folks while continuing with her artwork in her spare time.

'You haven't told Scott, have you?' Mum had asked.

'Not yet.' When Pops's solicitor had told them about their inheritance, Mum had made Holly promise not to tell Scott about it for at least a couple of weeks. 'Pops left that money for you, Holly, not for Scott. Take your time and think about what you would like to do with it,' she'd pleaded.

Holly had agreed because it was such a massive amount she felt that she needed time to get her head around it, but that didn't stop her feeling guilty. She didn't like having secrets from Scott. They were a couple, they were supposed to share things. Mum was right though, she needed to think about it and use the money wisely, like Pops would have wanted.

She yawned. Maybe they could use it to rent a bigger flat, or even put the deposit down on their very own home.

Or get married. That would be a dream come true.

She got into the car and set off for the short journey to Sunshine Lodge. She had a treat for the residents today.

'I've got something you all might like,' Holly announced as she walked into the lounge, carrying the big cardboard box of Pops's books. She put the box down on the table by Sid and Bert, two of the residents. 'Take a look.'

Sid leant forward and peered into the box. 'Books,' he said. He picked up the hardback lying on top and his face lit up. 'It's about the aircraft used in the Second World War.' He flicked the book open. 'Hey, my father used to fly one of these.'

'Let's have a butcher's.' Bert leant over the side of his wheelchair to look at the book with Sid.

'Look at all these photos.' Sid flicked excitedly through the book.

Holly smiled at them. 'I thought you'd like it. There's other books about the Second World War too, and the history of Britain, life of Winston Churchill.' She took a couple of the books out of the box and laid them out on the table. Pops's dad, Holly's great-grandfather, had been a pilot in the Second World War and Pops was very proud of him.

'Is there one about the Wrens?' Joan asked, slowly getting up and making her way over to the table. 'Women did their bit in the war too, you know. My mum was a Wren.'

'Oh, don't start her off. Joan was a feminist before it became trendy,' Sid said with a mock-groan.

'Of course there is!' Holly held out a book about women in the war.

Joan took it and sat down on the nearest chair to look through it. 'This looks good!'

'So does this. My mum used to make this cake.' Pat was flicking through a wartime cookbook.

Soon a group of the residents were gathered around the table, poring over the books and reminiscing. As she watched them, tears welled up in Holly's eyes. Pops had treasured his collection of books and would want them to be read by people who would appreciate them, who had lived through the same time in history as he had. She remembered

Pops sitting in his comfy old armchair by the fire, glasses perched on the end of his nose, reading his books and telling her about his teenage years growing up during the war. Nanna, too, had loved reminiscing, and trying out the recipes from her old cookbook, baking Holly cakes and treats that she and her mother had made when Nanna was a child. 'You can't beat the old ways,' Nanna had always said. 'Nothing was wasted then and we were grateful for simple things like clothes on our backs and food in our bellies. Not like now when everyone is always wanting more.'

'These are smashing, Holly love. Where did you get them from?' Sid asked.

'They were all my grandad's.' Holly kept the tears in check as she replied. 'Mum and I finally got around to sorting out his room yesterday and I thought you would all like these books.'

'Your grandad's? Are you sure, love? I know how fond you were of him,' another care assistant asked.

'Pops would love to know that his books are bringing pleasure to other folk,' Holly told her.

'Look at this book, Sid. It tells you all about the aircraft operating in the First World War. Oh, my dad had such tales to tell. He was a gunner, you know.' Agnes had tottered over to look at the box of books too. She turned back to Holly, her face wreathed in a big smile. 'Thank you, lass. You're such a kind soul.'

'Heart as big as a dustbin lid, that's our Holly.' Sid took out his hankie, wiped his glasses and peered at the book again. 'I wouldn't mind reading that after you, Bert.'

Holly felt someone touch her elbow and turned around.

'This is very kind of you, honey.' It was Neisha, the supervisor. 'How are you all coping? How's your mum?'

'We're okay. Pops had a good life, you know, and he'll be happy now with Nanna. He loved her so much.' She sniffed. 'But I do miss him. I miss both of them.' She took a tissue out of her pocket and wiped away a tear.

Neisha put her arm around Holly's shoulders. 'You will, honey. It's only natural. He's only been gone a few weeks.'

'I know. I feel like I've got a big hole in my life,' Holly told her. Neisha was one of those people you could say anything to: she was a motherly Jamaican lady with a big smile and an even bigger hug. The residents loved her, and the staff all knew they could confide in her. 'I miss seeing him every day, having a cup of tea with him and listening to his stories. Company was what he wanted most, especially after Nanna died.'

'Remember that he's still with you, in your heart.' Neisha patted her hand comfortingly.

'I know, but I wish he was here in person,' Holly said sadly. Her life felt so empty without Nanna and Pops in it.

When she checked her phone at lunchtime she was pleased to see a grovelling apology text from Scott, promising to make it up to her that evening. She felt her heart soften. He hadn't meant any harm; he'd had a bit too much to drink and now he was sorry. She knew he would be. Scott loved her, she was sure he did. Just like she loved him. She'd fallen in love with him as soon as she'd set eyes on him in the nightclub that Susie, her then-flatmate, had persuaded her to go to. When Scott had asked her for a dance Holly had been over the moon. She could hardly believe her luck when Scott had actually phoned the next day, as he'd promised, and asked her to go for a drink with him. With his smooth good looks, designer stubble and carefully coiffed blond hair, Scott could have taken his pick, and she couldn't believe he'd actually chosen her, mousy little Holly.

'You're not mousy, you're gorgeous,' Susie had told her. 'Scott's the lucky one!'

'What if he goes off me?' Holly had asked. She didn't have a good track record with the men in her life.

Susie had considered this thoughtfully. 'In my experience, guys like Scott do tend to like "feminine" women, so maybe you should change your image a bit? Put on a bit more make-up, let your hair down instead of tying it back, and stop living in jeans and jumpers?' she had suggested. And who was Holly to argue? It was Susie's makeover – doing her make-up and loaning her a sexy dress before they had gone out that night – that had first attracted Scott to her, after all. So Holly had continued with her new image whenever Scott had asked her out.

When Scott's flatmate had moved out, Scott had asked Holly to move in, pointing out that it made sense as they had been dating for almost a year, she spent most of her time there and they could share the expenses. It was perfect timing as Susie and her boyfriend, Liam, wanted to live together, so Liam moved in when Holly moved out. Holly was ecstatic. Now she and Scott were a proper couple. It was a bit of a strain keeping up the new image, though, and sometimes Holly really longed to slip back into her comfortable jeans and baggy jumpers, or shorts and colourful T-shirts, and to wear no make-up like she used to, but Scott was worth it.

She loved him and wanted to marry him more than anything in the world. The trouble was Scott showed no sign of wanting to commit any further.

'Why don't you propose to him?' Susie had suggested when Holly had confided in her.

'It's not as romantic,' Holly had replied. It was true, she did want Scott to be the one to go down on one knee, the full works. But the main reason she didn't propose was because, deep down, she wasn't sure Scott would accept. Then she would know that he didn't love her as much as she loved him. And that would break her heart.

Chapter Three

Holly's spirits soared as the smell of spaghetti bolognaise wafted over to greet her as soon as she opened the front door. She loved spaghetti bolognaise, which was a good thing as it was Scott's signature dish – make that his one and only dish. He really was sorry about last night and had cooked dinner to make it up to her. Perfect. Now they could both sit down and share the meal, with a glass of wine, and have a romantic evening.

Scott walked in from the kitchen, wrapped his arms around her and gave her a kiss on the lips – a real smacker of a kiss, not the quick peck they usually exchanged unless Scott had a night of passion on his mind. 'Sorry about last night, babe,' he said when they finally came up for air.

He looked really sexy, all spruced up in his new Hugo Boss shirt and skinny trousers. He was obviously planning a special night. If his clothes and the meal didn't spell it out, that kiss did. *OMG, is he going to propose?* Holly's insides melted as did all her annoyance at Scott's behaviour last night.

'Let's forget it,' she said, smiling at him.

'Dinner will be ready in ten minutes,' he said softly, his eyes holding hers.

She traced her fingers teasingly across his cheek and flashed him a brilliant smile. 'Perfect. I'll go freshen up and get changed.'

She had a mega-quick shower then rummaged through her wardrobe for something spectacularly sexy to wear, ignoring her favourite distressed jeans and loose-knit lemon jumper that were folded, neglected, on the shelf. Finally, she decided on a tight black dress, her skimpiest underwear and hold-up sheer black stockings.

A record ten minutes later she was dressed, had refreshed her make-up and was applying scarlet lipstick when Scott shouted, 'I'm serving up now!'

'Coming!' A quick spray of Passionate Nights perfume and she was ready. She studied her reflection in the mirror. Did she look alluring enough? The sort of woman Scott would want to keep in his life forever? This could be the most important night of her life, the night Scott proposed. Her heart soaring with happiness, she walked into the lounge. The table was covered with their best white tablecloth, with a vase of six red roses in the middle and a glass of red wine by each plate. God, how she loved him.

And Scott adored her too. She knew that Mum didn't think Scott was right for her, and neither had Pops. 'He's a nice lad but not for you, Holly,' he'd told her several times. 'He's not ready to settle down yet. You need a young man who will take care of you, cherish you.'

Pops meant well, but his generation was different. Just because a guy didn't open doors for you and sometimes went out on his own with his mates, it didn't mean he didn't love you. You had to give people space, not try and tie them down: that's what Holly believed. Scott adored her.

She could see that by the endearing way he was looking at her now.

'You look gorgeous, babe.' His eyes feasted on her as if he couldn't get enough of her. This was going to be some night.

'Thank you. You look fantastic too.'

'Sit yourself down,' he said, and he actually pulled out a chair for her.

'This looks delicious,' Holly said, gazing at the table as she sat down.

'Nothing's too much trouble for you, babe.' Scott disappeared into the kitchen and came back a couple of minutes later with two plates of spaghetti bolognaise – carefully dished out with the sauce in the middle and the spaghetti surrounding it – balanced precariously in each hand. Holly had to sit on her hands to stop herself from jumping up and taking one off him, knowing how clumsy he was. She watched anxiously as Scott walked very slowly to the table, put one plate down in front of her and the other at the place he'd set for himself opposite. Then he sat down, picked up his glass of wine and held it out. 'To us.'

A warm glow of love gushed through her entire body, right to the tips of her toes. 'To us.' She met his gaze as they clinked glasses, their eyes locked. *Oh my God, he is going to propose! He really is!* Had he already bought the ring, she wondered, or were they going to choose it together?

She ate the meal, floating on a cloud of happiness. They chatted amicably about their day but she could tell Scott wanted to say something. He kept fidgeting with the cuff of his shirtsleeve and looking at her as if he was going to speak then changed his mind. *How sweet, he's trying to pluck up the courage,* she thought. *I'll wait until I've accepted then tell him about Pops's gift, and we can use his money for the wedding. We could even get married this summer.*

'I'll clear up,' Scott said when they'd finished the meal. 'You have another glass of wine and put your feet up.'

I bet he's hidden the ring somewhere and is going to fetch it, then he'll get down on one knee and pop the question. Holly could hardly contain her excitement. 'You are spoiling me tonight,' she said as Scott refilled her wine glass.

'That's because I love you,' he said, bending over to give her a big kiss on the lips before picking up the plates and disappearing into the kitchen.

Holly practically skipped over to the sofa, running possible proposal scenarios through her mind and working out how she would accept. This was a big moment. She wanted to make sure it was memorable.

Finally, Scott came back in... with his jacket on.

'Are we going out now?' Holly asked, puzzled. She got to her feet. Perhaps Scott was whizzing her off to a cocktail bar to propose. Maybe even Jorge's, where they'd gone for their first date. *How romantic!*

Scott looked a bit awkward. 'Well... er... I promised the lads that I'd go out with them tonight. It's Paul's birthday.'

She could hardly believe her ears. She stared at him, mouth open, while her mind processed his words. He was going out with the lads. Again.

'But the meal, all this...' she finally managed to squeak out, waving her hand at the now bare table.

'That was to say sorry for last night, and for tonight. I didn't want you to feel like I'm neglecting you.'

'I've got all dressed up. I thought we were having a special night in.' *I thought you were going to ask me to marry you!* her mind screamed but she wasn't going to humiliate herself by actually saying the words.

He flushed, fidgeted and glanced at his watch. 'I'm sorry, babe, but I've really got to go. I'll make it up to you. We'll go out tomorrow for the day, I promise. We'll go to Primrose House.'

Primrose House was Holly's very favourite place. It was a beautiful old house surrounded by a garden of primroses, and set in gorgeous grounds with a lake and wood. Scott wasn't very fond of it so he'd be making a massive effort if he did take her there.

'See you later. I won't be long. I promise.' He kissed her on the cheek and then was out the door. Holly was left staring at it, not knowing whether to scream or cry.

Chapter Four

Two more glasses of wine later and she furiously messaged Susie, who messaged back:

Oh, Hol, that's awful. You must be gutted. Scott is so selfish and irresponsible. He doesn't deserve you. You should ditch him.

Holly replied.

I love him.

I know you do but he doesn't seem to care about you or your feelings. I'm so sorry, hun, but I've got to go now. Me and Liam are at a club. I'll call you tomorrow. Hope you're OK'

Out at a club. That's where she should be – dressed like this – but she hadn't been invited, had she? Scott was on another night out with his friends and hadn't wanted Holly along. The meal was just to butter her up, and the smart shirt and trousers weren't for her.

Face it, Holly, she told herself, *Scott has no intention of proposing. He doesn't want to commit to you. He's enjoying his life exactly as it is.*

And he'll probably come home in the early hours, drunk again.

Susie was right. Scott didn't care about her. He never considered her wants or needs yet she always made such a big effort for him. She was a 'jeans and jumper, hot chocolate and slippers by the fire' kind of girl but had tried so hard to change, to be more outgoing, dress more glamorously, go to nightclubs when she'd have preferred them both to have a cosy night in in front of the TV then been ignored by Scott most of the evening while he messed around with the lads.

It was time she stopped putting up with Scott's selfish behaviour, she thought, pacing around restlessly. She should leave him.

Leave him?

The unexpected thought stopped her in her tracks. She had never thought of leaving Scott before, but right now she felt like it even though she loved him. Let him come home to an empty flat and a goodbye note from her and see how he felt!

Maybe he wouldn't care. At least then he could go out with his mates without feeling guilty.

Then Pops's words came to her: 'Never make a decision while you are upset, tired or angry. Sleep on it.' Well, she was all three, so, yes, she would sleep on it. She loved Scott, she didn't want them to be over. Scott would make it up to her tomorrow. They'd spend the day at Primrose House, and then they'd sit and watch a film. After all, he didn't know she'd thought he was going to propose, did he?

She poured herself another glass of wine then went into the bedroom to remove her make-up and get ready for bed. She didn't expect to sleep, but the wine had a soporific effect and sunlight was streaming through the curtains when she awoke. She turned over. No Scott. He had probably come back late and was snoring on the sofa again. Bang went their day out at Primrose House; he'd be too hungover.

Holly pulled on her dressing gown and walked into the lounge, anger boiling up inside her. She was sick of Scott treating her this way. She was going to wake him up right now and tell him exactly what she thought of him.

But Scott wasn't on the sofa. He wasn't in the kitchen or bathroom either. In fact, there was no sign that he'd even been home at all.

She looked at the clock: 11 a.m. She couldn't believe how late she'd slept in. *You were tired and upset and had too much wine,* she told herself.

Eleven o'clock, though. Scott had been gone all night and half the morning. Where was he?

She checked her phone. No missed calls. Wherever he was, he was probably sleeping it off. She picked up her phone and dialled him but it went straight to answerphone.

Maybe he was lying hurt somewhere, she thought in panic. It had been raining all night: he could be unconscious in a ditch, soaked through.

Don't be silly. Scott was with a bunch of friends – if something bad had happened, you would have heard by now.

Holly sat down on the sofa, her mind racing. What if something had happened to all of them? Or something had happened to Scott on the way home and his friends didn't know?

Then another thought snaked into her mind. What if he'd spent the night with someone else?

No, he wouldn't. Would he?

He'd had a drink and was out with the lads. He was all togged up, wasn't he? Best Hugo Boss shirt, best aftershave…

No, he wouldn't.

Where was he, then?

Anger and fear were conflicting inside her as she flitted between feeling furious and sick with worry. Scott had never stayed out overnight before. There had to be a good reason. She should at least wait and see what had happened. She'd give him until twelve. Wherever he was, he would surely contact her soon, apologising.

She got dressed, had breakfast and started working on her latest design – a pattern of various woodland leaves – but it was difficult to concentrate and she kept looking at the clock as the minutes, then hours, passed by.

When her phone finally rang with the familiar tune announcing that it was Scott, Holly was so overwrought that she snatched it off the table and almost dropped it. The call died. Damn. She pressed 'call back'.

'Scott…'

'Babe, I need your help…'

Her chest tightened in panic. Something had happened to him. It was a good job she hadn't walked out – he was in trouble. Her heart was pounding as she asked anxiously, 'What is it? Are you hurt?'

'I'm okay, babe. I'm not hurt but I'm stranded.'

'Stranded?' she repeated, her mind racing. What had happened? Had he been kidnapped? Mugged? Wandered off from his mates and got lost?

'Where are you?' she asked

'Amsterdam.'

What? 'How…' she stammered, confused.

'We went back to Paul's last night and had too much to drink, then Paul and Floyd had this mad idea of booking a flight to Amsterdam. There was one going early this morning. So here we are. It sort of just happened.'

'Amsterdam? You're in Amsterdam?' God, she sounded like a perishing parrot but she couldn't get her head around it. All the time she'd been sitting here worrying about Scott, he and his mates were in bloody Amsterdam! 'How did you do that without your passport?' she asked.

'Er… luckily I had it on me because we were going to book a lads' holiday for the summer. But the thing is we couldn't get a return flight until midnight,' he continued in the contrite, pleading tone he always used when he'd done something he knew would upset her. 'So I'm stuck here until then. Can you pick me up from the airport later, please, Holly?'

What a bloody nerve! He'd booked a flight to Amsterdam with the lads, was going to spend all day there and seriously expected her to do the hour's drive at midnight to pick him up? And he was planning a week away with them too. Without her.

'You went with Paul and Floyd so why can't you come back with them?' she demanded.

'Paul's brother's picking him and Floyd up in his work van but there's no room for me. I told them it'd be okay, you'd come and fetch me. You will, won't you, Holly?'

Something snapped. He must think she was so stupid she'd put up with anything. 'No, I bloody well won't. You can get yourself a taxi!' she said furiously.

'Don't be like that, babe, you know how much I love you. I promise I'll never do anything like this again.' His tone had just the right amount of remorse and charm in it, which had won her over so many times in the past. Not this time. She'd had enough.

'I don't care if you do. You can do what you like in the future because I won't be here to see it. We're over, Scott. I'll be gone by the time you get back.' Then she slammed the phone down and burst into tears.

Chapter Five

'You need to sit down and think about what you want out of life,' Holly's mother said after listening to her pour her heart out for over an hour and supplying her with a box of tissues, two cups of very strong coffee and a plate of chocolate biscuits.

'I want… wanted… Scott,' she gulped, grabbing another tissue to dry her eyes. 'But he obviously doesn't want me.'

Rachel Parkes gently placed her hand on Holly's and squeezed it. 'Scott isn't right for you, Holly. He has a lot of growing up to do. He lets you down time and time again and will keep doing so. You deserve better.'

'I thought he was going to propose to me,' Holly wailed. 'Then I was going to tell him about Pops's money and how we could spend some of it on a lovely wedding.'

'Well, I'm glad you didn't tell him about the money. Scott wouldn't have wanted to spend it on a wedding; he'd have wanted a flash car and a few holidays. It would have been gone in no time,' Rachel said firmly.

Mum was right. Holly knew she was. But that didn't stop it hurting.

'I know you're upset, love, but you've done the right thing. Scott isn't the one for you.'

Holly sniffed and dabbed her eyes again. 'I thought he was. I wanted him to be. I wanted us to get married, have a family…'

'Not every marriage is as happy as Nanna's and Pops's, Holly. Stop looking for love – let it find you.' Rachel gently squeezed Holly's hand. 'Focus on what you would like to do with your life because that's what Pops left you the money for. He wanted you to live a little, to have the chance to do the things you've always wanted to do. You don't need a man to make you happy, love.'

Her mum was right. She didn't need a man in her life. She was sick of putting up with their thoughtlessness, of trying to please them. From now on she was going to live her life her way.

If only she knew what her way was.

Scott apparently couldn't believe that Holly had actually ditched him. He bombarded her with phone calls and WhatsApp messages all day, begging her to pick him up from the airport, promising to make it up to her. She sent him one message in reply – in all uppercase to make sure he got the point – that they were over and she was staying with her mum and stepdad. Finally, Scott's messages stopped. No doubt he'd got someone else to pick him up from the airport and was busy planning his next escapade with the lads.

'I know you're upset but honestly you're well shot of him, Hol. He's far too immature. You deserve better,' Susie said when Holly phoned her later that evening and filled her in about finishing with Scott. 'What are you going to do now? Stay at your mum's for a bit?'

'Yes, until I sort myself out.' Holly paused. 'Mum said I should use Pops's money to make my dreams come true, like Pops wanted. The trouble is I don't know where to start. I guess I could rent myself a nice flat, and maybe work part-time so I can build up my Dandibug online shop and start making my own website…'

'That's boring! You can do that anytime. No, you need to use that money for experiences. Memories. Things you can look back on when you're older. Why don't you make a list of all the things you'd really like to do? Then you can see how many of them you can make come true,' Susie suggested.

'I haven't got a list of things I want to do. Have you?'

'You bet I do! I can think of loads of stuff I want to do. Travel the world, buy a designer handbag, go shopping in Harrods…' Susie rattled off, eagerly. 'But this isn't about me, it's about you. There must be some things you really want to do. Everyone has secret dreams.'

Do they? All she'd ever thought she wanted was to get married and have a family. How sad was that? Too sad to confess to Susie. 'I've never really thought about it,' Holly said lamely.

'Well, think about it now. It'll take your mind off Scott. I tell you what – you've got tomorrow off, haven't you? Meet me at Coffee & Cake at lunchtime and I'll help you work on it.'

Well, she couldn't say no to that, could she? Coffee & Cake was her favourite café; besides, she really needed Susie's input. With her and Scott finished, Pops and Nanna both gone, and her mum and stepdad Owen busy running their antiques shop, an empty future loomed ahead and Holly had no idea how to fill it.

Chapter Six

At lunchtime on Monday, Holly and Susie sat in the popular coffee shop near Susie's office, drinking cappuccino, eating chocolate fudge cake and working out Holly's dream list.

'Don't worry about putting things in order of importance,' Susie suggested. 'Write down the stuff you'd like to do most and then see how many of them you can tick off by this time next year. They don't all have to be big things,' she added, 'they can be small stuff like getting a tattoo – me and Liam got tattoos together over the weekend. Look.' She held out her wrist to show Holly a musical note with an 'L' at the top of it and an 'S' at the bottom. 'Liam has the same, but his note has an 'S' at the top and an 'L' at the bottom.' A dreamy look came over her face. 'It was Liam's idea. He said we make great music together.'

Holly tried hard not to be jealous. Susie was a great friend and she deserved to be happy, and Liam was definitely not the sort of guy she fancied, but she couldn't help feeling a bit narked that Susie was getting her 'happy ever after' whereas Holly's life was now a love-free zone.

'Sorry.' Susie withdrew her wrist. 'That was a bit thoughtless of me when you're heartbroken over Scott.'

'It's fine. I'm over Scott. Well, I'm working on it,' Holly corrected. 'And I don't want another guy in my life. Ever.' That didn't sound convincing even to her ears so she quickly changed the subject and focused on the task at hand: her dream list. 'Tattoos aren't really my thing, but I've always wanted a dog. I'll write that down.'

'See, that's one thing already. And how about travelling?' Susie suggested. 'Everyone wants to travel more. I've heard of companies giving people a year off to travel now. You don't get paid, of course, but they hold your job open to return to at the end of the year.'

Holly chewed the end of her pen as she thought about it. She'd been on a couple of holidays abroad with her mum and her grandparents and taken her car through the Channel Tunnel to France last year with Scott to visit his sister, but that was the extent of her travelling. Not a lot to show for twenty-seven years on this planet. It would be good to see more of the world. 'Good idea. Actually, I'd love to live in another country for a bit,' she agreed, adding it to the list.

'Well, travelling and living in another country can be lumped together as one. But you need to travel before you get a pet, cos it's a bit difficult to travel with one,' Susie pointed out. She glanced at her watch. 'Got to go, I'm due back at work in five minutes.' She grabbed her bag and umbrella from under the chair, her coat from the back of it, and stood up. 'Why don't you carry on writing the list and you can fill me in tonight?'

'I will, thanks for your help.' Susie had got her thinking. Holly ordered another cup of coffee and wrote down all the ideas now buzzing in her mind of things she would like to do. She'd love to learn another language, learn to dance – a proper dance – expand her Dandibug shop so she could be totally self-employed, go on a motor yacht, go snorkelling, try fifty different flavours of ice cream instead of playing it safe and sticking to her favourite mint chocolate chip, ride a horse and ride on the back of a motorbike – actually, she wouldn't mind having a horse or a motorbike. And she'd always wanted to visit one of those underground caves, with huge stalagmites and stalactites, that she'd seen in a documentary; they fascinated her. And she wanted to get over her fear of heights... Before long she'd filled one side of an A4.

She sipped her coffee as she read through the list; she had no idea she was secretly so adventurous! Mind you, she needed to narrow it down a bit. Pops had left her enough money to take a year out and make her dreams come true, so maybe she should choose twelve things that she really wanted to do and try to achieve one a month. Surely that had to be doable?

She studied the list; some of the things could be combined if she made them more general.

Finally, she had a list of twelve things:

1. Get a pet
2. Live in another country
3. Be self-employed
4. Ride on the back of a motorbike
5. Visit an underground cave
6. Learn to speak another language fluently
7. Go on a motor yacht
8. Go snorkelling
9. Learn to dance
10. Get over my fear of heights
11. Try fifty ice-cream flavours
12. Be ME

Maybe number twelve should be number one. She'd changed her image for Scott, tried to be what she thought he wanted her to be, and the relationship still hadn't worked out. Well, she was never going to change her image for anyone again. If they didn't like her as she was, they could leave her alone. She wouldn't bother to rewrite the list, though; it didn't matter what order she did the things, as long as she did all of them by this time next year. She took her diary out of her bag, flicked to today's date – 12 February – and wrote: 'Starting my "dream list".' Then she flicked to the end of the diary, circled the same date on next year's calendar, drew an arrow from it and wrote in the margin: 'Dream list ends.'

Holly smiled ruefully as she read through the list again. If anyone had asked her to write that list two days ago, 'get married to Scott' would have been at the top of it. Well, not now. She was going to stop looking for love and fulfil her dreams instead.

Chapter Seven

Holly's phone, lying on the table, beeped to announce an incoming message. She peered at the screen. It was from Scott again. She picked up the phone and swiped the screen to read it.

Sorry, babe. I know I messed up. Please don't be mad at me. You know I love you. Come home. I miss you. xx

A little bit of her started to crumble. How she longed to feel Scott's arms around her, his lips on hers, to hear him whispering how sorry he was and how he couldn't live without her and wanted to marry her. Then the new Holly piped up. The only thing he missed was Holly tidying up after him, cooking his meals, doing his washing. He didn't really love her. Not the way she wanted to be loved anyway.

Scott thought he could charm her into coming back, like he always did. Well, not this time. He could get one of his mates to share the flat with him. He spent more time with them than he did Holly. She had to make sure she didn't soften towards him and there was only one way to do that.

She typed back:

We're over, Scott. And I'm going to block your number so you can't contact me again.

Then she blocked his number. She blocked him on Facebook and WhatsApp too. It was time she took control. Scott was out of her life. Forever. From now on the only person she was going to please was herself.

The first thing she had to do was find herself somewhere to live. Then she could concentrate on her dream list. As much as she loved her mum and stepdad, she didn't want to live with them any longer than she had to.

She looked out of the window at the rain pouring down. She could do with going somewhere there was no chance of bumping into Scott. Make a whole new fresh start. Perhaps she should change her job too. She enjoyed working in the care home but what she really wanted to do was something artistic. To have her own business. Maybe she could use Pops's money for that?

Suddenly she had the answer: she could visit Fiona and Pablo. She had gone to art college with Fiona and they had remained friends, even after Fiona had married her Spanish partner, Pablo, last year and moved to Spain. Pablo, a sculptor, had been made redundant from his day job at the art museum and Fiona was tired of teaching art at the local college, so they had bought a *finca* – a house in the country with land around it – called Las Mariposas in the Andalusian countryside. They intended to run it as an artists' retreat during the summer, and they were busy refurbishing it. Fiona had invited Holly and Scott to visit them but Scott wouldn't go. 'I want to go on holiday to the beach, babe, not in the middle of the sticks,' he'd said.

Well, Holly could go, maybe spend a month or so there. She could help Fiona and Pablo get their *finca* ready and work out what she wanted to do with her life. It might even give her inspiration for some new designs.

She picked up her phone and emailed Fiona to ask if it would be okay if she came over for a couple of weeks soon, briefly telling her about the break-up with Scott. Tomorrow, when she went into work, she'd hand in her notice. She was sure that Neisha would understand and give Holly her blessing.

Fiona's reply arrived late that night:

Brilliant! Can't wait to see you and catch up again! Come for as long as you like. In fact, why don't you get away from it all completely and stay till the summer? The retreat will be open the beginning of July and you could run some art courses for us.

Holly read and reread the reply. Why not? She could spend the next few months in Spain then come back and look for a new job and flat. If she liked living in Spain, she could rent somewhere there herself. Pops's house-sale money would be through in another couple of months at the latest, and she'd have a month's wages due from work. Plus there were her Dandibug earnings, and she could still sell her goods online when she was away. The old Holly would have said no, she couldn't do it. But the new Holly wanted to take this chance. The new Holly wanted to throw caution to the wind and live her life a little. She bit her lip. It was scary but exciting too. *Just do it!*

She emailed back:

I'd love to! I have to hand in my notice at work but then I'll come over. I'll be there next month.

She picked up her dream list and drew a red tick by 'live in another country'. *That's one off the list already, Pops.*

Chapter Eight

March

Holly was tired, hungry and lost. She pulled over and once again studied the map she'd printed out from the Internet. According to this, she was about fifteen kilometres away from Las Mariposas, Fiona and Pablo's *finca*. But where was it? The road was deserted, she'd hardly seen any cars for the past fifteen minutes and the sun was starting to go down. Soon it would be dark. She really, really wanted to find Las Mariposas before that happened.

She got out of the car, shielded her eyes from the sun and looked around, jogging on the spot to keep warm – despite the brightness of the sun there was a real nip to the air. She was surrounded by high, shrubby mountains with a smattering of sugar-cube houses dotted here and there. It was a beautiful view, one she'd seen lots of times during her journey here, but right now she wasn't in the mood to appreciate it. She'd been driving for hours, with only a couple of stops, and she wanted to pull into Las Mariposas, park the car and relax. Fiona had said their *finca* was just outside the village of Reino, and according to the map, the white village on the mountainside ahead was Reino. There were no other houses in sight apart from the ones perched high on the hills.

Surely Fiona didn't live in one of those?

Don't be silly, Fiona and Pablo wouldn't live up there, she told herself. *They're planning on running an artists' retreat. No one would want to come to a retreat high up in the mountains.* Besides, Fiona would have warned her. She knew Holly hated heights.

She had to ring Fiona and get more directions. She was tired and wished now that she'd flown over to Málaga then got a taxi to Fiona and Pablo's place, as her mother had suggested, instead of driving to Portsmouth, catching the ferry then driving down from Santander. She'd driven around France when she was on holiday with Scott and hadn't found driving on the right side of the road rather than the left a major problem so it had seemed a good idea at the time. She loved her little yellow Mini and would need transport when she was in Spain, so why not take it with her? She could fit Nanna's sewing machine and lots of other things she might need in the back and the boot. Not to mention the list of things Fiona had given her to bring, stuff that was difficult or expensive to get in Spain: Marmite, Cadbury's chocolate, custard, paracetamol…

Mum and Owen had tried to talk her out of it, pointing out that she could have her things shipped over, and Susie had given her a lecture about the dangers of travelling alone, but Holly was determined to do it. Even though she had to admit to being a little bit nervous, this was the new Holly, the live-life-to-the-full Holly, who wasn't scared to try anything – well, almost anything. And so far, she'd managed fine. The drive down from Santander to Andalusia hadn't been too bad and the views were spectacular. It was when she'd hit Andalusia itself that the trouble had started. The journey had turned into a nightmare, and the road had several times, without warning, wound up into the mountains. She'd been petrified, although at least the road was wide and there was a low barrier running along each side. Not like these mountain tracks.

Damn it, Fiona wasn't answering.

Holly switched to her Google Maps app and studied it, her phone battery was low so she'd left using the app until she had to. It didn't recognise Fiona's address so she keyed in 'Reino', and according to the app it was definitely the village she could see right ahead. So, where the hell was Fiona's house? And why wasn't she answering the phone?

Suddenly Holly's phone buzzed to life and she eagerly slid her finger across the screen. 'Fiona?'

'*Hola*, Holly. How are you doing? Are you almost here?'

'I'm lost.' She hoped her voice didn't sound as wobbly as it felt as she told Fiona what road she was on. 'I can see Reino ahead but where is your place? There's nothing but a few scattered houses that are far too high up for any reasonable person to want to go to.'

Fiona chuckled. 'I'm afraid we are a bit high up, hun. WhatsApp me your location so I can see where you are then I'll message you right back.'

She finished the call, selected Fiona's contact on WhatsApp and shared her location with her. A message from Fiona zinged back saying that they were only ten minutes away and sharing their location.

I'll keep the location live so I can track you, and don't worry about the road up the mountain: it's not as narrow as it looks and it's very safe. We travel up and down it all the time!

She'd evidently forgotten all about Holly's fear of heights.

Holly studied the location Fiona had sent to her phone then looked at the mountains on her left. According to this she had to take the track up to the left of the middle mountain. And she had to drive for ten minutes.

Ten minutes up that horrendous track!

She took a deep breath. It couldn't be that bad or Fiona and Pablo wouldn't live there. And they certainly wouldn't be thinking of running an artists' retreat there. No one would want to come to it if they had to travel along a dangerous track high up a mountain, would they?

She got back into her car, opened Fiona's location in Google Maps, and put the phone into the holder on the dashboard so she could see the map clearly. *Stop panicking, Holly. You can do this.*

She crossed over to the left and turned up the track, gripping the steering wheel and keeping her eyes focused on the narrow road ahead. She drove slowly, trying not to think about the fact that there were no barriers.

The road went up and up and up and got narrower and narrower. Holly was sweating like mad and her heart was thud-thudding in her chest but she was coping… until she made the mistake of looking to the left. *Oh my God!* It was a sheer drop down to the valley below. One sharp turn, one swerve to avoid a down-coming vehicle, and she'd be plunging down, crashing into the main road below. And there was absolutely no chance she would survive.

She was trembling so much she felt like she was going to be sick, and her Mini had almost come to a standstill. She gritted her teeth and clenched the steering wheel in a vice-like grip, so tight her knuckles were white. She couldn't believe she was actually doing this. She hated heights. Fiona knew she hated heights. Why hadn't she warned her?

She couldn't turn around so she had to carry on.

Deep breaths, Holly. Breathe in. And out. In. And out. Pretend it's a normal road you're driving along. Do. Not. Look. Down. Focus on the road ahead. You can do this. People drive this track all the time so it must be perfectly safe even if it is steep and narrow, she told herself as she slowly, cautiously drove up the track, hoping to goodness that she wouldn't meet a car coming down.

The app's auto-voice suddenly broke through her panicked thoughts to tell her that she was to take a turn to the right in 200 metres then another turn and she would reach her destination.

Hoorah!

She took the turn to the right – thankfully away from the nasty drop and onto another narrow track through some bushes. Now all she had to do was turn to the right again and she was there. She relaxed and took the right bend. *Oh shit, I'm a little too wide!* A motorbike was speeding along the other way and she was heading right for it. Holly slammed on her brakes, screeching to a halt as the biker swerved past, making a rude hand gesture as he did so. Holly was so overwrought, shaken and furious that she wound down the window and shouted back at him, 'Slow down, you bloody idiot!'

He paused and looked back as if he'd understood what she was saying. Holly briefly had a chance to take in dark eyes and what would have been a handsome face if he hadn't looked so angry before he zoomed out of sight around the bend.

Charming! Okay, so she felt bad about yelling abuse at him, and yes, she was a bit out to the centre of the track, but how dare he be so rude? He was the one who had come speeding along far too fast for a narrow track like this. It would have been his fault if they'd crashed. What if he'd come along a little earlier when she was going up that narrow bit of the track? He could have gone into her and knocked her right off the mountain. She shuddered. It didn't bear thinking about.

Chapter Nine

As soon as he was out of sight around the bend, Matias Alvarez pulled over to the side of the road and braked. He took a deep breath, then another. That had been close, too close. And the car – a yellow Mini with a huge sunflower on the door, would you believe? – was a right-hand drive. Another stupid British tourist, not used to driving on the right.

What was the stupid woman doing up this track anyway? Most people went on to Reino; the only ones who came up here were usually residents, and there were only a handful of them. Had she got lost? Perhaps she was visiting the young couple that had moved into Las Mariposas when the elderly couple had sold up and moved to the coast last summer. He'd caught a glimpse of the driver: pretty and quite young. Perhaps he shouldn't have sworn at her – she'd looked petrified – and he had been coming around the bend a bit fast; his mind had been on his last conversation with his father. He should have known better than let that distract him.

She'd been over on his side of the road, though, and they could have both been severely injured. Or killed.

Composed now, he restarted the bike and continued on his way down the track, slower this time in case anyone else was coming up. Once at the bottom, he headed for Marbella.

❋

'You have reached your destination. Your destination is on the left,' Google Maps announced.

Holly looked around. To her left was a huge pair of rather imposing white iron gates. *Gosh, is* this *where Fiona and Pablo live?* It was a lot different to the one-bed flats they'd each had back in the UK. She pulled up and got out, reaching for her jacket in the back; Fiona had warned her that it could be chilly this time of year, so she'd packed a jacket, jeans and jumpers too. She took her phone out of the holder on the dashboard then walked over to the gates. A tiled nameplate saying 'Las Mariposas', decorated with a border of colourful butterflies, was on the right side of the gate. This was the correct place, then. She'd looked up the meaning of the name: the butterflies – pretty. She peered through the bars of the gate. All she could see was a long path and lots of bushes. She'd have to ring Fiona. Again. She was just about to dial her number when a young woman – dressed in jeans and a sweatshirt, her dark hair in two long plaits – came down the path. The woman saw Holly and waved. It was Fiona.

'Holly! You made it! I was about to check if I could see you.' Fiona unlocked the gates and screeched them open. Then she dashed out and gave Holly a big hug. 'It's so good to see you.'

Holly was so pleased to see her friend, and to still be in one piece, that she almost burst into tears.

Fiona looked really concerned. 'What's the matter?' she asked. 'What's happened?'

'I thought I was going to fall off that horrible mountain track, that's what.' Holly tried to hold back the sobs but one escaped. 'And then an idiot came racing along on a motorbike and I almost crashed into him.'

'Oh, you poor thing.' Fiona gave her another hug. 'I never thought to warn you about the track, we're so used to it. I don't think twice about driving along it – it's quite wide, as wide as a normal road, and it's got a smooth surface. If you forget how high it is, you're fine.'

'Well, I don't want to go back down it ever again! I think I'm going to say in your *finca* for the entire time I'm here,' Holly said, shakily.

'Forget about that now. Come and have a cuppa and chill out a bit. Drive in through the gates and along the path , there's plenty of space to park on the right,' Fiona told her.

A cuppa and a chill-out were just what she needed. Holly got back into her car and drove slowly through the gates and up the path. A sprawling white house, buried in a nook in the mountainside, surrounded by trees, came into view on her left. At the front of the house was a terrace with some steps to one side, a gorgeous fountain feature, a seating area, a large swimming pool and sprawling gardens. Holly could see outbuildings at each side, a smaller house and more trees – the smell of citrus was so powerful she knew that they were orange and lemon trees before she spotted the fruit dangling from the branches. She guessed the rest were fruit trees too. *Wow!* She hadn't expected Fiona and Pablo to live in a place like this!

Holly parked the car, got out and automatically pressed the remote lock, although she was pretty sure no one would be stealing it here. Fiona was already closing the gates behind her.

'This is fantastic. Is all this yours?' she asked incredulously, wondering if maybe Fiona and Pablo lived in the smaller house she could see in the grounds.

'Yes, it's perfect, isn't it? What with the big house and the small *casita* in the grounds, we have enough room to put up ten guests, at least – more if they share a room – and there's loads of parking space.' Fiona flicked back a stray lock of dark hair that had escaped from the messy plaits.

Holly whistled. 'Wow! How on earth did you afford this? Did you win the lottery or something?'

Fiona grinned. 'Would you believe we got this for the same price as both our flats, plus Pablo's redundancy money?' When Fiona had moved in with Pablo, she had kept her flat and rented it out.

'You mean you don't have a mortgage? You actually own it?'

Fiona grinned. 'Yep. Mind, we're absolutely skint now so we've got to do all the repairs ourselves. Can't afford to pay anyone else. We've had to take part-time work too. Pablo works in a bar in the village and I teach English most mornings.'

'Is there much that needs doing?' asked Holly.

'There was loads. We've been working on it every spare minute we could since we moved here. We've cracked the big jobs now so what's left is mainly cosmetic, sprucing it all up a bit.'

'I can help,' offered Holly. 'I don't mind. Call it in exchange for you putting me up.'

'Would you really? Thank you, hun. We could do with another pair of hands. How long can you stay for?'

Holly shrugged her shoulders. 'I'm going to see how it goes. I bought a one-way ticket, like you suggested.'

'That's great!' Fiona looked delighted. 'It's so lovely to have the company. You can have a room in the big house if you want but I wondered if you would like the little studio apartment so that you can have your own space to think and create? There's plenty of space there for your art materials and crafty stuff.' She pointed to some steps leading down from the terrace. 'It's down there, so not far from the house.'

Her own apartment? Holly hadn't expected that. She'd expected to be sharing the house with Fiona and Pablo, and it had worried her a little that they might get under each other's feet. She had never dreamt of having her own apartment, and right by the pool too. She imagined getting up every morning, having breakfast on the terrace then going for a swim. It sounded too good to be true.

'Really? Are you sure?' she asked.

'Of course. It's only small, with one bedroom, but it's yours as long as you want it. We're not using it or planning on having guests stay in it yet.'

You bet I want it! 'That's perfect, thank you.'

'Leave your luggage in the car for a bit and come and have that cuppa, then I'll show you around,' Fiona told her. 'Pablo's at work but he'll be back soon. Now, would you like coffee or fresh orange juice? The juice is from our own oranges – I squeezed some this morning.' Fiona opened a huge wooden front door and led the way through a long lounge with dark wooden furniture into a big kitchen. Dark wooden cupboards lined the kitchen walls and a big dresser stood along one wall, full of brightly coloured Spanish plates, cups and bowls. A heavy wooden table surrounded by eight chairs stood against the wall in the corner.

'Definitely orange juice please!' Holly said. 'But first do you mind if I have a glass of water? My throat feels like sandpaper.' She took a glass from the draining rack and turned on the tap with a 'C' on it. Then two things happened: hot water spurted out of the tap and Fiona snatched the glass out of her hand. 'Don't drink the water!' she shouted. 'And "C" is for hot, "F" is cold – *caliente* and *fría*.'

'What?' Holly stared at her, stunned. 'Why can't I drink the water?'

'Because we don't have town water, we get it from a well. And it's got too many nitrates in it. We drink bottled water.' Fiona opened the huge fridge in the corner of the kitchen and took out a small bottle. 'Here.'

'You mean you have to lift the water up with a bucket?' Holly unscrewed the top and took a long swig.

'No, it's an underground well, really deep down. The water is pumped up from a borehole with an electrical pump into a huge tank. I'm not really sure how it works, it's all automatic – mind you, it's a bit of a bummer when we have a power cut as that means the pump doesn't work so we have no water.'

Holly didn't like the sound of that. You couldn't have a shower. Or go to the loo. Or do any washing. 'Does that happen often?' she asked worriedly as Fiona poured two glasses of orange juice.

'It's happened a couple of times, but luckily it hasn't lasted long, we always keep a couple of big bottles of drinking water in stock, and have a gas hob so at least we can have a warm drink and cook a meal. We're going to get a generator as soon as we can afford it.' Fiona handed her one of the glasses. 'Now tell me all about Scott. I can't believe you two are really over. I thought you were mad about him.'

Holly took a sip of the cold drink, savouring the delicious, citric taste before replying. 'I was but now I'm mad *at* him.'

'Want to talk about it?'

She shook her head. 'I'm all talked out, to be honest. Do I still care about him? Yes. Will I go back to him? No. I guess that about sums it up.'

'So definitely over?'

'Definitely. And I'm officially off men for at least a year.' She'd had one boyfriend after another since her teens, hoping each one would be 'The One'. Well, she didn't want a guy in her life any more. She wanted space to do what she wanted, to live her life for herself for once, not to please someone else.

Chapter Ten

When they'd both finished their orange juice, Fiona took Holly on a guided tour. The house was like a mansion, with a double bedroom and bathroom downstairs, as well as the lounge and kitchen and five more good-sized bedrooms, three bathrooms, a living room and kitchen upstairs. The downstairs rooms were all decorated and furnished fairly well but the dark wooden furniture was chipped in places. The upstairs rooms, where Fiona said the guests would be staying, all needed a coat of paint and had dark wooden shutters at the windows. All the rooms were furnished with the same worn but beautiful dark furniture as downstairs and metal-framed beds. There was also an annex with two large bedrooms and a bathroom.

'They're spacious rooms, and I love the dark furniture,' Holly said as they stood in one of the annex bedrooms. 'Where did you get it from?'

'It came with the house. People usually sell the houses furnished over here – they often leave everything except personal possessions behind. Which was lucky for us, it would have cost us a fortune to refurnish this house. And it's not bad, is it? I know it needs tidying up a bit.'

'It's great. Like you said, it just needs a bit of sprucing up, and you could do with a few pictures, cushions and stuff to brighten up the rooms.'

'That's what we thought. We want to run retreats from July to September, which is almost four months away, so hopefully that gives us enough time to do something with the rooms and tidy up the *casita* – the other little house in the grounds – too.'

'I can help you. I've brought my sewing machine with me. I can make you some cushions and throws, if you want.' Holly's mind was racing with ideas already: there was so much scope with rooms of this size, and dark wood was a great background. 'Do you have any particular style you want the rooms in? And do you want them all to be the same, or different?'

'Different furnishings but all a bit chintzy, you know, kind of Laura Ashley to make people feel they're in the country – which, of course, they are,' Fiona told her.

'That sounds perfect. And what about the furniture? Dark wood looks gorgeous when it's varnished and polished and makes a good background for any colour. We could sand them down and paint them pastel colours though, and I could stencil some designs on them, if you'd rather?'

'We're going to give it all another coat of varnish – we like the dark wood too. It's very Spanish and goes well with the blinds.' She sat down on the edge of the double bed. 'We're grateful for anything you can help us with, if you're sure you don't mind.'

'I'd love to,' Holly assured her. 'This place has a lot of potential. I think you could turn it into a fantastic artists' retreat.' She was feeling really buzzy about the whole project. This was just what she needed. Something artistic to work on. Something that would keep her busy and take her mind off Scott.

'Me too! Now let me show you your apartment.' Fiona led the way downstairs and out into the courtyard at the front to the huge terrace and pool. There was another fountain, and dotted around the grounds were several seating areas and beautifully sculptured statues. It really was an amazing place, Holly thought. She could hardly believe that her friend lived in a house like this.

'I love those statues – did the owner leave those too?' she asked.

'No, Pablo made them. They're gorgeous, aren't they?' Fiona said. She turned to the steps running down by the side of the pool. 'The apartment's down here. It's only small and basic but it's pretty and I think you'll like it.' Fiona led the way down the steps. There was a bit of courtyard outside with some colourful plants and a chipped white bench placed under the window. Pretty, as Fiona said, and private.

Fiona unlocked the door and they walked into a spacious room with an archway leading to a small kitchen with a very tatty yellow gingham curtain on a rail running under the yellow tiled worktop. The wall over the worktop was covered with the same tiles. The other walls were whitewashed and a couple of dusty pictures hung here and there on rusty nails.

Okay, so it needed smartening up. That was no problem. 'What's behind the curtains?' Holly asked.

'Nothing.' Fiona pulled the curtain to one side to reveal brick pillars with empty spaces in between. 'The pillars support the worktop – it's concrete with tiles on top – so underneath can be used for storage. We'll put some shelves across when we have time, but we need to get the other rooms ready first.' She pointed to a huge dark wooden dresser in the corner, with double cupboards at the bottom and several shelves. 'You could use that for food, and to put your crockery on. We can give you some crockery, there's lots in the house. Or you can pick some up for a few euros at the local market if you'd rather.'

'That would be great. If you could give me the basics – a cup, saucer and plate – for now then I'll get some from the market later.' She quite fancied buying some colourful Spanish cups, saucers and plates for the dresser shelves, like the ones in the kitchen in the main house. Her mind was already racing with ideas to pretty up the apartment. She could replace that gingham curtain and get a couple of shelving units to put under the worktop. Fiona opened a door to the left of the kitchen. 'This is the bathroom.' The bathroom was small with a washbasin, toilet, bidet and shower.

A narrow wooden flight of stairs at the back of the lounge led up to a mezzanine floor: a white-walled bedroom. The only furniture was a black iron double bed, already made up with a patchwork bedspread, and a very scratched dark wooden wardrobe and dressing table.

'I've put clean sheets on the bed and left you a change of bedlinen in the cupboard over in the corner. I know it looks a bit scruffy but you can paint the walls, wardrobe and dressing table, put pictures up, make new curtains, blinds, whatever,' Fiona said. 'That's if you want to. You can live in it like this if you'd prefer. Or have a room in the house.'

'I'd love to stay here,' Holly assured her. She was already imagining the wardrobe and dressing table sanded down and painted a soft blue, decorated with flower and leaf stencils, a matching bedspread and curtains, a couple of Spanish pictures on the wall... 'It's fantastic. I really love it.'

Fiona looked pleased. 'I thought it was perfect for you. Shall we take a quick look around the grounds now? We've got acres of woodland and fruit trees so I'll leave you to explore all that yourself, if you want to, when we're at work. I'll just show you around the gardens, as we call them, and the other buildings.'

'Sure. I can't wait to see it all.' She had never imagined Fiona and Pablo living in something like this.

They walked around to the rear of the house, where the extensive grounds backed onto mountains. Here there were numerous fruit trees, a vegetable garden, a rockery and a fountain. Scattered around were lots of nooks and crannies for people to sit: a bench under a tree, a table and two chairs in a clearing between two orange trees, another bench beside the fountain. It was idyllic.

'This is fantastic, I can imagine people sitting here, sketching or writing – is the retreat for writers too?' Holly asked.

'Yes, writers, artists and sculptors,' Fiona said. 'I'm so glad you like it.'

There were also several storage buildings and sheds. Holly was overwhelmed with it all. A place like this would have cost a small fortune back in the UK. She gazed around in wonder. 'It's beautiful. I can't believe all this is yours.'

'Neither can we,' Fiona replied. 'It takes a bit of time to get used to not having drinking water on tap, and the winter was hard – the *finca* is difficult to keep warm, there's not much central heating over here. And it does need a lot doing to it. But we love it. And we'd be so grateful if you want to stay for a while and help us. You'll soon forget Scott living out here.'

'Scott who?' Holly said with a smile.

Fiona was right: a few months in Spain was just what Holly needed. And thanks to Pops she could do it. She didn't have to worry about earning a living and could help her friends get Las Mariposas ready for their guests. She was determined to use his gift to turn her life around. No more Miss Pushover. From now on, she was going to do what she wanted and seize life with both her hands.

Chapter Eleven

'Matias, you are here.' His mother came out to greet him then looked him up and down, taking in the crash helmet in his hands and his jeans and T-shirt. 'Don't tell me you have come on that bike.' She almost spat out the word 'bike'. 'How can you forget so easily how dangerous they are? And I expected you to wear something more suitable for a meeting with your father. He will not be pleased.' She spoke in her native English, as she always did when she and Matias were alone.

Matias shrugged irritably. 'What does it matter what I wear?' He looked around the spacious hall, with its shining, tiled floors and marble stairs leading up to the second floor, where he and Camila had their own suite of rooms when they were children. He pushed away the memories and turned his attention back to his mother. 'Where is Padre?'

'In his study. I will let him know you are here.' Helena Alvarez swept her piercing blue eyes over him. 'Why don't you go and change first? There are still some of your suits hanging in the wardrobe in your room. Your father would appreciate it.'

'Padre has to accept me for who I am, not who he wants me to be,' replied Matias. Then his tone softened. '*Lo siento,* Mamá, but how I live my life is up to me.'

Helena shook her head and sighed. She reached out her hand and lightly touched Matias's cheek. 'I want you to be happy, Matias, and I know you have suffered terribly. But your father is so disappointed. This hurts him very much. He wants to hand the company over to you when he retires, for the family business to carry on. And you are trained for it.'

'It's not what I want to do any longer. Surely you can understand? You defied your parents to marry my father.' His mother had come to Spain for a holiday with her parents, fallen in love with his father and refused to go back home. He found it difficult to imagine his parents as love-struck teenagers who'd run away so they could be together. They were so stiff and formal – especially his father.

Helena sighed again. 'I did, and I do not regret it. I loved your father and wanted to be with him. With you it is different, Matias: you are turning away from your career, from what you are trained to do. You are throwing it all away to be a gym instructor!'

'I never wanted to be a lawyer or work in the firm. I did it because Padre expected it of me,' Matias told her. 'Please try to understand, Mamá, that I want to live my life my way.'

Helena nodded. 'I understand, my son, and I have tried to explain, but your father—'

'Is used to getting his own way.' Matias leant forward and kissed his mother on the cheek. 'Don't worry, Mamá. I don't care if he disinherits me. I have no interest in what I can gain from your deaths. I prefer you to be alive, and to make my own money.'

Helena smiled. 'Stubborn. Like your father. That is exactly what he said to his father when he was forbidden to marry me.' She patted his hand. 'No doubt it will all work out. Your father loves you very much. He will come around eventually. But be prepared for a bumpy ride before he does.'

'Helena! Has Matias arrived yet?'

Matias turned towards the sound of the familiar voice coming from his father's study. 'I will go and see him now.' He started to walk across the tiled hall.

Helena nodded. 'Matias…'

He turned. 'Mamá?'

'Be polite and patient. For me,' she added, pleadingly.

Matias took a deep breath. It was difficult to be patient when his father was so dogmatic and opinionated. 'I will try.'

Antonio Alvarez was looking out of the window as Matias walked in. He made no movement until Matias said, '*Buenas noches,* Padre.'

Antonio turned slowly, his eyes resting disapprovingly on Matias's jeans and T-shirt.

The conversation that followed in Spanish was not a pleasant one. Antonio Alvarez made it clear that he disapproved of Matias's lifestyle and new career choice, that he had been patiently hoping Matias would come to his senses but if he didn't return to the family firm instantly, then he would hire another lawyer, and Matias would be written out of the firm, and out of his will.

For his mother's sake, Matias kept his tongue and his temper in check. He merely nodded and said, '*Como desea*, Padre,' then turned and walked out of the room.

His mother was waiting anxiously at the bottom of the stairs. 'Well?' she asked.

'Out of the firm and out of his will,' Matias told her. He kissed her on both cheeks. 'Don't worry, Mamá. I don't mind. I will see you soon.'

She clung to his hand as he went to walk away. 'Don't be a stranger, Matias. You and Camila, you are all we have.'

Matias had no doubt that Camila would be delighted he had walked away from Alvarez Abogados, and that Camila's husband, Salvador, would be replacing Matias on the board, but he didn't care.

He kissed her hand. '*Hasta pronto*, Mamá.'

*

After Fiona's tour Holly fetched her suitcases from the car and took them to the studio apartment. She couldn't believe this was going to be her home for the next few months; it was so adorable.

Fiona followed her in, carrying a box. She placed it on the table and proceeded to take out some tea bags, half a jar of coffee, a carton of UHT milk, a few slices of bread in a plastic bag and some butter in a small plastic container. This was followed by a mug, a dish, a plate and cutlery. 'I've brought you these in case you want a snack or a cuppa late tonight or in the morning,' she said, opening the fridge and placing the milk and butter in it. 'I'm at work all day tomorrow but I can take you shopping in the evening so you can stock up on anything you want. Until then, feel free to help yourself to anything in the house.'

'You mean we'll have to go down into the village?'

Holly must have looked as scared as she felt because Fiona quickly added, 'I know you're worried about driving down the mountain track but I promise you you'll soon get used to it.'

'I hope so.' The thought of going down that horrendous narrow mountain track again – especially in the evening – totally freaked her out. *Pablo and Fiona do it all the time,* she reminded herself. Besides, Fiona would be driving this time so if Holly closed her eyes until they got down to the bottom, then maybe it wouldn't seem so bad.

'Right. I'll leave you to settle in. We'll be eating in an hour so come over and join us. Pablo will be back then.'

'Thanks. I'll unpack the essentials, have a shower, then I'll be over.' She felt really hot and sticky.

'Sure – and remember: C for hot and F for cold,' Fiona said as she opened the front door. 'See you in a bit. Come around the back way, the kitchen door's open.'

An hour later, after messaging both her mum and Susie to let them know she'd arrived safely, having a quick shower and unpacking any clothes that would crease, Holly went over to the main house where Pablo was laying the kitchen table and Fiona was pouring red wine into three glasses.

'Hollee.' Pablo held his arms out wide and kissed her on both cheeks, Spanish fashion, his face wreathed in smiles. 'I am delighted you are here. It is good to see you again.'

'Thank you for inviting me over. You have an amazing home.' She sniffed appreciatively. 'Something smells delicious.'

'It's home-made lasagne and garlic bread, and home-grown salad,' Fiona said proudly. 'Sit yourself down, it'll be ready in a few minutes.' She held out a glass of wine. 'Want one?'

Did she ever? 'Thank you.'

'I hope you're both hungry, I've made quite a lot.' Fiona opened the oven and stepped back from the blast of hot air that swooshed out, before lifting out a large Pyrex dish containing a bubbling, golden-brown lasagne followed by freshy baked garlic bread.

Holly's tummy rumbled and she almost salivated: it looked and smelt so delicious. She hadn't realised how hungry she was – but it had been hours since she'd eaten and then she'd only had a sandwich.

Fiona put the lasagne down on the table, and Pablo brought over the garlic bread, then they both sat down. 'Tuck in,' Fiona said.

It was a fantastic meal. The food was delicious and the conversation entertaining. Fiona and Pablo took it in turns to relay the various things that had gone wrong since they'd bought the *finca* – and there were several.

'The water pump broke not long after we moved in and we had no water for days,' Fiona told her. 'We were getting water out of the pool to flush the loo and using bottled water to wash in. Now we always keep some big urns full of water in the shower room outside, just in case.'

'Gosh that must have been awful!' Holly exclaimed. She couldn't imagine having no running water.

'Another time it rained heavily for two days and we had leaks everywhere,' Pablo told her. 'We had buckets all over the place trying to catch the water. And the mountain track was so muddy we were scared to drive down it.'

'Goodness! I bet you wished you'd never moved here, didn't you?'

Pablo reached out and took Fiona's hand; they smiled at each other then turned to face Holly. 'Yes, there have been times we have briefly felt like that, but then we go outside and look at our beautiful home, at the mountains, smell the fresh air and we know we have done the right thing.'

'And although we're both working hard at the moment, we spend a lot more time together than we did back in the UK. We're living our dream, so it makes it all worthwhile.'

They both looked so happy, so much in love, that Holly felt a slight twinge of envy. If only things had worked out with Scott. She swatted the thought away. She didn't need a man. She was going to make her own happiness.

'It is a gorgeous place to live,' she said. 'And now I'm here to help so we'll soon get it ready for the retreat.'

'You're a star, we could do with another pair of hands,' Fiona told her. 'I'm afraid you'll be on your own a bit though, as we're both working. But I'll be back at two thirty most days. I hope you won't be bored.'

'I won't. I'll have a mosey around the place, if that's okay, see if I can get some ideas for designs for the bedrooms.' Then it registered what she had said. 'How are you going to get back home if Pablo is still at work? Do you have two cars?'

'No, but we have a motor scooter too. Pablo will use the van tomorrow because he wants to get some paint so we can tidy up the bedroom walls.'

Holly gawped at her. 'Are you serious? You go down that horrible track on a motor scooter?'

Fiona shrugged. 'It's fine. I do it all the time.' She scraped up the last of the lasagne with her garlic bread. 'Let's sit out on the terrace when we've all finished. It's a mild night, too nice to stay indoors.'

They all mucked in with the washing-up – Holly washing, Fiona drying and Pablo stacking everything away – then went out onto the front terrace. It had gone a bit chilly so Pablo put the patio heater and light on and they sat talking and drinking wine under the starlit sky. It was a perfect evening.

Holly felt very happy as she let herself into her little studio apartment much later. She fell asleep as soon as her head touched the pillow. And she didn't think of Scott once.

Chapter Twelve

Holly slept soundly all night, not waking until ten the next morning. The travelling over the last couple of days had taken it out of her and she felt like she could have slept all day, but Fiona would be home in a few hours and she wanted to have some ideas for the guest rooms to talk to her about, so she yawned, stretched and went for a shower. Once dressed, joyously wearing her jeans and old blue shirt – the old Holly was back! – she went to make herself a cup of tea. She automatically turned on the tap with C on it before realising her mistake, and picked up the huge bottle of water by the fridge to fill up the kettle instead. This was going to take some getting used to.

After a breakfast of tea and toast she finished unpacking her clothes then stepped outside. It was a gorgeous day – a bit chilly and windy but the sun was shining and the sky was blue. She'd take a walk around the grounds first then go into the *finca* – Fiona had given her a key – and sketch some ideas for prettying up the bedrooms.

It took her a good hour to cover the grounds, although she didn't venture too far into the woods. Then she remembered that she'd left her sewing machine and a couple of boxes in the boot of her car so walked down the driveway to fetch them. As she opened the boot of her yellow Mini, she heard a dog barking. She looked around and saw a little white and gold Shih Tzu barking at the gate. *How cute!* The dog saw her and barked again, wagging its tail madly. Was it lost? It was wearing a pink collar from which a silver name tab dangled so obviously was female and belonged to someone. Shame. If it was a stray, maybe they could have kept it. She'd love a little dog like this. Mind you, she wasn't sure how a dog could possibly wander up this mountain and get lost, so she presumed it belonged to a neighbour. Fiona had said there were a few other houses scattered about, and that bad-mannered guy on the motorbike must have been visiting someone. The dog barked again then sat down and whined. It looked so cute with its teddy-bear face and button eyes; its coat was shiny and it appeared well-looked after.

'Hello, girl, are you lost?' she asked softly.

The dog whined and patted the ground with her paw.

She looked friendly so Holly slowly put her hand through the fence. The dog licked it. 'Aren't you a little sweetie?' Holly said, smiling.

She opened the gate and the dog bounced in, wagging her tail. She stood in front of Holly, her tongue out, panting, as if begging for a drink.

'What's up, girl? Do you want some water?' she asked.

The little dog sat down, tongue hanging out.

'You're beautiful, aren't you?' she said, gently stroking her head. She licked Holly's hand then started panting again. 'Poor thing, you're hot. Stay here and I'll get you some water.'

The dog followed her as she walked towards the house. She searched through the shed and found an old plastic container, which she filled up from the outside water tap – surely animals could drink the water – and put it down for the dog, who lapped it up greedily.

'I knew it. You're thirsty. I wonder who you belong to,' she said as the dog continued to lap up the water. When the little Shih Tzu had finished drinking, she sat in front of Holly, tail wagging. She knelt down and stroked her gently with one hand while reaching for the dog tag with the other. *Luna* it said on one side of the tag, and there was a phone number engraved on the other.

'I guess I'd better phone this number and let your owner know you're here, hadn't I, Luna?' Holly whispered. 'I bet they're really worried about you.'

'Luna!' a male voice suddenly shouted. 'Luna! *¡Ven acá!*'

The dog's ears pricked up and she got up and bolted across to the drive, down to the still-open gate, where a tall, dark-haired Spanish man was standing.

It was the same man on the motorbike Holly had almost crashed into yesterday, only he wasn't wearing a crash helmet today, so she could see that he had thick dark hair, cropped short, just enough stubble on his rugged, handsome face to be sexy rather than scruffy, and gorgeous tawny eyes. The tan shorts and olive vest he was wearing made his toned calves and bulging biceps clearly visible. This man obviously worked out on a regular basis, and he looked good for the effort. Not that she fancied him. In fact, she was going to stop staring at him right now.

The man said something to the dog – Luna – as she trotted to his side, tail wagging. He bent down to stroke her, his tone gentle. Then he stood up, glared at Holly and snapped something in Spanish.

Holly wracked her brains for the Spanish for 'I don't understand' but couldn't remember it so she shrugged and held her palms up, hoping that translated as, 'I have no idea what you're talking about.'

The man muttered something under his breath then demanded in perfect English, laced with a Spanish accent, 'What are you doing with my dog?'

His dog! She hoped the expression on her face wasn't as shocked as she felt. She could hardly believe that such a hunk of a guy owned such a dainty little dog. She would have said a boxer, Dobermann or German shepherd were all more his type.

'She was barking at my gate and I thought she was lost so I gave her a drink of water,' Holly replied defensively.

'It didn't occur to you to phone the number on the dog tag? It must have been obvious that Luna belonged to one of your neighbours,' the man snapped.

His tone irritated her but she tried to keep her cool. 'I was going to phone the number when you called. I only arrived yesterday. I don't know any of the neighbours,' she added in way of explanation.

His thick eyebrows knotted together in anger. 'Yes, I know, I saw you arrive. You almost knocked me off my motorbike – and were extremely rude. You British tourists are a menace. You shouldn't be allowed to drive over here until you've had lessons driving on the right side of the road and have passed another test!'

What a cheek. Okay, she had sworn at him but he could have killed her! She placed her hands on her hips and glared back at him. 'And you should watch your speed when you're going down a narrow mountain track.'

'I was not going fast! And you should drive on the correct side of the road,' he retorted, a muscle twitching furiously in his cheek. 'Now if you don't mind, I'll take my dog back home.'

'Be my guest! Maybe you should keep your gate locked if you don't want your dog to get out!'

'My gate *is* locked. She must have wriggled out through a gap in the fence when I wasn't looking.' He snapped his fingers. '*Ven*, Luna!' Then he turned and marched down the path away from Las Mariposas.

The dog immediately followed him. *What an ignorant man!* Holly walked out of the gate to see where they were going and saw him heading towards a house, over to the left and set back a bit. She'd been too busy staring at Fiona's place yesterday to notice it. This house was white too, smaller than Fiona's, surrounded by a falling-down fence and tall white gates. She couldn't see much of the house itself but it looked a bit shabby. Did the man live there by himself, she wondered, or did he have a partner? She felt sorry for them if he did – he didn't seem a very pleasant man… even if he was hot. 'Beauty is as beauty does,' Nanna used to say. The guy might be good to look at but Holly didn't fancy being on any closer terms with him. As far as she was concerned, the less she saw of their hunky but bad-tempered neighbour, the better.

Chapter Thirteen

So he had been right: the Englishwoman was visiting the couple who lived at Las Mariposas. Matias stormed back to his aunt's *finca*, Luna at his heels. Now, not content with almost knocking him off his motorbike, she was now trying to steal his dog.

You were *driving too fast, it was your fault too,* he reminded himself. And she was only giving the dog some water. Plus, Luna wasn't actually his dog, she was Tia Isabella's, though his aunt had left the little dog at the *finca* while Matias was living there because dogs weren't allowed at the apartment she now lived in. At first Tia Isabella had been heartbroken that she couldn't take Luna, but on Matias's last visit she had admitted that life was easier without Luna to look after as she had often been too tired to walk her, and she knew that Luna would miss being able to run around the vast garden of this house. He would probably have to find a new home for her when he sold the house. He would be renting an apartment again and even if dogs were allowed, Luna would hate being penned up all day while he was at work. He'd tried to persuade his mother to take Luna in but she had refused: his father didn't like pets in the house. He didn't really like anything that made a mess or didn't do as they were told. He'd only just tolerated Matias and his sister Camila when they were growing up.

He thought back to the young Englishwoman at Las Mariposas. She was pretty, with honey-brown hair that danced around her shoulders in delicate waves and blue eyes – one slightly darker than the other, he'd noticed – dazzling out of a sweet, heart-shaped face. She'd looked hurt when he'd first shouted at her, then he'd seen the anger spark in her eyes. She seemed kind but not a pushover. Maybe he'd been a bit hard on her. It wasn't like him to snap so much. He was letting this argument with his father get to him.

*

Holly closed the gate, went back inside, made herself a cup of coffee and took it with her as she had another tour of the house – avoiding Fiona and Pablo's bedroom, of course. She was determined to help as much as she could to get the *finca* ready for guests. She wondered what rooms they would let out first: the spare rooms on the top floor, or the *casita* in the grounds. She guessed it would be the rooms on the top floor and the annex. The *casita* needed the most work.

The morning flew by. Fiona had said she would be home about two thirty and it was almost that now. Should she prepare some lunch? Holly opened the fridge in the huge kitchen and found eggs, salad, cheese and ham, and a crusty loaf in the cupboard. That would do a simple but tasty lunch. She couldn't keep eating Fiona and Pablo's food, though; she had to get some in for herself, which meant going shopping with Fiona that evening. She hated the thought of going down that mountain track, and certainly didn't want to make the journey in the dark.

Well, you've got to do it, she told herself sharply as she washed the lettuce – remembering just in time to use the bottled water. *You can't expect Fiona and Pablo to keep supplying you with food. And you can't hide away up this mountain. Besides, getting over your fear of heights is one of the things on your list so you've got to get over it and that's it.* Perhaps she could persuade Fiona to go shopping tomorrow morning. If she was working, maybe Holly could go down with her, then come back with her in the afternoon when she'd finished work. At least it would be light then.

She chopped the lettuce, tomatoes, peppers and cucumber into a bowl, added grated carrot and tossed it all in olive oil. She'd laid the table for two and was just slicing the bread when Fiona came in.

'Hey, that looks nice. Thanks, hun. I'm starving.' Fiona put her bag down on the sofa. 'How's your day been?'

'Good, apart from a run-in with your grumpy neighbour.'

Fiona raised an eyebrow 'Really? Do you mean the guy over the back? He only moved in a couple of weeks ago. We've barely seen him. What happened?'

Holly filled her in on the episode with his dog. 'Honestly, I was only giving the poor dog a drink. Anyone would think I was going to kidnap her.' She wrinkled her nose. 'And he's the same guy who was speeding around the bend on his motorbike yesterday – he made out that was my fault too! Then he had a rant about how British tourists shouldn't be allowed to drive over here without taking another test.'

'Oh dear.' Fiona washed her hands at the kitchen sink and reached for a towel. 'Take no notice of him; most Spanish people are really welcoming. We'll go down to the village tonight for shopping, then to the bar where Pablo works so you can meet some of our friends.'

Holly chewed her lip. 'I thought it would be nice to stay in and have a chat again. Then maybe I could come down with you in the morning when you go to work and have a bit of a look around the village, get some shopping in.'

Fiona studied her. 'You're scared of going down that track, aren't you?'

'Yes,' admitted Holly. 'To be honest the thought of going up and down it is freaking me out. I know I've got to do it, but I'd rather do it in the daylight.'

'I know how you feel, hun, I was the same. But believe me, you'll get used to it. Just sit in the back and close your eyes – we'll be on the main road before you know it. She pulled a chair out and sat down at the table. 'You'll soon be whizzing up and down the track in your little Mini wondering why you were so frightened.'

Holly thought that was highly unlikely. She was going to need a camomile tea before she did this trip and something stronger once she was down in the village so she could face the trip back up again.

Pablo came home an hour or so later and finished off the salad and crusty bread they'd left for him, then they all set to painting the walls of one of the guest rooms white.

'There's a big market on Saturdays – I thought we could go there one weekend and pick up some material for the rooms. Do you fancy it?' Fiona asked.

'That sounds great. I can get some bits for my apartment too.'

'Let's see if we can make it next weekend.' Fiona glanced at her watch. 'Now how about we eat down in the village? We can get a cheap bowl of pasta where Pablo works. Then we can do the shopping.'

Holly could feel her heart pounding already. 'I don't think I can do this,' she said to Fiona. 'Could you get my groceries for me if I give you a list?'

'Honestly, Holly, it won't be any easier if you leave it until another day. It'll just get harder because you'll build it up in your mind, and in the end you'll convince yourself that you can't do it.'

That's pretty much how she felt right now. 'But it's dark outside. I'll be okay – well, better – if we go in the daylight and Pablo will be able to see clearer. There are no barriers on the road,' Holly pointed out. 'One wrong move and we'll go plunging down to the ground.'

'Stop worrying! It's as wide as any other road; there's plenty of room for us and another car to pass us coming down.' Fiona reached out and touched Holly's hand reassuringly. 'I do know how you feel. I was like that at first. We both were. But it'll be fine. I promise. The trick is to look ahead, forget about the drop and focus on where you're going.'

Holly thought about the close call with their neighbour. If she'd encountered him on the main track and swerved to avoid him… *But you wouldn't have swerved, you'd have stopped, and so would he,* she told herself.

'Okay, but remember I'm sitting in the back, behind Pablo.'

Ten minutes later they were all in Pablo's van heading down towards the village. Holly closed her eyes firmly, fought down the urge to scream, 'Let me out,' and sat on the edge of her seat, clutching the door handle – she couldn't say why, she just felt safer that way. Fiona chatted away, obviously in an attempt to take Holly's mind off things, but Holly barely replied; she was too busy inwardly chanting, 'Please let us get down safe, please let us get down safe,' and making all sorts of promises to a God she wasn't even sure she believed in, if they managed the trip safely.

'We're at the bottom now – that wasn't too bad, was it?' Pablo asked.

Holly opened her eyes and looked out of the front window. They were on the main road running towards the village. Thank goodness, now she could breathe easily. And she wasn't going to think about going back up again.

Pablo parked the van in a big car park and led the way downhill, into the town. Reino was so quaint, with pebbled streets, ornate tiles on the bottom walls of many of the houses they passed, benches dotted about here and there where people sat chatting, a pretty water fountain in the middle of the square, and exquisite black iron railings on the balconies of the flats over the shops they passed. Holly was amazed at how busy it was. It was starting to get dark now and the streets were bustling. People, young and old alike, were sitting outside cafés drinking, eating and chatting. Children were playing around nearby.

'Is it always this lively?' she asked.

'Yes, the Spanish close for a siesta in the afternoon – especially during the summer months when it's so hot – then come out as a family in the evening.'

'It's fantastic. Which bar do you work in, Pablo?'

'That one on the corner. We'll go and have something to eat there. I don't start work for an hour,' he replied.

'Then we can go to the shops,' Fiona added.

The bar was busy already, and a group of people waved to Pablo and Fiona as they approached.

'Let's join them; they are some of my students and Felipe, another tutor,' Fiona said. They pulled up another couple of chairs at the table and Fiona introduced Holly. 'She's staying with us for a few months.'

'*Hola*, Holly,' one of Fiona's students said.

Fiona ordered their meal – a plate of pasta each – and they sat chatting to everyone for a while in a mix of broken English and Spanish.

'I'm so sorry I can't speak much Spanish,' Holly apologised to the man sitting next to her, who Fiona had introduced as Felipe.

'It is no matter, we like to practise our English,' Felipe replied.

'And I want to improve my Spanish. I'm going to take Spanish classes,' she told him as she polished off her plate of pasta.

'Then come to my class. I am a Spanish tutor,' he said, smiling broadly to reveal very white teeth. 'You are staying here for a while, yes?'

'I'm here through the summer,' she replied. 'And I'd love to come to your classes. Thank you.' Perhaps she could travel down with Fiona until she got used to driving up and down herself.

Felipe picked up a serviette from the container on the table, took a pen out of his pocket and wrote down the days and times of his classes on it then handed it to Holly. 'You are welcome to join us any day,' he said.

'*Gracias.*' Felipe was making such an effort to speak in English, the least she could do was use one of the few Spanish words she knew. 'I'll have a think when I go back home and see what days are best.'

'You don't have to come the same day every week. Any day you wish you can join us,' he told her.

'That'll be great.' Felipe seemed nice and it would be good to get to know the others too. She really wanted to embrace her life in Spain, and learning to speak another language fluently was another thing on her list.

Fiona turned to Holly. 'Are you ready to go? Remember we need to get some supplies from the supermarket. We can bring them back here and put them in the fridge until Pablo has finished working.'

'Sure.' Holly pushed her chair back and went to stand up. As she did so, Felipe stood up too and kissed her on both cheeks. 'I look forward to seeing you soon, Holly,' he said.

'Er, yes. Me too.' *What a lovely guy!* Then she suddenly became aware that someone was staring at her over Felipe's shoulder. Sitting at a table a few metres away was their hunky but bad-tempered neighbour and a very pretty Spanish woman. The woman was looking at her mobile but the guy was staring at Holly, and from the expression on his face he wasn't very pleased to see her. What was it with him? Why did he dislike her so much?

Chapter Fourteen

'What is the matter? You look troubled,' Felipe asked, concerned.

'I've just spotted our neighbour and I've had a couple of run-ins with him. He doesn't look very pleased to see me here.'

The guy had turned away now and was chatting to his companion, who was gazing into his eyes as if she was totally in love with him. Maybe she was.

'Run-ins?' Felipe raised his eyebrows questioningly. 'Matias has run into you? On his motorbike?'

'No, I mean… disagreements,' Holly explained. So his name was Matias. 'You know him, then?'

'*Sí*, he used to spend the summers here, at his aunt's house, when he was a child. Sometimes he would come down into the village and hang around with a few of us but he is a bit older than me; we weren't really friends. I haven't seen him for years. The house, it was – how do you say? – falling down, so his aunt has moved out.'

No wonder the house looked so shabby. 'So is he living there now?' she asked. If he was, she was going to do her best to avoid him. She didn't want any more unpleasantness.

Felipe nodded. 'I have heard that Matias works in a gym in Málaga and he is renovating the house so it can be sold.'

A fitness instructor, eh? No wonder he looked in such good shape. 'Well, I'd better be going. I'll drop in at one of your Spanish lessons soon,' she promised.

She turned to look for Fiona, who had stopped to talk to a couple at the next table. As Holly walked over to join her, she heard a loud laugh and glanced over to see Matias, head thrown back, dark eyes twinkling, roaring with laughter as he talked to the man at the next table. She stared at him, unable to believe the transformation that the laugh had made to his face. *What a shame he doesn't laugh more often,* she thought as she turned away and joined Fiona. Maybe he did. Maybe it was just Holly he disapproved of.

✳

She seemed to be everywhere, this Englishwoman. He wondered how long she was staying. He'd seen her look at him then look away. She was with Felipe, the language tutor, and the couple from the villa next door. He guessed she was here for a holiday, so maybe a week or two.

'Why are you staring at that woman? Who is she?' Sofia asked in their native Spanish, an edge to her voice.

Matias tore his gaze away. 'I don't know. She turned up at the house next door yesterday and almost drove into me when she was coming up the track, then I found Luna in her grounds this morning – she was giving her some water.'

'So why is it that you can't take your eyes off her?' Sofia pouted her cherry-red lips. 'Do you fancy her?'

'Of course not!' Matias snapped. 'I was looking because I recognised her, not staring! You're being ridiculous, Sofia.'

'Well, what am I supposed to think when you bury yourself in this godforsaken place and refuse to come back to Marbella, to your home, your job?'

'I've told you. I am helping my aunt, like she helped me. When everyone else turned their back on me.'

'I didn't know you then,' whispered Sofia, leaning over and placing her hand on his. 'I would have looked after you. I wouldn't have walked away like Natali did. I would look after you now, if you would let me. Why don't you let me move in with you?'

Matias scowled at the sound of his former fiancée's name and eased his hand out from under Sofia's. 'I have told you, Sofia, I don't need anyone to look after me. And I don't intend to live with anyone ever again. I thought you understood?' He furrowed his brow. The last thing he needed was Sofia getting serious. She was beautiful, and fun most of the time, but he didn't want her – or anyone else – as a permanent fixture. It had been a mistake living with Natali, giving her his heart. He wouldn't be doing that again.

'Okay, okay. Let's not spoil the evening.' Sofia snuggled up to him. 'Why don't we have one more drink then go back home and have an early night?'

Normally, Matias would find that an enticing proposition, but as he watched the Englishwoman talking and laughing with a group of people, the unwanted thought crossed his mind that he would rather spend the night with her. He thrust the thought away, picked up his glass and downed his drink. 'I have a better idea. Let's go back now – there's a bottle of wine cooling in the fridge. I am tired of drinking alcohol-free beer.'

✳

The smell of fish hit Holly as soon as she walked through the supermarket doors and there, on the left, was a huge counter displaying a variety of seafood. 'I didn't know so many different fish existed,' she said.

'I know, I was surprised too. I always thought of cod, haddock and plaice and that was about it,' Fiona replied. 'Do you like fish? Do you want to get some?'

'I'd love some salmon.' Holly picked up two fillets of salmon and put them into her basket. 'I'd like some salad stuff and pasta and rice too – they're all great standbys for meals.'

There was a huge variety of fresh fruit, vegetables and meat in addition to the fish. Although she didn't know much Spanish, Holly found it fairly easy to identify everything.

She watched as Fiona put a box of hair dye into her trolley. She'd forgotten that Fiona's hair was really light brown, like hers, and she dyed it black. 'I wouldn't mind colouring my hair,' she said, impulsively.

'Go for it. What colour do you want to be? Blonde, auburn, black?' Fiona pointed to the array of boxes. She tilted her head to one side, considering, then said, 'I think blonde would suit you. It would bring out the blue of your eyes.'

'I'm not sure. I'm scared of it going wrong. You hear such stories…' She'd read one once about a woman having her hair coloured at the hairdresser's and having such an allergic reaction her face had swollen up.

'I use this all the time, it's fine. But you need to do a patch test first.' Fiona picked up a box of dye. 'Look, here's a golden-blonde one; it's not that much lighter than your colour now. Why don't you try it? You can always put a brown dye on if you don't like it.'

Holly hesitated. Blonde sounded good – a lot better than her mousy brown. *Take a chance, Holly, stop being so scared to try things.* She put the colourant into her basket. 'You'll have to translate it for me. I don't want to get it wrong.'

'I'll do it for you, if you want,' offered Fiona.

'Thanks.' She did want. She trusted Fiona to make a better job of it than she would.

Once they'd paid for their shopping they took it back to the bar, where Pablo placed the fresh food in the fridge while they sat and chatted a little more about life in Spain, waiting for his shift to end. Holly noticed a couple of stray dogs hanging about and Fiona told her that sadly there were lots of stray dogs – and cats – and many of the British adopted them, sometimes taking in half a dozen or more. Holly could understand why: she felt sorry for the dogs, who had now wandered off. She felt like adopting them all.

It was almost midnight when they set back up the mountain trail and, once again, Holly sat in the back, and closed her eyes. Not that she could see anything; it was too dark.

'Wake up, sleepyhead, we're home!' Fiona said, shaking her gently.

'What, already?' She must have dozed off.

'I can see you're getting used to this track,' Pablo jested. 'Good to know my driving is so smooth it sends you to sleep.'

Holly yawned. Gosh, she was exhausted. It must be something to do with the mountain air. She couldn't wait to get to bed.

Then she realised that she hadn't thought of Scott all day, a sure sign that she was getting him out of her system. Coming to Spain had been a brilliant idea.

Chapter Fifteen

Luna was back the next morning after Fiona and Pablo had gone back to work, tail wagging and barking at the gate. Holly walked over to her, put her hands through the bars and stroked the dog's soft coat. 'You'll get me into trouble with your master, you will,' she said softly. 'You know how he hates you coming here. Hates me.' She really had sensed the dislike coming from Matias; it had felt personal. Fiona had said that she and Pablo had hardly spoken to him but when they'd met him he was always a bit off. He obviously had a thing about tourists coming over.

'Never mind; if you don't tell him, I won't,' Holly whispered as the little dog licked her hand, tail still wagging. 'Stay here, girl, I'll go and fetch you a treat.' She'd picked up a bag of doggy treats yesterday from the supermarket, hoping that she might see Luna again – or another stray dog. She'd love a pet and was hoping a cute little stray dog might find its way up the mountain and wander into Las Mariposas, but she guessed that was unlikely, so she'd settle for sharing Luna as long as Matias didn't catch her doing it.

She came back with a couple of treats and put her hand through the bars, then opened her palm, keeping her fingers straight so that Luna could easily reach the treats lying there. 'Here you are, girl.' Luna trotted over, quickly scoffed them up then sat down by the gate and stared at Holly as if to say, 'Please let me in.'

'Don't give me that look. You know your master won't like it,' Holly scolded her.

No sooner were the words out of her mouth than she heard Matias call the dog. Luna pricked up her ears and trotted off.

Honestly, why doesn't Matias fix that fence if he doesn't want the dog to get out? It's simple enough. She shrugged her shoulders. Oh well, she'd better get cracking with some work. She wanted to start on the wardrobes. Pablo had brought paint and varnish back with him yesterday.

She spent the morning sanding and varnishing the huge wardrobe in the bedroom where they'd painted the walls yesterday. She'd just finished when Fiona came home.

'This is looking fantastic,' Fiona said, gazing around the bedroom. 'You're a miracle worker, Holly.'

Holly had to admit that she was pleased with how well it had all come up. 'I'll do the dressing table later,' she said. 'Then if we get some material at the weekend, I can make a bedspread and some cushions.'

'That would be fantastic,' Fiona said. 'It's a shame we can't buy rolls of material of your designs. I was looked at your Dandibug online shop at the weekend and your designs are amazing. I love the woodland fern one, and the sunflower one too. It would be fab to have curtains and bedspreads in your designs.'

'Hey, that's a brilliant idea! I'll look into it.' She'd never thought of having her designs printed on rolls of fabric, as well as mugs, cups, phone cases and notebooks but there must be a way she could do it. 'I could create some new designs, based on the Spanish countryside. I could sell them on Dandibug too so people could use it to make their own furnishings.'

'Finish our rooms first, though, won't you?' Fiona joked.

'Of course I will. In fact, Las Mariposas could be my showcase. I could take photos when we've finished the rooms and use them for advertising. If you wouldn't mind that?'

'No way. It'd be fab publicity for us too! Pablo isn't working tonight so how about we check out your designs and see which ones we'd like for the rooms?'

'Sure. And I'll research how I can get them printed onto material and delivered to us.' This was exciting. If she could really make this work, she might actually be able to be fully self-employed. She gazed around the bedroom, imagining her designs on the bedspread, cushions, maybe even curtains too; they would brighten up the dark wooden blinds.

'Let's have some lunch and sit by the pool,' Fiona suggested. 'It's always warmer outside than it is inside in Spain. The houses are made to keep out the heat rather than keep it in.' She suddenly looked worried. 'I hope you haven't been cold? I never thought to tell you that's there's a gas heater in the hall you could wheel in and put on.'

'I'm fine. I am hungry, though. Shall I do lunch? I bought some fusilli pasta yesterday; do you fancy some with herbs and tomatoes?'

'Sounds good,' Fiona agreed. They walked out of the room, closing the door behind them, and went down to the kitchen. Holly nipped over to her apartment to make the pasta while Fiona squeezed some oranges to make a jug of fresh juice.

They sat outside to eat and Fiona was right, it was far warmer than inside. 'When do you usually go in the pool?' Holly asked. 'I can't wait to have a dip.'

'You might be able to go in the end of next month if it's warm, although a lot of people don't go in the pool until June. It depends how brave you are!'

'It was lucky you came over in the summer last year – at least you managed to use the pool a bit,' Holly said. 'It must be fantastic to get up every day and have a swim.'

'It is. And believe me, July and August are so hot all you'll want to do is go in the pool every day.'

'The guests will enjoy that,' Holly said, tucking into her pasta.

'Talking of guests – before I forget, we're expecting a delivery tomorrow. We've ordered a new shower for one of the bathrooms and couldn't fit it in the van. They'll ring the bell on the gate to let you know they're here.'

'Of course. Although I can't speak much Spanish,' she reminded Fiona. 'I'll have to rely on the Google Translate app on my phone if they ask me questions.'

'I doubt if they will. All you have to do is sign for it. I'll WhatsApp them our location before I go to work in the morning so they know how to find us.'

When they'd finished lunch, Fiona announced that she was going to colour her hair.

'Shall we do mine too?' Holly said. She was quite excited about going blonde. It would be a whole new look.

'We'd better do a patch test first. Best to play it safe. You have to leave the patch test for twenty-four hours, so we'll do yours tomorrow when I come home from work.'

She guessed Fiona was right. She could wait another day.

Fiona did the patch test just behind Holly's ear. 'Don't wash it off,' she said. 'If you haven't had an adverse reaction by tomorrow afternoon, then you'll be fine to colour it.'

Once Fiona's hair was done – and she was right, it was a very simple process, she just put the colour all over her hair, left it for twenty minutes then washed it off again – Holly went to spend a little time in the studio apartment while Fiona prepared her lesson for the next day.

She wanted to do some research on printing her designs out on material and soon found a few sites that offered that service. It seemed simple enough: you uploaded your designs, selected whether you wanted it printed on fabric, wallpaper or paper, then ordered the amount you wanted. A company called Sundial seemed the best: the printing service was quick, there was no minimum order and they delivered all over the world. They took commission, of course, but it was a good way to start up and see if the idea was viable. She couldn't wait to tell Fiona.

Holly told Fiona and Pablo about it as they sat out on the terrace that evening. 'So if you like any of my existing designs, I can order them to be printed onto fabric and make the furnishings out of them,' she explained. 'Do you want to take a look now? See if there's anything you fancy?'

'Yes please! It sounds brilliant. We could have a different design for each room – then we could name the rooms things like the Wildflower Room and the Fern Room,' said Fiona enthusiastically.

Holly fetched her laptop and clicked onto her Dandibug shop page. Fiona and Pablo 'oohed' and 'aahed' as they checked out the designs, which made her feel quite proud… Scott had always dismissed them as her 'little hobby'.

'Wow! Fiona said you were talented but I wasn't expecting these. I love this woodland design,' Pablo exclaimed.

'This blossom pattern is gorgeous too,' Fiona said. They both pored over the designs and finally selected eight they wanted.

'When we've finished all the guest rooms in the house, we'll do the two rooms in the *casita*,' Fiona said. 'It won't matter if we use the same fabric we've used for rooms in the house.'

'I'm going to do some new designs – a purple bougainvillea and something else, I'm not sure yet. I'm calling it my Spanish collection. Maybe you could use those for the *casita*,' Holly suggested.

Fiona and Pablo were delighted.

'This is so kind of you, Holly. You must accept some payment from us,' Pablo insisted.

She shook her head adamantly. 'No way. You're providing me with accommodation, which more than pays for these. Besides, as I told Fiona, this can be my showcase. Las Mariposas is the guinea pig for my new business.'

They were all on such a high that they sat chatting until late in the evening, Fiona and Pablo holding hands and excitedly finishing each other's sentences as they told Holly of their plans for the retreat: Fiona would be running art classes and Pablo pottery classes, then they would both run classes on creative writing. 'We want the students to have something complete to take home with them – a painting, a small sculpture, a short story,' Fiona explained.

'It sounds wonderful,' Holly told them. She was so excited to be part of their adventure.

Chapter Sixteen

The next day Fiona and Pablo were both at work again so Holly spent the morning opening an account on Sundial then uploading her designs to their website. That done, she decided to check on the patch test Fiona had done behind her ear. She pushed her hair back and checked in the mirror to see if there was a rash. It looked fine. She glanced at her watch. It had been twenty-four hours now and there was no reaction, so she could safely put the dye on. Fiona had a couple of private students this afternoon, though, so wouldn't be back until five. Well, she didn't have to wait for Fiona, she could do it herself.

Ten minutes later the hair dye was smoothed all over her hair. Actually, it looked more of a deep purple than blonde but she tried not to panic, remembering the odd colour of Fiona's hair dye when she'd smoothed it on last night. She checked her watch. Ten more minutes to go. She'd make herself a cup of soothing camomile tea then it would be time to wash it off.

She sat down at the kitchen table to drink the tea, constantly glancing at the clock to check the time. Right, two minutes to go. She got up to go over to the sink when suddenly the kitchen was plunged into darkness. For a moment she stood there, stunned. Then she realised the bulb must have gone. Even though it was daytime it was crazily dark inside with the shutters closed. She grabbed her mobile off the table and switched on the torch then went over and opened the shutters, throwing daylight into the room. That was better. She'd see if she could find where Fiona and Pablo kept the replacement bulbs as soon as she'd washed this colour off her hair. She opened the blinds at the window by the sink to let in more light and turned on the water tap. It creaked and a few drops of water trickled out, then nothing. What had happened? Confused and a bit panicky, she turned the tap off then on again. Still no water. She hurried along to the bathroom and tried the tap there. No water.

Fiona said their water came from a well. Had it run dry?

Holly quickly messaged Fiona to tell her what had happened and ask what she should do. A couple of minutes later a reply zinged back:

We must have had a power cut, hun. Remember I told you it affects the water too. Hopefully it will be back on soon.

But I've got hair dye all over my hair and I'm supposed to wash it off NOW Holly typed back.

Her phone rang. It was Fiona. 'Oh no, hun. That's a bummer. You'll have to use bottled water. There's a couple of bottles in the kitchen, but I'm not sure there is enough to wash all the colour off.' She paused. 'Hang on, we've got some huge urns full of water in the outside shower room – you could use those to wash it off.'

'*Cold* water?' Holly shuddered at the thought.

'I know it's not ideal but you need to wash the colourant off; if you leave it on too long, your hair could turn out an odd colour. Or worse,' she pointed out. 'I'm really sorry, Holly, but I've got to go. I'm parked outside my next student's house and I don't want to keep them waiting.' Then she was gone.

There was nothing else for it then; she had to wash her hair with the urns of cold water. Holly went to the outside shower room at the back of the house and opened the door. Six massive containers of water stood in one corner – and they looked too heavy to pick up, never mind pour over her hair. She really regretted putting this dye on her hair now. She checked the time – it should have been washed off almost ten minutes ago. What if she had an allergic reaction and her face puffed up? Or the chemicals made her hair break off? She could go bald.

Calm down, Holly, she told herself, *you're overreacting.* She dragged one of the huge urns over to the sink. Damn, she'd forgotten to bring a towel. The hand towel hanging at the side of the sink would have to do. She couldn't wait any longer.

TRINNNG!

Damn. That was the bell at the gate. It must be the delivery men. What a time to call. She wrapped the towel around her head and went to the gate.

And there, standing outside, was Matias.

Great, that was all she needed when she had her hair wrapped up in a towel which was probably splattered in hair dye. What the hell did he want? Had Luna escaped again and he thought she was here?

'*Hola,*' she said cautiously.

'Do you have electricity?' Matias demanded. 'Mine is cut off.'

'No. Fiona thinks it's a power cut,' she replied, hoping he would hurry up and go. 'We have no water either,' she added.

'Me neither and I need some. I'm in the middle of mixing cement and it will go hard without water. Do you have any to spare?'

'We have some big storage bottles. You can have one if you want,' she replied, trying to ignore her itching head and the growing fear that the dye – which should have been washed off ages ago – was now causing a reaction. Her whole head was probably bright red.

'Yes, please. I will return it tomorrow.'

There was no way she could carry that huge urn of water over to the gate so she had to let him in. 'You'll have to fetch it, it's too heavy for me,' she said as she unlocked the gate.

He nodded and followed her to the shower room. She pointed to the big containers. 'Take your pick.'

He looked at the urn with the top off that was perched on the stool, then at the plug in the sink. 'You were about to use some?' His eyes drifted to the discoloured towel on her head then lingered on the blob of deep-purple dye on her forehead she'd just spotted in the cracked mirror. 'You are colouring your hair?'

'Yes, and the dye should have been washed off over ten minutes ago so I was going to use the water out of that container.'

He raised an eyebrow. 'You were going to keep refilling the sink with cold water?'

'Do you have any better ideas?'

'Yes, I do. Bend over the sink and I will pour water over your head.'

Holly stared at him. He was offering to wash her hair? She couldn't let him do that! He was right, though; she was going to struggle if she had to keep filling the sink with that bottle. And she'd already got the towel all messy.

'Really?' she asked.

'Yes, but be quick. I need to do my cement.' He picked up the bottle as if it contained a couple of litres instead of several gallons. 'Take the towel off your head and bend over the sink,' he said briskly.

Nice manners! She needed this dye off quickly so she unwrapped the towel, noticing his eyes widen as they flitted to her hair. 'It looks a funny colour until it's washed out,' she said defensively.

He nodded and she gritted her teeth as he poured a torrent of icy-cold water over her hair. She was shivering from the top of her head to the tips of her toes, and it was all she could do to stop herself from screaming

'There, it is all off. Do you have a gas hob?'

'Er… yes,' Holly replied, confused. Why did he want to know that?

'Then I suggest that you boil some water in a kettle on the stove so you can rinse your hair in warm water. You are shivering so much I'm afraid you might catch cold.'

Like I need to be told that! Holly thought as she squeezed the icy water out of her hair. All she wanted was to get into the kitchen, wrap a clean towel around her head and sit by the gas heater. She grabbed the not-too-clean hand towel and wrapped it around her head again, trying to stop her teeth from chattering as she mumbled her thanks.

'If I could just take one of the urns, I will refill and return it as soon as the water is back on.' He went to grab a bottle when a shout from outside made them both turn towards the open door.

'*¡Hola!*' It was a man's voice.

'Are you expecting someone?' Matias asked.

'A delivery,' Holly replied. *Honestly, could this day get any worse?*

'Do you want me to deal with it while you go and get yourself a dry towel?' he asked.

Yes!! Then Matias could deal with any awkward questions the man might have. 'Please. I'll be back in a few secs.'

She stepped outside and saw a delivery van parked in the drive, with a man standing by it. The man shouted something in very fast Spanish and Matias replied equally fast. Holly left him to it and ran over to the kitchen, anxious to warm some water to swill her hair. She found a clean towel and heated some of the bottled water in the kettle on the stove then poured it into the bowl in the sink. She sighed with relief as she leant over and rinsed her hair in the warm water. That felt wonderful.

'Sorry, I did knock but you didn't hear me. I've signed for the delivery and the driver has left it by the outside shower room. I hope that is okay,'

Matias's voice made her jump. She reached for the clean towel, wrapped it around her head and turned to face him, He was standing in the doorway, staring at her.

'Yes, that's fine. Thank you.'

'At least you have stopped shivering,' he remarked. 'I bet that is the first time you've had to wash the colour off your hair with cold water. This is life in rural Spain. The electricity is unreliable.'

'It's the first time I've ever coloured my hair, and I think it might be the last,' she said. She smiled at him. 'Thanks for your help.'

He paused, still staring at her hair, then shrugged. 'Your hair was pretty as it was, but I guess you wanted a change.'

He obviously didn't approve of her dying her hair blonde, probably thought it was a bit bimbo-ish. Well, it was none of his business.

'Yes, I did. Brown is boring,' she retorted defensively.

'Then I will get back to my concrete. I will return the water urn tomorrow. Thank you for it.'

'You're welcome,' she said. He nodded in acknowledgment and walked out.

Well, that was a turn-up for the books, she thought. Matias had actually been rather pleasant this time – but then he had come to borrow some water, so perhaps he thought he had better be.

She went into the bathroom to get the conditioner, unwrapped the towel from her head then gasped in horror at her reflection in the mirror. No wonder Matias had been staring at her hair. It wasn't blonde. It was orange.

Chapter Seventeen

'Where have you been? I woke up and you had gone. Then I went to have a shower and there is no water or electricity. And what are you doing?' Sofia demanded as she stood in the back doorway watching Matias pour water into the pile of cement in the wheelbarrow, a thick white towel wrapped around her body. 'I can't believe you are actually mixing cement,' she said, answering her own question. Then her eyes narrowed. 'What's that on your arm?' She stepped closer and scrutinised it. 'It looks like hair dye.'

'I need to cement in the fence post, Luna keeps getting out,' Matias told her. 'But the water went off when I was mixing so I went to borrow some from our neighbours. The Englishwoman was colouring her hair. I guess some of the hair dye must have rubbed onto my arm.'

Sofia looked suspicious. 'You would have to get very close for that to happen,' she said sharply. 'What exactly *were* you doing there?'

Matias shrugged. Sofia was getting too possessive; they weren't an item, as much as she wanted them to be. He'd been really clear and honest with her about wanting to keep things casual, and she'd agreed wholeheartedly. They just went out – and to bed – together now and again. He didn't ask her to account for what she did when she wasn't with him, and he didn't expect to have to answer to her either. 'The Englishwoman…' He really had to find out her name instead of referring to her as 'the Englishwoman' all the time. 'She was frantic, the dye should have been washed off her hair ages ago and she only had huge urns of cold water which she couldn't lift so I helped her.'

'You washed her hair for her?' Sofia repeated, in disbelief.

'It's no big deal. I helped her in return for one of the urns of water.' He continued mixing the cement.

'I don't think I like my boyfriend washing another woman's hair,' Sofia snapped.

His eyes rested on hers. Her face was contorted in anger and she was clutching the towel tightly around her.

'I am not your boyfriend, Sofia. We have agreed that this… this is just a casual thing. We are both free agents.'

'I was hoping we had become more than that. That you would come to your senses and return to Marbella, work with your father again,' Sofia retorted. 'You had a good career, a nice home, and you threw it away to live here.' She threw her arms wide to encompass the house and the towel dropped to the floor, leaving her standing there naked. She stepped forward, her eyes on his face. 'Matias, we are good together,' she said, her tone now soft, wheedling. 'Please come back to Marbella with me.'

This was what she had been hoping all along, Matias realised. Sofia, the daughter of a family friend, had hooked onto him a few months ago. She had been soft, supportive, hung on his every word. And at the time he'd been lonely, wanted someone by his side, someone who understood why he had walked away from his old life. He thought Sofia had understood, but no, she had wanted him for what he used to be, not what he was now. And all the time she had been pretending to be supportive she had been playing him, hoping she could talk him into going back to Marbella.

He stepped back. 'I will never go back to Marbella or be a lawyer again, Sofia.' Then, more kindly, he added, 'I think it is best if you and I finish. Then you can find someone who you really want to be with, who will give you the life you want.'

Sofia looked furious. 'You don't fool me, Matias! You are ditching me because you fancy that little Englishwoman! Well, you are a fool. She will return home soon enough, and then where will you be?'

'I am not ditching you, as you call it, but it is not working between us. You obviously want more out of this relationship than I can give you. I will call a taxi now and ask it to come in an hour. That should give you time to dress and pack your things.'

He turned and walked away over to the patio, leaning back against the outside wall while he calmed down. He was a fool to get involved with Sofia; he should have seen that she was playing the long game. As for her absurd claims that he fancied the Englishwoman next door… It was ridiculous. Yes, she was pretty, gorgeous actually, and feisty, and determined…

His mind cast back to her bright-orange hair. Had she meant it to be that colour, he wondered, or had the colour gone drastically wrong? He'd wanted to ask her but couldn't bring himself to, not wanting to see the smile disappear from her lovely face if it wasn't the colour she had wanted. Camila and her friends had often coloured their hair in dramatic colours when they were younger. How he remembered his father's face when Camila had walked in with deep-purple hair. She had looked odd but she had loved it. The Englishwoman would look beautiful with any colour hair, he thought – even orange.

'I've phoned for a taxi myself and it will be here in fifteen minutes,' Sofia shouted. 'Don't let me stop you from getting on with your cement-mixing.'

✳

'Actually, it looks quite cool,' Fiona said when she came home and saw how distressed Holly was. The electric had finally come back on and she'd washed her hair several times and only managed to tone the tangerine down a little. 'If you'd texted me, I could have bought another dye.'

Holly shook her head. 'I'm never dyeing my hair again.' She dreaded what colour it would turn out if she put another dye on it. Probably bright green knowing her luck! 'I'll just have to stay in the house until it fades.'

'My friend Claire will take a look at it for you. She's a mobile hairdresser. She trained and worked in one of the top salons in Manchester until she and her partner, Ash, moved over to Spain a few years ago. Want me to contact her?'

Holly considered this. It had taken her years to pluck up the courage to dye her hair and now it had all gone wrong. What if this Claire made even more of a mess of it? But then she couldn't leave it like this, could she?

She nodded. 'Yes please.'

After a long conversation with Claire, Fiona said that the hairdresser could get rid of the orange but Holly's hair would then be light brown and she'd have to rest it for two weeks to give it time for the hair's natural moisture to be restored before she could get it to blonde. All this only to return to the same mousy brown! 'Do you want to book an appointment with her?' Fiona asked. 'She can pop in on Saturday.'

It looked like she'd have to go around like this for at least a couple of days. She wouldn't be going anywhere, that's for certain. There's no way she wanted anyone to see her like this. Matias already had, she remembered. No wonder he'd been staring at her. 'I guess that's not long to wait. Thanks,' she said.

'Why don't you embrace the orange?' Fiona suggested. 'It's not too bad. And you carry it off well. Maybe you could go for an edgier cut. I'll do it for you if you like.'

Holly looked at her warily. 'You've got no hairdresser training,' she pointed out.

'I know but I always cut my own hair,' said Fiona. 'Look, what harm will it do? Claire will come along on Saturday and tidy it up if you don't like it, as well as turning you back to brown.'

Oh, what the hell. This new life is all about taking chances, isn't it? 'Go ahead – but I don't want it short, mind,' Holly warned her.

'I promise,' Fiona said, disappearing into the bathroom and coming back out a minute later with a pair of hair scissors.

Holly crossed her fingers as Fiona told her to sit on a stool then draped a tea towel around her shoulders and started to pin up sections of her hair. Suddenly she was filled with doubt. What if Fiona made it look even more of a mess?

Snip. Snip. Snip.

It was too late to change her mind now. She closed her eyes and prayed Fiona wouldn't get scissor-happy.

Fraught minutes crawled by. Finally, Fiona put down the scissors. 'There,' she said triumphantly. 'You look amazing. Hang on and I'll get you a mirror.'

As she disappeared into the bathroom, Holly looked down at the locks of orange hair over the floor and gulped. There seemed to be a lot of hair there.

Fiona returned with a large make-up mirror. 'Take a look,' she said.

Holly plucked up her courage and peered into the mirror. She hardly recognised herself. Fiona had layered her hair so it framed her face and fell in soft feathers around her shoulders. The new cut – and colour – defined her cheekbones somehow, and her eyes seemed brighter, rounder. It made her look – and feel – more outgoing, fun, livelier.

'Well?' Fiona asked.

She nodded slowly. 'I like it. Thank you. You've saved my life.' She paused. 'Do you mind cancelling Claire? I think I'll keep it like this for a bit.'

A huge smile spread across Fiona's face. 'Of course not. Embrace the orange, that's what I say. And when you get fed up of it, Claire will fix it for you.'

Holly wasn't sure that she wanted to stay like this forever, but right now, she did. She'd had the same hair and hairstyle for years. Scott had liked long hair and would have sulked at her new hairdo; he liked her to be feminine, wear a dress, have long hair, always wear make-up. Well, Scott had gone, and here was the new Holly. She briefly wondered what Matias would think, remembering how his eyes had widened with shock when she'd pulled the towel off her head. *Who cares what he thinks?* She was done with trying to please a man.

Matias came around to return the huge container of water the next morning, when Fiona was home. Holly was sitting by the pool as he walked down the path with Fiona, explaining in excellent English that her friend had lent it him.

'Yes, I heard all about the water disaster,' Fiona told him as she opened the shower room door so he could put the urn inside. 'Holly told me.'

'How is her hair?' he asked.

'It's fine, thank you,' Holly said, standing up and enjoying seeing the surprised expression on his face as his eyes rested on her new hairdo.

He looked a bit awkward then replied, 'That is good. I must get back to my work then,' and he was off.

'He's a bit of a hunk, isn't he?' Fiona asked as soon as Matias had disappeared from earshot.

'Shame he's such a grump,' Holly said, remembering the incident on the motorbike, and with Luna. Mind you, he had been helpful washing the colour off her hair, even if he had been a bit abrupt. 'Felipe said his name is Matias and he works in a gym in Málaga,' she added. 'Apparently he's doing up his aunt's house. She's moved to the coast and wants to sell up.'

'Really? An old lady used to live in the house when we first moved in. Matias only appeared a few weeks ago. I thought he must have bought it. He must commute to Málaga for work.'

'I guess it's easier for him to live here while he's doing it up. Kind of him, isn't it?' Holly said thoughtfully. *He must be really fond of his aunt to give up so much of his time.* Matias was a bit of a mystery, that was sure. Still, she had more important things to think about than their rather stroppy but dishy neighbour.

Chapter Eighteen

Holly had her first Spanish lesson with Felipe the next morning – another thing to tick off her dream list. She travelled down with Fiona as she ran English lessons in the same building, a former convent that had been taken over by the council. It was a really old building, a bit austere, but then Holly guessed nuns were supposed to make sacrifices and live in poverty, weren't they? She wondered what had happened to them when the convent was sold. Had they all been sent to live in other convents? The history behind old buildings had always fascinated her.

'See you lunchtime,' Fiona said as she opened her classroom door. Felipe's classroom was on the next floor, and Fiona had lessons all morning, so they had arranged to meet for a coffee in the café in the square at lunchtime. Holly was looking forward to having a walk around the village a bit after the Spanish lesson. She waved to Fiona then hurried up the stairs; she was a little late.

Felipe was writing something on the blackboard when she walked in. He turned around and smiled. 'Ah a new student. Take a seat, please.'

He didn't recognise her with this new hairdo. 'Hi, Felipe. It's Holly. Fiona's friend. I had a bit of a hair disaster yesterday,' she said cheerfully.

His face registered surprise then his eyes twinkled. 'So I see. But it isn't a disaster. It suits you. You look very pretty.'

His praise made her glow inside. The way he said it, and looked at her, made her feel that he meant it. *He's just being kind,* she told herself. *Besides, you're supposed to be off men. Nothing wrong with having a friend though,* she thought as she sat down.

'Trying to go blonde, were you?' the middle-aged woman next to her asked kindly. 'I tried that last year and my hair went green.'

'Oh no!' Holly replied sympathetically. 'Did it take long to get back to your normal colour?'

'A couple of weeks. Your hair looks fine though. Felipe is right, it suits you. You're young and pretty enough to carry it off.'

'Thank you,' she said, feeling pleased and slightly embarrassed by the compliment. The next hour and a half went quickly. Felipe was a good teacher, gearing the lesson around words and situations they might need in everyday life. The first half of the lesson involved naming certain items of food, and the second half was role-play, in which Felipe was the greengrocer and the students all had to be customers, buying at least three items each. It was fun and useful. Holly was surprised to discover that she recognised quite a few of the phrases, and even managed to ask for a few items in Spanish when it was her turn to be the customer.

'Very good, Holly. You can speak Spanish, I see.'

'*Un poco,*' she replied, flushing with pleasure at his praise.

Afterwards, the other students invited her to join them for a coffee in the square, practising their Spanish as they ordered *café con leche* (coffee with milk) – although when Holly saw that churros and chocolate were on the menu, she couldn't resist ordering some, pointing at the picture on the menu and saying, *Esto, por favor* (This, please), which made the others smile.

'This is delicious,' she said, dipping the sugary churros in the hot melted chocolate.

Felipe watched her with a grin on his face. 'I see you are a chocolate-lover, like me.'

'You bet, and I've been dying to try this.' Holly tucked into her treat with delight.

They all had a chat and a laugh, exchanging stories and experiences, then Fiona and her class came along and they ended up staying for lunch. It was gone four before Fiona and Holly set off home. As Fiona drove up the narrow mountain path, Holly thought how much her life had changed in a week. She had barely thought of Scott, and when she did it was with a quiet sadness, not with tears. She realised now that he wasn't the right one for her. She was so grateful to Pops for giving her the chance to make a new start and determined not to waste a moment of it.

The next morning, Fiona and Pablo left for work straight after breakfast and Holly felt a little restless. They'd offered to take her down to the village with them so she could have the walk around she'd intended yesterday, but she declined, not wanting to hang about until they'd both finished work. She had so much to do. She wanted to draw some new designs – a Spanish collection, vibrant and colourful, inspired by the flowers here rather than the delicate pastels she usually used. So she packed a bottle of water and a couple of biscuits along with a sketchbook and pencils into her small backpack then set off up the mountain.

It was a beautiful, crisp day. The end of March was still usually very cold and wet in the UK, but here it was bright and warm; she wasn't sure if she'd need a jacket, so she tied one around her waist just in case. She glanced to the left, over at Matias's house, as she closed the gates behind her but there was no sign of life. She guessed he was at work, at the gym in Málaga. She half-wished Luna had escaped again; it would be good to have the company of a dog on her walk. As soon as this year was over and she was settled somewhere, she was going to get a dog, she decided as she headed up the mountain, taking care to walk at the side of the track to avoid any vehicles coming down.

She paused for a moment to admire the view below and around her. Wildflowers were budding here and there, and green leaves covered the shrubby bushes. She bet it was beautiful here in the summer.

She carried on up the track and around the corner then stopped as she heard a dog barking. It sounded like Luna. It was! The little Shih Tzu suddenly bounded around the corner, tail wagging, barking happily. She came to a halt at Holly's feet, looking up expectantly.

'Hello, girl, what are you doing out here? Have you escaped from the garden again?' Holly asked, bending down to stroke the little dog. As she ran her hand gently over her head, Luna turned and nuzzled her nose into Holly's hand. She was such a gorgeous little dog.

Then Matias came running into view, looking sizzling in a black-and-red running vest that showed off his bulging muscles to perfection and black shorts with a red trim that revealed long, toned, suntanned legs. He'd obviously been out for an early-morning run. He really was a fitness fanatic. Wasn't working at a gym enough for him?

He came to a stop just in front of Holly, still jogging on the spot. His eyes rested on her hair… Was that actually a smile playing on his lips? 'Good cut, it suits you. So does the colour.'

'Thanks.' She didn't know what surprised her the most: the smile or the friendly words. Had he had a personality transplant? He looked so different when he smiled – friendly, approachable. Nice. She wondered what he'd be like when he let his hair down, chilled a little with a glass of wine maybe. If he did chill, that was. She tried not to look at that hot body under the tight vest and shorts and wonder what he was like in bed. She was off men. Totally.

'Are you staying here long?' he asked.

Gosh, he was actually striking up a conversation with her! 'For a few months. I'm helping Fiona and Pablo get the place ready for guests. They're running an artists' retreat in the summer.'

'Nice if you can take so much time off from work.'

Okay, he was back to being Mr Disapproving again. Holly immediately bristled. Who was he to judge her?

'Actually, I am still working. I'm a designer and I run my own business,' she replied loftily. 'Now, if you'll excuse me, I'm off for an inspirational walk. My next collection is based on the flowers and plants of Spain.' She stuck her nose in the air and walked past him. Who the hell did he think he was? He wasn't exactly Mr Dynamic Business Man, was he? Working in a gym and strutting around in his running shorts and vest as if he was some sort of famous athlete.

She was in such a bad mood she walked for longer than she had meant to, and when she finally stopped stomping and sat down for a rest and swig of water, she realised that she was about halfway up the mountain. The view was stupendous. As she looked down to the sweeping valley below, littered with trees, shrubs and colourful houses scattered here and there, she felt a wave of peace flood over her. What did it matter if Matias was off with her? If Scott hadn't loved her enough to marry her? If her hair was orange instead of blonde? She was here, in this beautiful place, making a fresh start. Pops had given her the gift of a new life and she wasn't going to waste it with negative thoughts. She was going to make the most of this year out, this chance to live without worrying about money, to be self-employed as she had always wanted to be.

She put her jacket over a patch of shrubby grass, took her sketchbook out of her bag then sat down and started to draw. A bougainvillea plant climbed over the page, purple flowers blooming out of the stalks; it would make a lovely design for a duvet cover. A cluster of oranges and lemons followed, and already she was imagining them made up into kitchen curtains, and the runner a lot of Spanish kitchens had under their worktops, like the gingham one in the studio apartment. Then a white hibiscus plant, an intricate pattern of blooms, stalks and leaves. She didn't know how long she sat there sketching, but when she'd finished she knew that these were going to be part of her new collection. She hugged her knees and looked around her, up at the trees growing up the side of the mountain and then down at the valley below. She'd only been here a short time but already she felt at home, as if this was where she was meant to be.

Later that evening, Susie video-called her on WhatsApp to ask how she was settling in. It was good to see her again, even if it was only on a phone screen. Holly had already had a quick chat with her mum the night before and let her know how she was settling in.

'Oh gosh – your hair!' Susie clasped her hand over her mouth, then moved it and nodded. 'Actually, it's good. I like it.'

'It was an accident. It was meant to be blonde but the electricity went off and we had no water,' Holly told her.

Susie's eyes widened again. 'Let's pour ourselves a glass of wine and then you can tell me all the goss,' she ordered.

So, Holly filled her best friend in on the exhausting journey and hor-rendous drive up the narrow mountain track, how gorgeous the house was, how happy Fiona and Pablo were, her hair disaster and learning Spanish.

'Wow! It sounds like you're really busy. No regrets, then?'

'None at all,' Holly said happily. 'Moving here was the best thing I could have done.'

'Well, I miss you, Hol, but I'm so glad you're happy. Besides, we can always have weekly catch-up chats like this,' Susie replied, leaning over so only her shoulder was visible then returning to the screen with a bowl of popcorn. 'And this way I get to keep the popcorn to myself!'

Holly laughed. She missed Susie. It was good to chat to her again.

'How many of your dream list things have you managed to cross off?' asked Susie.

Holly thought about it. 'Well, I'm living in another country and I'm going to start my own business. I'm learning Spanish too,' she added. 'So that'll be three.'

'And you're getting over your fear of heights cos you have to keep travelling up and down that mountain track, so that's four,' Susie reminded her. 'You should keep a memory book, take some photos and keep souvenirs of the things you do. A record of what you did with your grandad's money.'

'I will – when I get it, Mum said it should be through in another month or so,' Holly told her. 'Next time we go to the shops I'll buy a scrapbook.' She'd write her list in the front of the book and tick off the items as she did them. She wanted to make sure that by the end of the year she had achieved everything she wanted.

When she'd finished talking to Susie, Holly studied the list she'd put in the Notes app on her phone for easy reference. Her eyes rested on one item: 'ride on the back of a motorbike'. Her thoughts immediately went to Matias. She imaged sitting behind him on the back of his red-and-black motorbike, her arms wrapped around his waist, her head buried into his back as they sped along, the wind blowing in her hair.

She shook her head. That definitely wasn't going to happen. There was no way she was going for a ride on the back of Mr Grumpy's motorbike, even if he asked her to, which was about as likely as pigs flying – she'd seen how he rode, far too fast. Maybe Felipe had a motorbike. She was sure he'd be a careful driver. She'd sound Fiona out and find out.

Chapter Nineteen

'Felipe rides a motor scooter, like me,' Fiona replied when Holly asked her the next day. 'You can ride on the back of my scooter if you want.'

Holly screwed up her nose as she poured fresh orange juice into two glasses. 'It's not the same, is it? Motorbikes are edgy and exciting. Motor scooters are…'

'Boring and safer,' Fiona finished for her. 'I'm surprised you want to do something so dangerous, Holly. It's not like you.'

'That's what my dream list is all about: stretching the boundaries, doing things that I'd like to do but normally wouldn't. And I've always wanted to ride on the back of a motorbike.'

'Well, you'll either have to get friendly with Matias next door and talk him into giving you a ride or wait until you meet someone else with a motorbike.' Fiona picked up her glass of juice. 'Shall we take this outside?'

'Sure.' Holly picked up her glass, grabbed a packet of cookies and followed Fiona.

They both sat down on the bench by the pool. 'What else is on the list?' asked Fiona.

Holly opened the Notes app on her phone and read out the list: 'Visit an underground cave, go sailing on a yacht, get a pet, go snorkelling in the sea, learn to dance, get over my fear of heights, try fifty different flavours of ice cream and, finally, be who I want to be – that's a work in progress,' she added. 'It just means that I'm not to change myself for someone like I did for Scott.' Saying his name didn't hurt as much now, she realised, although now and again an image of his face flashed across her mind and she felt a pang in her heart for the good times they'd had together. If only they had lasted.

Fiona peered over and read the list again. 'Have you started trying out the ice creams yet?' she asked.

Holly shook her head. 'I'd forgotten that one.'

'Well, that's one you can start on.'

It made sense. Things like riding on the back of a motorbike, visiting a cave and swimming in the sea could wait until the weather was warmer. Do the easy ones first. She'd take a look at the ice-cream flavours tomorrow when she went to the village. She wanted to pick up the ingredients to cook a special meal for Fiona and Pablo, to thank them for putting her up.

'I'll cook supper tomorrow night,' she said. 'Pablo isn't working in the evening, is he?'

'No, and that's great. We look forward to it.' Fiona took another swig of her drink. 'How are you getting on with designs? Do you have anything to show me yet?'

'I've made a couple of sketches,' Holly told her. 'Hang on a sec and I'll get them.' She put her glass down and hurried down the steps to her apartment, picked up her sketchbook and returned with it. She flicked to the page where she'd drawn the bougainvillea and hibiscus. 'What do you think?'

'They're gorgeous. I can just imagine these on bedspreads and curtains. The rooms will look fantastic.' She wrapped her arms around

Holly in a big hug. 'I'm so pleased you came to help us. I don't know how we'd manage without you.'

'I told you I'm glad to help. I'm so grateful for you putting me up and giving me time to sort my life out.' She closed the sketchbook. 'Now, come on, let's get cracking on those rooms. We want to make this place look wonderful for your guests.'

✳

'You're doing well, Richie, really well,' Matias said, patting the young man on the shoulder.

'Thanks to you, mate.' Richie looked up at Matias, his eyes full of emotion. 'I felt hopeless until I met you. Felt like my life was finished, that I'd never be able to do anything.' He swallowed. 'You've made me feel that I'm still worthwhile. That I have a life worth living.'

Matias felt a lump form in his throat as he remembered how depressed Richie had been when he'd first come to the gym. It was as if he'd given up on life – becoming paralysed from the waist down in a work accident had hit him hard. Now he was training regularly and had developed a keen interest in wheelchair basketball.

'I'm glad I could help you, but you did all the hard work, Richie. You're the one who's changed your life around. I'm proud of you.' Matias placed his hand on the younger man's shoulder and squeezed it affectionately. 'See you Friday. And remember, keep doing those exercises.'

'I will.' Richie nodded. '¡Adiós!'

Matias watched as Richie took the brakes off his wheelchair and headed for the doors.

He thought back to his own accident, five years ago. The one that no one thought he would come back from and for a long time had left him in a wheelchair. He couldn't remember much about the accident itself, only a car speeding around the corner on the wrong side of the road, brakes screeching, a big bang, then falling, the bike crashing on top of him, pinning him down…

It had been a long, painful fight back to health and had taken all his courage to get back on his motorbike again. His experience had left him determined to help others in the same situation, so when his compensation money had come through, he had put it into this gym. He provided equipment that could be easily accessed by customers of all abilities, and ensured that he and another member of staff were trained fitness instructors for people with disabilities.

His father and mother looked on it as his 'pet project', a sort of hobby; they didn't understand what this gym meant to him, how important it was to him to give these people hope, goals to achieve, to make them feel better about themselves. He had been there once, crippled, helpless, a life of despair ahead of him. Only luck, enough money to pay for the best medical care and sheer determination had pulled him out of it. Not everyone had the chances he had. For others, all the money and determination in the world wouldn't make them walk again, but he could give them their pride back, show them that their life was still worth living. And the look on a client's face when they finally achieved – or even surpassed – their fitness goal was worth more than winning any court case. He wasn't saying that what his father did wasn't worthwhile: people needed lawyers and his father was a good, fair one. But Matias had been to hell and back and it had changed his outlook on life. He couldn't help that. He just wished his father would understand.

He'd had a message from his mother again this morning:

Please come to lunch on Sunday. Camila and Salvador will be there too. Let us remain a family even if we differ on things.

He would like to go for his mother's sake but he couldn't. He knew that if he was in the same room as Camila, Salvador and his father, he wouldn't be able to keep hold of his tongue and he didn't want any more upset. He texted back to say he was sorry, he was busy but would visit soon.

※

Holly had spent the evening looking through Spanish cookbooks, trying to decide what dish to make. She wanted something easy but traditional.

'Why don't you do a paella?' Fiona suggested. 'That's a traditional dish and you can get all the ingredients from the supermarket in the village.'

Holly read the recipe. It looked simple enough. 'That sounds a good idea,' she said. 'And I'll make some sangria to go with it.'

'*Muy bien*. I look forward to that,' Pablo told her. 'Paella is one of my favourite dishes. Perhaps we could invite Felipe too? Make an evening of it?'

'That'll be great.' She liked Felipe, although it put more pressure on her to get the paella right. *You can do it, just follow the recipe,* she told herself. *And if it goes wrong, laugh!*

She plucked up the courage to drive down the track herself the next morning, got the shopping and drove back up again, feeling very proud of herself. Yes, she was still nervous, but she had learnt to look in front of her, not down, and to take it slowly when she got to the bends.

She'd decided to cook a simple three-course meal, so she prepared a starter and dessert too. For the starter she was doing *gambas pil pil* – prawns with garlic and chilli; she'd checked with Fiona that everyone liked seafood – and Spanish lemon cake for dessert. It looked simple enough: lemon yoghurt, sugar, flour, eggs, baking powder and olive oil all mixed together and baked. Nanna had taught her to cook as a child and she'd always enjoyed it. She was sure she could handle this.

When Pablo and Fiona came home, bringing Felipe with them, the chicken and seafood paella was cooking away nicely on top of the stove, the lemon cake was in the oven, all the ingredients were ready for the *gambas pil pil* – she had cooked the prawns earlier to make it easier – and she had made a jug of sangria and put it in the fridge to cool down.

'Something smells nice,' Felipe said, kissing Holly on both cheeks. 'Thank you for inviting me to join you.'

'It's only paella,' she told him. 'And I warn you, I've never made it before so you are all my guinea pigs.'

Felipe clutched his stomach with his hands. 'No one warned me,' he groaned and Holly playfully hit him with the tea towel.

'Let me serve up the sangria while you cook the *gambas*,' Fiona offered, taking the jug of fruity liquid out of the fridge and over to the table, which Holly had laid earlier. 'Sit down, guys.'

'Do you have Coke or *cerveza sin alcohol*?' Felipe asked. 'That sangria looks *deliciosa*, but I have to ride down that track later.' He'd come on his motor scooter.

'I'll give you some to take back home with you so you can have a nightcap,' Holly told him.

It was a fun evening, and no one minded that the rice was still a little hard and the lemon cake a little wet in the middle. They all toasted Holly on her success and Felipe said that they must come around to his one night for a meal too.

'You like cooking?' Holly asked.

'It will be a barbecue, but that is fun, *sí?*' Felipe said with a smile.

'That sounds great,' Holly agreed.

It was almost midnight when Felipe finally left. They had sat outside after the meal, drinking sangria – Coke for Felipe – and chatting in a mixture of Spanish and English. It was the best evening Holly had spent for ages.

As Felipe mounted his scooter, Holly suddenly remembered that she'd promised him some sangria to take home. 'Hang on!' she shouted and raced back to the kitchen. She grabbed an empty jam jar off the shelf – Fiona collected them to put marmalade in, although she hadn't yet had time to make any – poured some sangria in it, making sure there were some bits of fruit too, and screwed the top on tight. Then wrapped it in a tea towel.

Felipe was waiting by the open gate, legs astride his scooter.

'Your sangria,' she said, placing it carefully in the top box. 'Enjoy it when you get home.'

'*Gracias*, Holly.' He leant over and kissed her on the cheek. '*Luego,*' he called and set off.

✳

Matias stepped back into the shadows as Felipe leant over and kissed Holly. So, they were together now. It hadn't taken Felipe long to make his move. He shrugged. What did it matter to him?

He waited until Felipe had disappeared down the mountain track and Holly had closed the gate before he continued on his jog up the mountain. Tonight he had found it difficult to sleep – again – and hoped some fresh air and exercise might help.

It did. He was weary when he finally crawled into his bed an hour later, and as he closed his eyes his last thoughts weren't the usual disturbing memories, but an image of Holly, smiling, the moon shining behind her as she stood at the gate, waving goodbye to Felipe.

Chapter Twenty

May

The next few weeks raced by and May was here before they knew it. Fiona, Pablo and Holly had worked hard getting Las Mariposas ready for their first guests at the beginning of July. All the walls had now been whitewashed, and between the three of them, they had re-varnished most of the dark furniture and it now looked shiny and bright. Holly had sanded down some less salvageable pieces of furniture and repainted them in pastel colours then decorated them with stencils. She'd also spruced up her apartment, painting a couple of crates white and placing one on top of the other, then slipping them under the kitchen worktop as makeshift cupboards. Fiona had taken her to the local market one weekend and Holly had bought some brightly coloured cups, plates and saucers and a couple of jugs. As soon as the material she'd designed arrived, she intended to make new curtains for the windows and replace the tatty gingham one under the worktop. She sent regular updates, with photos, to both her mum and Susie about how she was getting on, what they were doing to the *finca* and the designs she created. They were both full of praise. 'Pops would be proud of you, Holly,' Mum had said. Holly hoped so.

Felipe had even dropped by to help one afternoon, mending broken hinges and door handles before going back down to the village with

Pablo when it was time for him to return to work in the bar. Felipe had asked Fiona and Holly to join them for a drink but they were too busy painting to want to bother getting washed and changed. 'Another day,' Holly told him and he'd smiled. He kissed Fiona first then Holly on both cheeks, his lips lingering a little longer on Holly's than they had on Fiona's.

'I think he fancies you,' Fiona said, teasing.

'Don't be daft, we're just friends. Anyway, I told you, I'm off men. This year is a man-free zone!' she replied. She liked Felipe but he didn't make her heart quicken like Scott had done.

And like Matias does.

She brushed the thought from her mind. She hadn't even spoken to Matias since the day after the Great Hair Disaster. Occasionally she heard his motorbike race by or caught a glimpse of him when they were sitting around talking at the bar, waiting for Pablo, but that was it. She hadn't seen Luna either; she guessed Matias had secured the fence now. She missed the little dog. She didn't miss Matias though. Her life was good as it was. She didn't need complications.

When the orange dye on Holly's hair had started to fade, Claire had coloured it again for her, a darker brown than her natural colour, and she loved it. Now that she was a brunette, and had a light suntan, she looked so different – and felt it too. Every day was busy; there were times when she thought of the old folks in Sunshine Lodge with a bit of a pang, but she was far happier than she'd ever been.

The weather was warm enough to use the pool now, and that was most afternoons. Holly's Spanish vocabulary had improved – thanks to the lessons with Felipe – to the extent that she could actually order a meal and ask for what she wanted in the shops, although sometimes all she could manage was, '*Quiero esto, por favor,*' then point to the item she wanted. And now the weather was warmer she was working her way through the variety of ice creams the local *heladerías* offered. Her current favourite was cookies and cream but salted caramel truffle came a close second. So, that was another thing she was working on from her dream list. She'd made no progress with the others yet. *It's only been two months, there's plenty of time,* she told herself.

Besides, the big thing she wanted to concentrate on was her design business, especially now Pops's inheritance had come through. Fiona and Pablo had chosen the designs they wanted for the rooms and they'd been pleased with the samples; the fabric was on order and she couldn't wait to see it. At last, she got the phone call to say that her material had been delivered to the post box address they used.

'I'll go and pick them up right now,' Holly told Fiona. 'Do you want to come with me or are you busy?'

'I'd love to come, but let's take the van. The fabric rolls might be too big for your Mini,' Fiona replied.

She was right, the rolls were too long for the Mini; it was a tight squeeze to get them in the back of the van. They were both really excited as they carried the fabric into Holly's apartment, unwrapped the first one and rolled it out onto the kitchen table. Holly gazed in awe as the fabric unfurled in front of her: purple bougainvillea and pale-green leaves on a duck-egg-blue background. It was the first time she'd ever seen one of her designs on material. It was overwhelming.

'That's totally gorgeous!' Fiona said. 'You're so talented, Holly.'

Holly gazed at the material, too choked-up to speak. She was so pleased with the way it had all turned out. She'd been worried: having a design printed on a roll of fabric was a lot different to having it printed on a mug or a cushion. She'd taken a chance but it had worked out, thank goodness.

'Hang on, let me take a photo. This is a special moment.' Fiona took her mobile out of her pocket and selected the camera. 'Hold up one end of the material and smile,' she said.

She took three photos, just to make sure, and immediately sent them all to Holly.

'You can put them in your memory book,' she said. She held out a length of the fabric. 'I can't wait to see this made up, it's going to look amazing.' She gave Holly a quick hug. 'It's so good of you to do this for us. We can't thank you enough.'

'It's a pleasure. You've given me a lovely apartment here in Spain in return, helped me make a fresh start. I couldn't have done it without you and Pablo. Besides, it was your suggestion to do this.'

Fiona smiled. 'Go on then, open the other rolls.'

Holly opened the rolls one by one, and Fiona snapped away as Holly held out the end of the roll to show the pattern on the material.

'I tell you, people are going to be falling over themselves to have you make them stuff – or even to buy the material themselves so they can make what they want from it. This is going to be really popular.'

'I hope so.' The one thing out of her whole dream list that she really wanted to come true was this, to have her own business. It meant so much to her and she was sure Pops would be pleased too. He and Nanna had been so proud of Holly's designs and had bought several of her cups and other items themselves.

When Pablo came home after his morning shift, he brought Felipe with him, and they both admired the material too.

'These are wonderful. I didn't realise you were such a good artist,' Felipe said. 'Are you going to sell this material? It will be very popular.'

'Thank you.' Holly was beginning to feel a bit embarrassed with all the compliments now. Although her family had always praised her designs, Scott had dismissed it as her 'hobby' and had never taken much interest.

They sat talking outside, drinking sangria – even Felipe as Fiona and Pablo had persuaded him to stay the night – and talking about their plans for the summer.

'Maybe one evening you will come out with me for a meal, Holly,' Felipe said.

Was he asking her for a date? Holly hesitated before replying. 'Why don't we all go out for a meal together to celebrate once the rooms are finished?'

She felt a bit bad when she saw the disappointed look cross Felipe's face, but she knew it was best to nip this in the bud. Felipe was a friend, nothing else.

'That sounds fun!' Fiona held up her glass. 'To Las Mariposas – and Holly's fabulous designs!'

They all raised their glasses and joined in the toast.

Chapter Twenty-One

Holly looked around the room with a mixture of pride and relief. She'd spent the last couple of days making cushions for the old pale-blue two-seater sofa out of the purple bougainvillea material, and matching bedspreads for the twin beds. She was chuffed with the results: bright and breezy, the soft furnishings had brought a touch of summer to the room. Although the dark wooden furniture had been sanded and polished and the walls whitewashed, it had needed something to give it a lift and the soft furnishings had done just that. She couldn't wait to see Fiona's and Pablo's faces when they came home from work. Right now, though, she fancied a dip in the pool. It was hot today, and she'd spent the last few hours bent over a sewing machine.

She changed into her bikini, grabbing a towel and a kaftan to cover up just in case Fiona or Pablo brought any of their friends home with them, and made her way over to the pool. Leaving the towel and kaftan, along with her phone, on the nearest sunbed, she dived in. The water was so refreshing and cool. She swam a couple of lengths then floated lazily on her back. This was definitely the life. She could stay here all day.

'*Woof! Woof!*'

That sounded like Luna. She hadn't seen the little dog for ages – Matias had obviously fixed the hole in the fence – but she recognised the bark. Had Luna got out again? Holly got out of the pool, slipped on the kaftan and flip-flops, grabbed her phone and walked over to the gate. There was no sign of Luna but Holly could definitely hear her.

Holly hesitated. What should she do? She opened the gate – they no longer locked it if one of them was at home – and stepped outside.

'*Woof! Woof! Woof!*' The barking became more insistent. In fact, it sounded almost desperate. What if the little dog was hurt? Matias could have gone out and left her in the grounds and she'd got stuck somewhere. Holly walked along the path to Matias's house. The gates were closed and Luna was at them, barking agitatedly.

She didn't look hurt but she definitely looked distressed. Maybe something had spooked her or she didn't like being left on her own. Holly peered through the gates. There was no sign of Matias; he must be at the gym.

'What's the matter, *chica*?' she asked, using the Spanish term for 'girl'. 'Are you lonely?' She put her hand through the bars and stroked the little dog's head. Luna immediately barked again then turned, walked away a little bit, turned back and barked again. *She wants me to follow her,* Holly realised. *Why? What's happened?*

She could see that the gate was unlocked. Should she go in? If Matias came home and found her in the grounds of his house, he wouldn't be very pleased.

Luna was standing at the corner of the house now, whining and yapping. She disappeared around the corner then came back again. '*Woof! Woof!*' she barked, looking directly at Holly.

She's definitely trying to tell me something, Holly realised. She made a split-second decision and slid the bar back on the gate to open it. Luna wagged her tail and disappeared around the corner again. Holly followed as fast as her flip-flops would allow her. She turned the corner to the side of the house then froze when she saw a figure sprawled out on the ground, a ladder and an upturned tin of paint. Matias. By the look of it, he'd fallen off the ladder and was out cold. Luna lay down beside him, resting her head on her paws.

A few quick steps and Holly was kneeling down beside him, on autopilot, feeling for a pulse, calling his name, as they'd been taught in their first-aid lessons at Sunshine Lodge. 'Matias! It's Holly. Can you hear me? Give me some sign if you can. Move your hand, wiggle your finger, anything.'

Matias lay perfectly still with his eyes closed.

Holly took a deep breath, fighting down the panic that was threatening to overwhelm her. His pulse felt strong and he was lying on his side, so at least he hadn't landed on his neck or his spine. But he was unconscious and could have a concussion. She looked up at the wall he had obviously been painting, a splash of white paint coming to a sudden halt near the top of it. It was quite a height to have fallen from. He could have broken all of the bones in his body. She shuddered. *Keep calm,* she reminded herself. He was breathing steadily, had a pulse and was practically in the recovery position, which was good as she was scared to move him in case he'd broken his neck or spine.

Don't think like that. He will be okay. He has to be.

'Matias! Mati!' She called his name a few times more but he didn't stir. She had to get him medical help and quickly. She grabbed her phone and, her fingers trembling, she keyed in 112 – the Spanish emergency number – praying one of the operators spoke English.

They did. After taking a few details, the operator warned her not to move Matias, to monitor his pulse and breathing, and to keep talking to him; he assured her that an ambulance was on its way.

Holly quickly texted Fiona to tell her what had happened then knelt beside Matias and kept talking to him, checking that he was breathing normally and had a pulse. Luna lay by his side, whimpering.

'He'll be okay, Luna,' she reassured the little Shih Tzu. At least she hoped he would. He looked deathly pale and still showed no sign of coming around. What if he had fallen on his back first then rolled onto his side? He could have hit his skull, broken his spine. Holly felt so helpless as she sat there, talking to him, knowing that his life could be in her hands but not knowing what more she could do apart from hold his hand and reassure him that help was on the way, just in case he could hear her.

It was twenty long minutes before the ambulance arrived.

The medics were marvellous, and Matias was on a stretcher and in the ambulance in no time. 'Is there anyone I should contact?' the female medic asked in heavily accented English.

'I have no idea. I hardly know him,' Holly replied, wishing that Fiona would hurry up and come home. Just as the ambulance doors were about to close, she saw her friend running through the open gates and down the drive.

'Holly? Is he okay?'

'I don't know.' She was shaking and felt ridiculously tearful. 'Do you think I should go with him? It seems wrong to send him on his own.'

'Yes, you go – you found him and the medics might want to ask you some questions. I'll look after the dog and contact Felipe to see if he knows anything about Matias's family.' Fiona grabbed Luna's collar. 'Let me know when you're ready to come home and I'll pick you up.' Then she noticed Holly's kaftan. 'I bet you haven't got any money on you, have you? You might want a drink or something at the hospital.' She opened her purse and took out a twenty-euro note. 'Here, this should tide you over.'

'Thanks.' Holly climbed into the back of the ambulance and sat by the still-unconscious Matias, now hooked onto a machine. Would he be okay? Did he have any family nearby? A girlfriend, ex-wife, a child? She realised that she knew nothing at all about him.

She had been sitting in the hospital waiting room for hours now. Matias had been immediately taken away to be seen to by doctors and Holly had been left sitting outside, praying he would be okay. Fiona had messaged a couple of times, once to say that she'd asked Felipe but he knew nothing about Matias's family apart from the fact that he thought they lived in Marbella, and had no idea how to contact them. Felipe didn't know the name of the gym Matias worked at or his aunt's new address either. So they still had no idea who to contact. It seemed to be taking a long time to treat him too and Holly was seriously worried, knowing that the longer Matias was unconscious, the more chance there was of complications. He could be brain-damaged. She couldn't bear the thought of Matias, so virile and active, not being able to walk, move, speak.

Finally a nurse came out and told her that Matias had regained consciousness, the scan had showed no signs of brain injury and Holly could go and see him. She was so relieved she almost burst into tears. 'Your girlfriend is here, Matias,' the nurse announced as Holly followed her into the small room, not sure what to expect.

Girlfriend? She guessed it was only natural for her to jump to that conclusion as Holly had come in with Matias and had been sitting outside all afternoon. Holly was relieved to find Matias sitting up in bed, looking tired but unhurt apart from his right wrist, which was bandaged up.

Chapter Twenty-Two

Matias opened his eyes wearily and looked over as the door opened. Girlfriend? Who was she talking about? Was it Sofia? Had they found her number in his phone and contacted her? He hoped not; she was the last person he wanted to see. He was astonished when Holly walked in. *¡Qué diablos!*

'Holly?' He stared at her in surprise.

'I found you,' she explained. 'I was in the pool and I heard Luna barking like crazy. So I went to see what was wrong with her.'

In the pool? So that's why she was wearing that flimsy kaftan. And standing by the window like that, the light revealed an enticing silhouette of her gorgeous bikini-clad body underneath. He must be okay if he could still notice things like that, he thought wryly. Although some would say he could be half-dead and still notice a beautiful girl. And there was no doubt about it, Holly was beautiful.

'You were unconscious for ages. Are you okay?' She sat down on the chair beside him, her eyes full of concern. 'I wasn't sure what to do. I mean, I've had basic first aid training but…'

'Whatever you did, it was exactly right because here I am with nothing but a headache and a sprained wrist,' he told her. 'It could have all been a lot worse if you hadn't found me and called for an ambulance. *Gracias.*'

Deep-blue eyes, one bluer than the other, gazed at him. 'Ouch!' She winced in sympathy. 'How long will it take to heal?'

'A couple of weeks. It is only a moderate sprain but he must rest it and take things easy for a while. He has had a nasty blow to his head and must stay here for tonight,' the nurse said in perfect English. 'I'll leave you to talk for a few minutes.'

'Don't look so worried – luckily I'm left-handed,' Matias said as soon as the nurse clicked the door shut behind her.

He could see the concern on her face as she looked at the bandage around his wrist and lower arm. 'How will you manage? What about your work in the gym? Is there anything I can do to help?'

'The gym is a problem but I'll find a way around it. I've had worse things happen.' There was something he wanted her to do for him, but how to ask her? He considered his words carefully. 'There is one thing you can do to help. I hate to ask but it is only a formality so I can get out of here and go home.'

Now she looked serious. 'Go ahead,' she encouraged him.

'The doctor doesn't want to discharge me as I live alone, and with a concussion there can be complications for a few days. They say I need someone to stay with me for forty-eight hours,' he explained. 'They already think you're my girlfriend so I wondered if we could pretend that you are and that we live together. Then they'll let me go home.'

'Is that a good idea?' she replied, nervously.

'Sorry, I don't mean to put you in an awkward position but I don't want to be in hospital any longer than I have to. Obviously, I'm not asking you to actually stay with me,' he added, in case that was what she was thinking. 'I am quite capable of looking after myself. I just want you to pretend, to back me up to the doctor.'

'Lie for you, you mean.' Holly hesitated. 'And if you do have complications, what then? Then I get the blame for pretending I was looking after you.'

He felt his face flush. Lying was a bit of a strong term for a little favour like this. 'It is only a small thing to ask.'

'It's a big thing,' she corrected him. 'And I think you should remain here until the doctor says you are fit enough go home.'

Now she was irritating him. All he wanted to do was get out of here; why couldn't she understand that? 'If you don't agree I will discharge myself anyway, but I would rather go with the doctor's blessing. It will make things easier if I need more treatment,' he said firmly.

She seemed to be considering this. She nodded. 'Yes, I reckon you are stubborn enough to do just that. I will agree on one condition.'

Matias raised an eyebrow questioningly.

'That I check in on you a few times a day and you promise to message me instantly, day or night, if you feel unwell at all. Deal?' She met his gaze full on.

¡Dios! A woman fussing over him was the last thing he needed or wanted. 'There is absolutely no need—'

'That's the deal. Take it or leave it.'

He guessed he had no choice but to agree. Once he got home he could make it clear to her that he didn't want her calling around and checking on him. '*Vale*, but for forty-eight hours only.'

At that moment the door opened and a doctor walked in. 'Ah, I see your girlfriend is here.' He held out his hand and Holly stood up to shake it. 'Matias has been lucky and there seems to be no sign of brain damage but we need to keep him overnight just to make sure. You would think he would be more careful after his other accident. It's a miracle he walked again then.'

*

The doctor's words left Holly reeling. What did he mean, it was a miracle Matias had walked again? What had happened? No wonder the doctor was reluctant to let him go home unless he had someone to look after him.

'Accident?' she repeated sharply. 'Matias hasn't told me much about that.'

'Really? Well, I think you should, Matias.' The doctor walked over to the end of the bed and looked at Matias's chart. 'Holly needs to be aware of possible complications. She must keep a close eye on you for a few days when you go home. We'll keep you here tonight as a *precaución*.' He put the chart back, nodded to them both and walked out.

Holly rounded on Matias as soon as the door closed. 'What did he mean?' she demanded. 'It was a miracle you walked again?'

He shrugged dismissively. 'I had an accident some years ago, but as you can see I am fine now.'

If something happened to him, it would be her responsibility: she was lying and saying she lived with him, fooling them into believing he had someone to look after him. 'Look, I'm worried about this…'

He reached out and touched her hand, the contact sending a tingle right up her arm. 'Please say you'll help me, Holly. I really don't want to stay in here any longer than I have to. You can come and check on me as often as you like.'

He looked tired, which was no wonder, and desperate. She could understand why: she hated hospitals herself.

'Okay,' she agreed.

Her phone zinged. It was a message from Fiona.

How's the patient, hun? Do you need a lift home?

She read it and glanced at Matias. *Should I leave him to rest?*

'Is that from your friends?' he asked. 'Please don't think you have to stay any longer. You have done enough and I could do with some sleep. I will see you tomorrow, *sí?*'

She stood up. '*Sí.* I will be back tomorrow.'

The nurse came back in then. 'It is time to take your blood pressure, Matias.'

'I will leave you to it. I'm going home now.' Better make it look like she really was his girlfriend. She leant over and brushed her lips against his. 'Take care, Mati. See you tomorrow.'

She saw his eyes widen, as if the touch of her lips on his had the same effect on him as it had on her. *'Adiós, querida,'* he whispered.

Goodbye, darling. The words were like a caress but she knew that, like her kiss, they were only because the nurse was watching.

Chapter Twenty-Three

Fiona picked Holly up from the hospital, and Holly filled her in about Matias's injuries, and his plan, on the way home.

'I don't think you should agree to this arrangement, Holly. What if something happens to Matias? There can be side effects from a concussion for a few weeks afterwards. He could become unconscious again, fall and have a bad injury,' Fiona pointed out.

'I know, I'm not happy about it but he's desperate to come home and said he'll discharge himself anyway.' She really didn't know what to do. 'Perhaps he's worried about Luna. I'll go to see him again tomorrow and offer to look after her, put his mind at ease. And I'll tell him he'll have to stay in hospital until the doctors say he is fit enough to leave.'

Holly's job as a care assistant had taught her how important aftercare was and there was no way she was going to agree to anything that could jeopardise Matias's health.

When she arrived at the hospital the next morning Matias was up, dressed and sitting on the side of his bed. A different doctor was reading through his notes and turned as Holly walked in. 'Ah, is this your girlfriend?'

'Yes, this is, Holly.' Matias beamed at her. 'I was just telling the doctor, Holly, how you were taking a couple of days off work to look after me.' He stood up, wrapped his undamaged arm around her, pulled her to him and kissed her full on the lips. Wow, she hadn't been expecting that! Nor had she expected it to feel so good to be this close to him, to have his arm around her, to feel his lips on hers. It was a proper kiss, not a peck like she'd given him yesterday, and she felt almost giddy, which was ridiculous. He was just acting a part, going along with the pretence that Holly was his girlfriend, and she had started the kissing business yesterday. And look at her now, eagerly kissing him back. It was as if she couldn't help herself. His eyes darkened as if he wanted more too and she quickly stepped back. After that display of affection, she couldn't blurt out that Matias was lying and she wasn't even his girlfriend, never mind not living with him, could she? *I bet that's why he did it.*

'I've been thinking, Matias, if the doctor feels you need to stay in here a bit longer, to make sure everything is fine, then we should listen to him.'

'But he doesn't.' Matias spoke to the doctor in Spanish, and the doctor quickly replied. Holly felt frustrated as she listened to them, wishing she knew the language better. She'd improved since she'd started taking lessons with Felipe, but not enough to understand conversations, especially when they spoke so quickly.

Finally they finished talking and the doctor handed her a leaflet. 'Please call for an ambulance for Matias in any of these circumstances.' He pointed to a list, which was fortunately written in both Spanish and English. 'Or make sure Matias sees the doctor if he is still feeling unwell.'

What could she do now? There was only one thing she could think of: persuade Matias to come and stay with them at Las Mariposas for a couple of days. She was sure Fiona and Pablo wouldn't mind; they had plenty of rooms.

'This is very kind of you,' Matias said as they walked down the corridor and out of the hospital.

'I don't feel that I had much choice and I don't like it. I hate lying,' Holly told him. 'The doctors seem to be really worried, especially as you had such a bad accident a few years ago.'

His face clamped in an 'I don't intend to talk about it' manner.

'Why don't you come and stay with us at Las Mariposas for a while? Fiona and Pablo won't mind.'

'I don't need anyone to look after me. I am not an invalid,' he said curtly.

'Look, this could be serious. If you lose consciousness…'

He sighed, swept his left hand through his hair and took a breath, as if to compose himself. 'I am very grateful to you, Holly, for finding me, calling the ambulance and taking me home today. But I am not stupid. I will not take any risks. And I have already promised you that I will message you if I am feeling ill, so can we please drop this?'

Honestly, he was infuriating, but what else could she do?

'Okay, well let me put my number in your phone then,' she said.

He looked as if he was going to protest but then took out his phone, silently handing it to her. She keyed in her name and number. 'Make sure you message or phone me every night before you go to bed and every morning as soon as you wake or I *will* be moving in and looking after you,' she told him.

He sighed. '*Vale.*'

They had reached Holly's yellow Mini now. Matias opened the passenger door before Holly could do it for him and slid into the seat. She closed the door and went over to the other side.

They drove home in silence. Holly was so aware of his body next to hers, of her hand grazing his knee as she changed gear, of the smallness of the car and the searing memory of *that kiss*, that she couldn't wait to arrive at Matias's home and drop him off.

'Thank you again,' Matias said as he got out of the car. 'I will be fine now.'

As much as she wanted to drive away and leave him to it, she knew she shouldn't without making sure he was okay.

'I think I'd better come in with you and check you have enough food to last you a few days because you won't be able to go out on your bike until your wrist has healed, and that Luna has food and clean water, and then I'll go home,' she said firmly.

'There is absolutely no need…'

She stood up to her full height, which meant she just about reached his nose. 'Look, I don't want to do this any more than you want me to, but you are not killing or injuring yourself on my watch. I used to be a care assistant. I've spent my working life looking after people so I'm sure I can look after you for a couple of days until you feel stronger and we're certain there's no sign of any adverse effects from the concussion.'

He nodded, sweeping his hand across his forehead, suddenly looking very tired.

Holly had messaged Fiona, who'd been looking after Luna, that they were on their way home, and she came out with the little dog. Luna immediately barked joyfully and hurtled over to Matias, who slowly bent down and stroked her. '*Hola, chica,*' he murmured softly to her then stood up. 'Thank you for looking after Luna,' he said to Fiona.

'*De nada,*' she told him, which Holly knew meant 'you're welcome'. 'How are you feeling?'

'A little tired,' he admitted.

Holly told Fiona, 'I'm going to make a cuppa and make sure Matias and Luna are settled okay, then I'll be back. I'll only be half an hour or so.'

'Sure. Give me a shout if you need anything,' Fiona said.

Once inside, Matias sank wearily onto an armchair in the lounge, Luna nestled by his feet.

'Rest for a moment and I'll make a cuppa,' she told him. 'I presume you want coffee?'

'*Sí, gracias*. Black with one sugar,' he said, his eyes closed.

She soon found her way around the kitchen and made two cups of coffee, but when she took them in Matias was snoring softly. She studied him for a moment. He looked so vulnerable and pale. He had obviously had a bad blow to his head. She wondered again what the accident was that had almost crippled him. She thought of him tearing about on his motorbike, and about him jogging along the mountain paths, so virile and strong. Whatever had happened it hadn't made him scared to take risks, that was for sure.

She put his coffee down on the table next to him and sat down on the other armchair, wondering if she should wake him. He probably needed something to eat too, and it might be difficult to make it himself even if the sprained wrist wasn't his dominant one. She hated the thought of leaving him on his own to cope. She'd give him five minutes then wake him and see if he needed a sandwich.

She glanced around the lounge as she sipped her coffee. It was a large room and it was evident a family had once lived here. Family photographs adorned the walls, tables, dressers. Communion photos, wedding photos. A beautiful painting of the Madonna and child hung over the fireplace, and a large crucifix was in the middle of an adjoining wall. It seemed that his aunt had a large family, so why was Matias, her nephew, living here and doing the house up for her rather than one of her sons or daughters? Holly got to her feet. Nestling the cup in her hands, she walked over to the photos to have a closer look, wondering if any of them were Matias. Then she spotted him: he looked about five or six but the eyes and the expression were definitely Matias. He was standing with a man, lady and mischievous-looking little girl. They must be his parents and sister. *Are they still alive?* she wondered. *And where is his sister?*

'Holly?'

She jumped at the sound of Matias's slightly slurred voice. 'I'm here.' She walked over to him, still nursing her coffee cup. 'You dropped off so I thought I'd leave you for a few minutes. You look so tired.'

He rubbed the back of his neck. 'I am. I thought you had gone,' he added.

'I was looking at the photos. Sorry, I didn't mean to be nosy but I love looking at family photos. All those memories. You are so lucky to have such a large family,' she added wistfully. Her mum only had one brother, Uncle Tim, who didn't have any children, and she knew nothing about the family on her father's side.

'Yes, but even seemingly happy families have their problems.'

It sounded like he'd had some sort of quarrel with his family but she didn't want to pry so decided to change the subject instead. 'Would you like something to eat before I go? I don't mind cooking you something.'

'Thank you. I will make myself something later. You have given up enough time for me. If you could just feed Luna and give her fresh water, I will go and lie down for an hour once I've drunk my coffee.' He reached out and took a sip from the cup. 'The dog food is in the cupboard underneath the sink and her dishes are in the corner by the gas bottle underneath the boiler.'

'Of course.'

Holly took one of the cans of dog food out of the cupboard, opened it, and placed the contents in the dog bowl. Luna had evidently smelt the food as she was now standing by Holly wagging her tail. Holly put the bowl down on the kitchen floor and poured some fresh water in the water compartment, and Luna tucked in eagerly. Leaving the little dog to eat, Holly washed her hands and went back into the lounge.

'Luna's eating and has fresh water. Are you sure there is nothing I can do for you?'

'No, thank you.' He stood up. 'I'm going to lie down.'

'I'll come back later,' she told him. 'Perhaps you could give me a key – or keep the back door unlocked, so I can get in if I need to. You know, in case of an emergency. Oh, and I'll need a gate key too.'

He looked exasperated. 'You are very kind, Holly, but I really am not an invalid. There is no need for you to come back, or to have a key.'

Boy, he was stubborn. But she could be too. 'The conditions of me pretending to be your live-in girlfriend so you could come home earlier than the doctors wanted are that I check on you morning and night,' she told him. 'I will, of course, message you first but if you don't reply I need to be able to get inside in case you've lost consciousness or are injured.'

He furrowed his brow and she could see that he was processing this. Finally, he nodded. 'Very well. Just for a couple of days, that's all.'

'Of course. I'm far too busy to play nursemaid for long,' she told him then wished she hadn't because it sounded like it was a burden to check on him. She smiled to take the edge off her words and quickly added, 'As soon as we're sure you've fully recovered from the concussion, I'll hand your key back.'

He went into the kitchen, opened a drawer and took out a bunch of keys. Then he selected one and tried to get it off the key ring, which was difficult with only one hand. Holly reached over, took the keys off him and wriggled off the one he wanted. 'I presume this is the front door key?'

'No, the back door,' he replied. 'And the small one is the gate key. You will need that too.'

She took the small key off the ring then put the rest of the bunch back in the drawer. 'I'm guessing these are spare keys, and you have copies too?'

'I do.' He frowned and gestured to the sling. 'I hadn't realised how much of a nuisance this was going to be.'

'Which is exactly why you need a bit of help. Are you sure you don't want me to do anything else before I go? Make you a sandwich?'

'Thank you but I'll be fine. I'll message you if I need help. I promise.'

It suddenly occurred to her that it might be difficult for Matias to message with only one good hand.

'Try it,' she said. 'Send me a message now.'

'What?' He looked puzzled and irritated.

'It's going to be pretty awkward to hold your phone with one hand and type in a message. I want to make sure you can do it.'

'Of course I can. My fingers and thumb aren't bandaged up. And I told you that I'm left-handed,' he snapped.

'Prove it.' Holly folded her arms and waited.

He rolled his eyes, shoved his left hand in his pocket and took out his phone then held it awkwardly with his right hand while he tried to type. It took him a while and she could see the mixture of frustration and determination on his face, but finally her phone pinged and there was his message:

Told you.

She smiled. 'Good. Now if you need anything, message me. Or phone if it's urgent. I'll come straight around.'

He nodded. 'Thank you, Holly. Goodbye.'

Talk about being abruptly dismissed. She could see that he was tired though so left him to rest.

'How's the patient?' Fiona asked when Holly returned.

'In pain, stubborn and tired,' Holly said, worriedly. 'I hope he's going to be all right. He really should have someone with him. He was out cold for quite a while.'

'He's an adult, Holly, and I guess you've left him your phone number in case he needs anything?' Fiona opened the freezer, scooped out some ice and popped it into two long glasses. 'Want a *tinto de verano*?'

'I'd love one.' She watched Fiona pour red wine into the glasses then top them up with lemonade to make the popular 'summer wine'. 'And yes, I've left him my phone number but it's a struggle for him to text with a sprained wrist. I've told him he has to phone or text me every morning or night for the next couple of days, otherwise I'll be around to check on him.'

Fiona handed her a glass of the cool, red drink. 'Then you've done all you can.'

Holly knew she was right but it didn't stop her worrying.

Chapter Twenty-Four

It wasn't until Holly was sitting outside on the terrace later that afternoon that she allowed her mind to remember and linger on that kiss. The feel of Matias's arm around her, holding her close, his lips on hers, soft and brief but with the promise of more, of a sensuality waiting to be unleashed. She shook her head. It was ridiculous to be so affected by such a brief 'just to convince the doctor' kiss.

'Are you still worrying about Matias?' Fiona asked, plonking herself down next to her and holding out a bag of crisps.

Holly took a handful and nibbled at them while she considered her answer. 'A bit. I'm wondering how he's going to prepare a meal, open a can or packets with a sprained wrist – you need two hands for that, really.'

'Getting undressed and having a shower would be awkward too,' Fiona said. 'Do you fancy playing nurse? He's quite a hunk, isn't he?'

Holly swatted away the image of lathering down Matias's naked body in the shower that instantly flashed across her mind. 'Of course I don't! He's injured, for goodness' sake. I was talking in a professional manner. I did used to be a care assistant, you know.' *For older folk, Holly, not hunky fitness instructors with bodies to die for.* No wonder her mind kept lingering over that kiss.

'Chill, I'm only teasing.' Fiona grabbed another handful of crisps and put them in her mouth before adding, 'Ask him if he wants to join us for a meal tonight, if you like. Pablo's not working and he's cooking risotto – there'll be plenty for four.' She got to her feet. 'Right, I'm off to help Pablo varnish those wardrobes. There's only three more guest rooms to get ready then we can start on the *casita*.' She paused. 'With all this panic about Matias I forgot to say how pretty the bougainvillea room looks. Pablo and I are so pleased with it. You're a star.'

'I'm so pleased. I'll start the furnishing for one of the other rooms tomorrow,' Holly told her as she typed in a message to Matias telling him that Fiona and Pablo had invited him to join them for a meal tonight. 'Hang on and I'll come and work in the same room that you're varnishing in, so we can keep each other company.'

They worked all afternoon, and Holly tried not to keep glancing at her phone in case a message had come in from Matias and she hadn't heard it.

'Not replied yet, then?' Fiona asked as Holly took her phone out of her pocket yet again.

'You don't think something's happened to him, do you? He could have fallen unconscious again.'

'I expect he's asleep,' Fiona replied. She pointed at Holly's phone as it suddenly pinged. 'I bet that's him now.'

It was. Holly read the message.

Gracias, but I am tired. I will fix myself something to eat here and have an early night. I'll message you tomorrow.

She relayed the message to Fiona. 'Do you think he's telling me not to message him later and check he's okay? If so, I'm ignoring it. We agreed he'd contact me every morning and night.'

'Stop worrying and give him a bit of space,' Pablo said, climbing down from the stepladder he'd been using to paint the top of the wardrobe. 'If it was me, I'd want to be left alone to rest.'

'And if he falls again…'

'I'm sure he'll be careful. It must have been a horrible shock to wake up in hospital with a sprained wrist and be told he has a concussion. He's not going to risk anything else happening, is he?'

'I guess not.' Perhaps she was over-worrying. She pushed all thoughts of Matias out of her mind and carried on with her sewing.

The evening went quickly. They ate the risotto and sat on the terrace for a while, sipping sangria and chatting. It was a lovely, warm spring evening. They even had a dip in the pool. Holly tried not to keep checking her phone to see if Matias had messaged. As Fiona said, he wouldn't take any risks, would he? She should really stop fussing.

Pablo yawned. 'I think I'm going to turn in, I want to do a bit more painting before I go into work tomorrow.'

'Me too.' Fiona scooped up her things and got to her feet. 'How about you, Holly? Feel free to sit out here a bit longer if you want to.'

'I'll just finish my drink then I'll turn in too,' Holly said. She still had half a glass of sangria.

'See you in the morning, then.'

'*Luego.*' Pablo waved as he walked over to the house.

Holly waved to them both then sat looking at the moon shining on the pool, sipping her drink as she wondered whether she should message Matias again or not.

He was an adult and had made it clear he didn't want her to fuss.

But he could be unconscious again.

She could at least message and make sure he was okay. She wouldn't be able to sleep otherwise.

She swiped her phone, selected his name and tapped in a message:

Hi, just wanted to check that you're okay before I go to bed.

Then she finished her drink and waited for a terse 'I'm quite capable of looking after myself' reply.

None came.

Should she phone him? Go and check? It was almost eleven thirty. He was probably asleep in bed and wouldn't be very happy if she walked in. No, she should leave it. Ignoring her screaming 'care assistant' instincts, she finished her drink and went to bed too.

She woke the next morning to sunlight streaming through the gaps in the blinds and no text from Matias. She sent him a 'good morning' text, asking how he was.

No reply.

She had a shower and pulled on cut-off denim shorts and a white vest then checked her phone. Still no reply. She was starting to feel a little panicky. What if Matias had fallen? He could have been lying there all night. Or if he'd gone into a coma... After all, that's what the doctor was worried about. She had to go and check.

She shoved her phone in her pocket, took Matias's house keys out of her bag and set off to check. There was no sign of life and no sound from Luna. She opened the gates and ran down the drive to the back of the house, then knocked on the door. 'Matias!'

She peered through the glass. Suddenly she heard Luna yap. She could just about make out the shape of the little Shih Tzu, but nothing else.

'Matias! Are you okay?' she shouted again.

No answer. She had to go in.

Her hand was shaking as she unlocked the door, wondering what she would find. She should have called around last night. What if Matias was lying injured, had been lying injured all night? She'd never forgive herself if anything had happened to him...

She raced across the kitchen, opened the door and stepped out into the hall. Which way should she go? She had no idea which rooms the doors led to. She raced along the corridor. 'Mati!'

She stopped and turned as a door opened on her right and Matias peered out, a towel wrapped around his waist, the bandage now off his arm and his bare torso wet. He'd obviously been in the shower, or bath. She gulped, wanting to throw her arms around him with relief that he was safe but feeling more than a bit awkward that she'd let herself into his house when he'd been showering – or bathing, whatever – and was minutes away from walking in on him naked.

Don't even think about that.

'What is it?' he snapped, obviously annoyed. 'What are you doing here?'

She swallowed, feeling suddenly awkward at the irritation in his tawny eyes, and she lowered her own eyes then wished she hadn't as they were now resting on the mass of damp dark hair on his chest, and now, as if of their own free will, they were going lower to the blue and white towel wrapped loosely around his hips...

She snapped her eyes back up to his face. 'I was worried. You didn't reply to my message last night. I thought you'd fallen or hurt yourself,' she gabbled. 'And what's happened to your bandage?'

'As you can see I am perfectly fine. I overslept. As for the bandage, I took it off so I could have a shower,' he replied. 'Now if you wouldn't mind leaving me in peace I'd like to get dressed.'

'Yes, of course. Sorry. If you need any help… I mean…'

Drat, that sounded like she was offering to dress him, and he obviously thought the same as he raised an eyebrow sardonically. 'Thank you, but I'm sure I can manage,' he said just as the towel slipped off his hip. He grabbed it quickly, holding it in the middle of his groin, managing to cover his modesty but revealing a flash of strong thighs. Before she realised what she was doing, she instinctively reached out, grabbed the towel and matter-of-factly wrapped it around him again, tucking a corner of the towel in the top to keep it secure. As her fingers touched his bare flesh, sending a tingle zinging through her, and her eyes rested on the scar running across his taut stomach muscles, she suddenly realised what she was doing and felt her cheeks burn.

'Thank you. You can go now.'

She'd obviously embarrassed him too.

'Sorry, I used to be a care—'

'Assistant,' he finished. 'Yes, so you keep telling me.' He sighed and wiped his hand across his forehead. 'Look, if you really want to help, maybe you could feed Luna and make a cup of tea while I get dressed – white with two sugars. And please don't come in and ask me if I need help, no matter how long I take!'

'I won't,' she promised. 'But shout if you do.'

He shook his head in exasperation then turned, revealing another deep scar running down his back, and went into his bedroom. *Are those scars from his other accident, the one he won't talk about?* Holly thought as she made her way back to the kitchen. She put the kettle on then got the dog food out of the cupboard and fed Luna, who scoffed the food up happily, wagging her tail. She was such a sweet little dog. 'I wish you were mine,' Holly said softly, stroking the Shih Tzu's head.

'You're so beautiful.' Luna wagged her tail faster, as if she knew what Holly was saying, and carried on eating.

Well, best to get on with making the tea. Holly glanced at her watch: twenty minutes had gone by. She guessed that Matias was having difficulty dressing himself with only one useable hand. She knew from her experience in the care home that things like buckling his belt and pulling a T-shirt over his head would be really difficult – but if she offered to help again, he would probably get mad at her. She picked up her cup – no sugar – and started sipping it, the hot liquid calming her down a bit. She guessed that's why the British always made tea in a crisis.

She heard the door open and glanced around. Matias was standing behind her, looking very frustrated; the belt of his jeans was unbuckled and he was wearing a T-shirt which he was trying to pull down at the back with his left hand. The bandage was still missing from his right hand.

'I think I could use a little bit of help with my buckle, if you don't mind,' he said.

'Of course.' She walked over, eased his T-shirt down at the back then bent down to buckle his belt, focusing on keeping herself completely professional and not even stopping to think how close she was to a very personal part of his body. And just how fit that body was.

'*Gracias*,' he said as, belt buckled now, she stood up.

'Where's your bandage gone?'

'It's in the bathroom. I'll put it on after I've drunk this,' he said, picking up his cup of tea. 'Thanks for this.'

She fetched the bandage from the bathroom. 'Let me put this on you, please. You need it to support your wrist, if only for a few days.'

He sighed as he held out his right hand. 'There is no need to fuss, Holly. I have had far worse than this.'

She guessed he was referring to his other accident. The doctor had said that he'd almost died.

'Thank you. Again,' he said as she carefully put the bandage back in place. 'It seems that all I do at the moment is thank you.'

He walked outside with his cup and she followed him.

'What happened?' she asked as she sat next to him on the bench, nursing the remnants of her own drink. 'With your first accident? It sounds like it was really bad.'

He gazed at the mountains ahead for a while and she thought he was going to ignore her question. Then he replied softly, 'It was. It almost killed me and then it completely destroyed my life.'

Chapter Twenty-Five

Holly listened as Matias, his eyes still fixed on the mountains ahead, his voice little more than a whisper, relayed how he was out on his motorbike one day when he was hit by an oncoming car on a bend: a British tourist had rented the car for the holidays and forgotten that he should be driving on the right side of the road, not the left.

So that's why he was so mad at me the first time we met, and so against tourists driving!

'Is that how you got your scars?' she asked softly.

'Yes. The motorbike was a write-off and the doctors thought I was too. I was unconscious for weeks, had multiple injuries, was told I would never walk again.' It was as if the words were being dragged out of him from somewhere deep down where they had lain buried for years.

She could hardly believe it. He was so fit, so strong, and still always racing about on his motorbike. 'How did you recover from that?' she asked.

'Sheer determination.' He turned to face her, and she could see the pain of the memory in his eyes. 'Enough money to pay for the best treatment. And love. But it was a long, hard road.'

'Your girlfriend pulled you through? Is that the woman I saw you with in the bar?' she asked. Why hadn't he contacted her this time, though?

A dark look crossed his face. 'No, that was Sofia, a friend. Natali, my fiancée at the time, made a quick exit as soon as she realised that I might never walk again. It was my Tia Isabella, my father's sister, who nursed me. Now I am repaying her by doing up this house so she can sell it and buy a *casa* on the *costa*.'

His aunt. So where were his parents? Holly wanted to ask more but knew from her experience in the nursing home that it was best to leave people to tell you things at their own pace. Not that Matias was anything like the old residents she had helped look after, but she guessed feelings stayed the same no matter how old you were.

'That was very kind of her. And incredibly inspiring that you not only managed to walk again but that you still ride about on a motorbike.' She could only imagine the determination and strength that must have taken. 'You're very brave.'

'I was in a dark place at first. I thought my life was finished. Tia Isabella, she took me to her home, encouraged me to exercise, gave me hope. And I was lucky that my injuries weren't as severe as the doctors feared.'

'What about your parents?' The question was out before she could stop it. She saw the shutters come down on those tawny eyes again and an ice mask slip over his face. He turned his gaze back to the mountains. There was a long pause before he replied, as if he was considering his answer.

'They were concerned, of course, but they were too busy with the business to nurse me. Although they paid for a top consultant and anything else I needed.'

'How many years ago was this?' she asked softly.

'Five years since the accident. It was three years before I could walk properly again.'

And now he worked in a gym and was renovating his aunt's house. He was amazing.

'Is that why you work in a gym? To make sure you keep fit by exercising?' she asked

He nodded. 'Partly. I've always been interested in physical fitness, and that helped me build up my strength when I thought I'd never walk again. The months I spent practically bedridden made me rethink what I wanted to do with my life. I walked away from my parents' law firm and retrained as a fitness instructor, specialising in fitness training for people with disabilities. I know how depressed I felt when I was disabled, and knew I wanted to help other people get as fit as they can, to help them achieve their full potential.'

She hadn't expected that! How wrong she had been. She had thought he was aloof, grumpy and obsessed with working out, when in truth he'd gone through a terrible ordeal, turned his life around and was now using his experience to help others.

'Your parents must be very proud of you.'

He shook his head. 'Not at all. They are mad at me for walking away from the family firm. I'm a trained lawyer. My father was hoping to hand the company over to me when he retires.'

He was a lawyer and used to work in his father's company? The surprises just kept on coming. 'But what you're doing is so worthwhile. I never realised…' She felt a bit awkward.

'You thought I was just a bad-tempered poser, eh?' He shrugged. 'Well, I admit I am a bit bad-tempered, but only when it comes to tourists driving over here without any experience, because that causes so many accidents.'

'I have got experience,' she told him. 'I drove through France with Scott.'

'Your boyfriend?'

'Former boyfriend. He preferred to go out clubbing with his mates than spend time with me. When he decided to take himself off on a spur-of-the-moment trip to Amsterdam with his mates I decided to take myself off too. And never went back.'

'Is that why you came to Spain? To get over him?'

She thought about this. 'Partly, but mainly to sort out what I wanted to do with my life.' She told him about her inheritance from Pops, her job at Sunshine Lodge, how Fiona and Pablo had invited her over to help get Las Mariposas ready for the summer. It all seemed so empty and self-centred compared to what Matias had been through.

He clearly didn't think so, as he replied, 'Then I have misjudged you too. I see now you are a caring person and not the thoughtless tourist I took you for. And I have to admit that I was going a little fast around that bend the day you arrived. I apologise.' He held out his left hand. 'How about we both make a fresh start?'

She smiled and shook his hand. 'Delighted to.'

They sat in silence, sipping their tea and gazing at the gorgeous mountain view. Holly could hardly believe that they had opened up so much to each other. It was as if the accident had brought them closer, given them a kind of bond. *Don't be stupid,* she told herself, *he just needed someone to talk to and you were there.*

They both jumped as her phone pinged with a message. It was Fiona:

Are you okay? I knocked on the door to your apartment but you don't seem to be in.

'Do you need to go?' Matias asked, turning to her.

'It's Fiona, wondering where I am. I'll send a quick reply.'

'Please don't let me keep you from your friends or work. I will be perfectly fine. I don't need a nurse, I promise.'

'Do you promise that you'll take it easy and won't start doing any renovating until your wrist's healed?' she asked him.

'I will be careful but I can't promise to do nothing – I will be bored. Careful exercise is good for me.' He got to his feet. 'Thank you for coming by. At least I am decently dressed now. A trained care assistant as a neighbour comes in handy.'

She got up too and smiled. 'I cared for elderly people but the basic principle is the same. Assist, be professional and try to respect their privacy.'

His eyes danced. 'You managed that well – not a hand out of place.'

She knew he was referring to when she had buckled his belt. She grinned back. 'Don't worry, I'm far too professional to take advantage of a patient.'

She picked up her cup but he shook his head. 'I'll take them inside. I can manage. You get on. And thank you for your time.'

She knew better than to argue with him. 'You're welcome. And if you get bored, pop around, see what we're doing to the *finca*. Fiona and Pablo won't mind – I think they're both at work this afternoon though.'

He leant forward and kissed her on the cheek, sending a little tremor down her spine.

'Thank you. I might.'

'*Luego*.' She waved, patted Luna goodbye and headed for the gate.

Fiona was waiting for her as soon as she got in. 'What happened? Did Matias message you for help?'

Holly explained about being worried when she had no reply from Matias so she went around to check, and how Matias had told her about his accident.

'Gosh, I had no idea,' exclaimed Fiona. 'That must have really shaken him up – and it's fantastic that he's been able to come back from that.'

'I know. I'm not sure if he wants it to be public knowledge, so you won't tell anyone, will you? And please don't mention it unless he does.'

'Of course not.' Fiona cast Holly a thoughtful glance. 'You're quite taken with him, aren't you?'

'Don't talk rubbish, I'm just helping him a bit until he gets on his feet,' Holly said defensively. 'Oh, and he can't do much at the moment so I told him to pop over here if he's bored. That's okay, isn't it?'

'Sure. Maybe we can even give him a hand with doing up his aunt's house when we've finished here.' Fiona pointed to some freshly picked lettuce and tomatoes on the table. 'Fancy a salad baguette for lunch?'

'Sounds great. I've got some feta cheese, I'll go and fetch it.' Holly hurried off to fetch the cheese from the fridge in her apartment, her mind still on Matias. Although he was putting on a brave face, he'd looked so pale and weak. *I hope he's going to be okay. I'll check on him again later,* she decided.

The afternoon passed quickly. By the time Fiona returned from work, Holly had hung up the new curtains in the woodland room and was putting the finishing touches on the bedspread.

'I absolutely love it!' Fiona squealed, clasping her hands in delight as she looked around the room. 'You've completely transformed this room. It's amazing.' She flung her arms around Holly's neck. 'Thank you so much.'

Holly had to admit that she was proud of her efforts too. The woodland leaf design had come out much better than she'd expected, and teamed with a fern-green rug and white accessories, the bedroom looked restful. Susie said the woodland leaf was her favourite when Holly had sent her a photo of it, and suggested that Holly print the design on wallpaper too. Holly was mulling that idea over.

Pablo arrived home a little later and he admired it too. 'You're very talented, Holly,' he said. 'I think you should run some courses too. Either on designing or making soft furnishings. Or both.'

Fiona clapped her hands. 'What a brilliant idea! Do say you will, Holly. We could take some photos of the rooms and upload them to our website. Then we could write a bit about all the furnishings being created by talented designer Holly, give a few links to your Dandibug shop and say you'll be running courses on designing your own soft furnishings. I bet that will bring people in!'

It was an exciting thought; her own business and running classes at a summer school too. It was what she'd always dreamt of.

'I'd love to,' she agreed.

Her phone suddenly vibrated in her pocket. She took it out and saw there was a message from Matias:

Just to let you know that I'm still alive but I might need help opening a bottle of wine later, if you're interested. Sparkling white?

She smiled.

'Is that from Matias?' Fiona asked.

'Yes.' Holly read the message to her and Fiona swapped a knowing look with Pablo before asking, 'And are you?'

'Well, I can't leave him to struggle, can I?'

Holly typed in:

Sparkling white is very okay! Shall we say eight o'clock?

She smiled as the reply *'Perfecto'* shot back.

Chapter Twenty-Six

Luna ran out to greet Holly, tail wagging happily, as soon as she opened the gates. 'Hello, Luna. I'm guessing your master is out the back.' Holly bent down to stroke the little Shih Tzu. Luna licked Holly's hand then trotted beside her as she made her way around to the terrace at the back.

As Holly had guessed, Matias was sitting on one of the wicker chairs, a bottle of sparkling wine in an ice bucket on the table and two glasses and a corkscrew on a silver tray beside it. A few large citronella candles were burning on the table, to keep the mosquitos away.

'*Hola*, Holly,' he said, getting to his feet and kissing her lightly on both cheeks – mere pecks but enough to make her senses jump to attention. 'I am afraid you will have to open the wine.' He looked down at his bandaged wrist. 'I can't hold the bottle firmly enough yet.'

'No problem.' She put her bag down on the table and picked up the corkscrew. Soon she had the cork out and was pouring the fizzy wine into the two glasses.

'Expertly done,' Matias told her. 'You are used to uncorking wine, I see.'

'My grandparents always liked a tot before they went to bed and they could never open the bottles. I tried to persuade them to buy the screw-top ones but Pops is…' she corrected herself, 'was very old-school. He preferred corked bottles. He always had a bottle ready for me to uncork when I visited them.' She turned away as unexpected tears sprang to her eyes.

'Your grandparents passed away recently?' Matias reached out and touched her hand comfortingly. 'I can see that you were very fond of them.'

She nodded. 'Nanna died two and half years ago and Pops died earlier this year. They were wonderful. My mum was a single parent – she's remarried now – so Nanna and Pops were my base, they looked after me whenever Mum was at work.'

'Like Tia Isabella. I spent my school holidays with her, in this house,' Matias replied. He picked up his glass, staring into the bubbles for a moment as if he too was lost in memories. Then he asked, 'You are an only child?'

'Yes. A much-loved one but as a single parent my mum was always busy. I'm glad I had Nanna and Pops.' She lifted her legs onto the chair and hugged her knees. 'I don't know what I'd have done without them.' She turned her head to face him. 'What about you? Do you have any siblings?'

'I have one older, *very bossy* sister.'

His emphasis on the words 'very bossy' made her smile. 'I take it you don't get on?'

He took a sip of wine before replying. 'We can manage to be polite if we don't see each other very often. My grandparents both died when I was very young. You are lucky to have been so close to yours.'

She swirled her finger around the rim of the glass as she thought how lonely her life would have been without Nanna and Pops. 'I know,' she replied, thoughtfully. 'And it's thanks to them that I'm here now.'

He gazed into her eyes. 'I think that you were also very kind to them and that they are paying you back? They want you to look after yourself a bit instead of looking after other people.'

She sighed. 'That's what Pops said. Mind you, I enjoyed working in Sunshine Lodge, the old folk are lovely and some of them have such stories to tell. It's wonderful to be over here though. I feel like I've been given a chance to start my life over again. I've even made a dream list of things I want to do this year.'

'This Scott you mentioned earlier, are you still heartbroken over him?'

'No. I'm over him now but I've no intention of getting involved with *anyone* ever again.'

'So you are not with Felipe? You seem to be… close.'

'I think that Felipe would like us to be close but he is a good friend, that's all. I told you I'm off relationships – I want to live my life how I choose.'

Matias took a long sip of his drink. 'Amen to that.'

She glanced swiftly at him. 'You have had your heart broken too. What Natali did was awful! You must have been devastated.'

His eyes darkened for a moment as if he was remembering the pain. 'I got over it, and like you I'm off relationships.' He held out his glass. 'To friendship.'

She clinked it with her glass. 'To friendship.'

Matias downed his drink then stood up. 'Now let us have another drink and you can tell me all about your dream list, and I will see if I can help you make any of your dreams come true.'

Holly held out her glass for him to fill, her eyes taking in the T-shirt clinging to his toned torso, the sleeves pulled over his muscled biceps, the thick mop of dark hair curling around his rugged, handsome face. She bet he'd made a few women's dreams come true in bed. She shook the thought of them both lying naked, caressing each other, out of her mind. They'd just raised a toast to friendship and that's all she wanted: to be friends… even if he was the hottest guy she'd ever met.

'You can help me with one of them, when your wrist is better,' she said.

He stopped as he was about to pour wine into her glass and looked up, his eyes just centimetres away from her. 'And what is that?'

'Let me have a ride on the back of your motorbike.'

She saw amusement dance across his face.

'I hadn't imagined you as a biker,' he said as he refilled her glass then moved onto his own.

'I'm not. But this is all about pushing me out of my comfort zone, doing things I'd love to do but am too scared. And riding on the back of a motorbike is one of them.'

'I'd be honoured.' He sat down.

She was chuffed – and a little scared. 'Thanks, Mati... I mean...' she stammered; she hadn't meant to shorten his name like that again. A lot of people didn't like their name shortened.

He leant over and lightly touched her hand. She tried to ignore the now-familiar fluttery feeling she got whenever he touched her. 'It is fine. I like it. Tia Isabella always called me Mati. You can too.'

She felt like he'd bestowed an honour on her and wasn't sure how to respond.

He removed his hand and leant back in his chair. 'And what are the other things?'

Holly relayed the list to him. 'So, left to do is ride on the back of a motorbike, go on a motor yacht, visit a cave, snorkel in the sea, learn to dance – and I still have quite a few flavours of ice cream to get through.'

'There were ten things on your list?' he asked.

'Twelve,' she admitted. 'The others were to get a pet...'

Just then Luna came trotting over, nudging Holly's hand with her nose.

'She likes you,' Matias said.

'I like her too.' Holly fussed the little dog. 'She is gorgeous.'

'Then you must share her with me until you go home. Now you have a pet. Although actually Luna is my aunt's dog, not mine.' He raised his glass. 'Another thing off your dream list.'

'Thank you. And when I go back to the UK and get my own flat I will get a pet of my own.'

'And the last thing on your list?'

Holly paused, wondering if it sounded stupid. 'To be who I want to be. To never change to please someone else again, like I did for Scott.'

Matias raised his glass. 'I'll second that.'

*

He'd never told anyone any of that stuff before, Matias thought as he lay in bed that night, long after Holly had gone home. Holly was so easy to talk to that it had all come out, especially after she had confided in him about her love for her grandparents, and how her selfish boyfriend had treated her. He was an idiot, this Scott, to let someone like Holly go. She was beautiful inside and out, loving and caring – she should be cherished.

And they were just friends. That was the deal they had made. Even as they had clinked glasses and said those words, 'to friendship', he had wanted to reach out and trace his fingers over her soft skin, to kiss her, to feel her body melting against his. He had wanted it so much. Too much. He didn't want to feel like this about another woman again. To care. That is why he had proposed a toast to friendship. So they both knew where they stood. To stop either of them expecting more, so they didn't complicate their friendship by slipping into a relationship.

Even though he desperately wanted to.

Chapter Twenty-Seven

A Week Later

Holly and Matias had fallen into an easy routine over the past week. Holly called around to have breakfast with Matias and see if he needed any help – which was usually no. After that first day he even managed to buckle his own belt – something she was quite relieved to see as it'd wreaked havoc on her 'we're just friends' resolution when she'd had her finger on his zip! He'd worked out a fitness regime and exercised every day, telling her that stretching and strengthening exercises were essential to his recovery. He'd even started doing odd bits of painting at his aunt's house, despite Holly's warnings to take it easy. 'I'm left-handed, I don't need to use my injured arm,' he pointed out, which wasn't strictly true but it was a waste of time arguing with him, and he certainly looked a lot happier when he was keeping busy.

Today when she walked in, she noticed that he had a real sparkle in his eye and looked very upbeat. 'Morning, Holly. Would you like a cup of coffee?' he asked. He had already filled the kettle, set out two cups and was showered and dressed.

'How are you today?' she asked.

'I am good. So good that tomorrow I'm going back to work.' He handed her a mug of coffee with his right hand. 'Shall we drink this outside? It is such a beautiful day.'

'Sure.' She carried the mug outside and sat down at the table on the terrace, her mind whirling. Matias worked as a fitness instructor. How could he possibly go back to work with a sprained wrist? The nurse had said it needed a couple of weeks to recover and it had only been one week. She chose her words carefully as he pulled out the chair opposite her and sat down. He was a proud man and she didn't want to suggest that he wasn't capable of doing anything.

'That's great but… you will be careful, won't you? If you put any strain on your wrist…'

'I won't, of course. I don't want to delay the healing time but it's almost better,' he pointed out. 'I have people to help who have a lot more serious disabilities to cope with than a sprained wrist. And before you ask, yes I am fit enough to ride my motorbike.'

That had been her next question. She nodded. '*Lo siento*. I worry too much…'

His eyes met hers and softened. 'It is nice to have a friend who cares.'

She smiled and tore her gaze away from those gorgeous eyes – which made her think of being more than friends – and transferred it onto the pool instead, where she could see an air bed floating. 'Have you been using the pool?'

'Yes, swimming is very good exercise. Why don't you come back over later and join me? Are you free? And Fiona and Pablo too, of course.'

She had a Spanish lesson with Felipe this morning then wanted to do some sewing this afternoon. She had planned on finishing the furnishings for another room today. It was tempting to have a dip in the pool with Matias though, and he was back at work tomorrow. 'I could come around about five?' she suggested. 'I have work to do before then. And I'll ask Fiona and Pablo, but I'm not sure what they're doing this evening.'

'That is perfect. How are you all getting on with the refurbishments? Your first guests arrive in a few weeks, don't they?'

'Yes, we have bookings all through July and August,' she told him. 'We've finished the *finca* and are now doing up the *casita* in the grounds. You must come and have a look when we've finished.'

'I'd like to,' Matias told her.

They finished their coffees and Holly went back to Las Mariposas, promising to come back later for a dip in the pool.

Maybe I should have told Mati to come around to us instead, she thought. It seemed a bit too intimate, just the two of them, clad only in their swimwear. She shrugged off the doubts. This was Spain. Everyone jumped into each other's pools over here. She'd lost count of the times Fiona and Pablo had invited friends back, and they'd come equipped with cans of beer, swimwear and towels. At first she'd felt self-conscious but now she didn't think twice about it. Well, with a bit of luck Fiona and Pablo would be free too.

She mentioned it to Fiona when she saw her in the corridor after her lesson had finished. They had both driven down in their separate cars as Fiona was working all morning and Holly wanted to get back so she could finish her sewing.

She was working on what Fiona had dubbed 'the sunshine room' today. Bright-yellow sunflowers with emerald-green leaves printed on a white background for the cushions and bedspread. The bright yellow was picked up in the lampshade and cushions and an emerald-green rug broke up the bareness of the floorboards, which Pablo had sanded down and painted white. All she needed to do now was add the pleated trim to the bedspread. That shouldn't take too long.

'Mati has invited us around this afternoon for snacks and a dip in the pool, about five o'clock. Do you and Pablo fancy it?' Holly asked as they made their way to the café in the square for a quick coffee.

Fiona sat down beside her, put her bag down on the floor by her feet and gave Holly a knowing look. 'You sure you two wouldn't prefer to be alone? Especially if you're only going to be in a bikini…'

'Of course not. I've told you we're friends, nothing more. Like me and Felipe,' she added.

Fiona shook her head. 'You and Felipe are friends, yes. You act like friends – although I think he wishes you were more than that – but you and Matias, you look at each other as if you want to be far more.'

Holly felt a flush creep up her cheeks. She was trying desperately not to think of Mati in that way and was sure he didn't think that way about her. She didn't want to complicate the friendship they had. 'We're friends and that's the way I want it to stay,' she replied. 'So it'd be great if you and Pablo came around too. I'm only staying for an hour or two. Mati starts work again tomorrow so he'll be wanting to get to bed early.'

'Okay, if you're sure, I'll pop around for a bit. I'm sure Pablo will too.'

Holly worked steadily all afternoon and had the room finished before Fiona and Pablo came home. She looked at it proudly. It looked so fresh and cheerful, with sunlight streaming in through the open blinds. Fiona and Pablo had sanded and polished the dark wooden furniture so it gleamed.

One more room to do, she thought happily. Then she could plan her courses and get cracking on tidying up her studio apartment. She loved that apartment and would be quite sad to say goodbye once summer was over. Still, if she prettied it up, then Fiona and Pablo could rent it out and that would be some payback for them allowing her to stay rent-free since March.

Matias texted:

Beer chilling.

Holly smiled and replied:

On my way.

Fiona and Pablo will follow when they get home, she thought. She pulled on her bright-yellow bikini, which she knew showed off her tan perfectly and was one of her most respectable ones, and slipped her multicoloured kaftan over it. Shoving a towel and her phone in a tote bag she set off.

Matias was already in the pool, floating on his back, in black swim shorts low enough to reveal the top of the scar running across his stomach. She watched for a moment, her eyes taking in the toned, tanned body, the wet, dark hair on his chest, the muscled biceps.

'*Hola*, Holly!' He waved and she was glad she was wearing sunglasses so that it wasn't evident she'd been staring at him. 'Jump in!'

Why not? It had been hot working up in the *casita* and she could do with a cool-down. She waved back. 'Just let me put my bag down.' She walked over to the table then, keeping her back to the pool, she stripped off her kaftan. It sounded daft but this way she felt like Matias wasn't watching her; it was just too personal to face him and strip down to her bikini.

✻

She really is gorgeous, Matias thought, his eyes lingering on Holly as she pulled the kaftan over her head, revealing a very shapely body clad in a sunshine-yellow bikini – almost the same colour as her car. His mind went back to when he awoke in the hospital to see Holly standing in front of him, in the same colourful kaftan and bikini, the light from the window revealing her shapely body underneath. He longed to make love to her, to feel her lips on his, to run his hands over her soft skin. But he wasn't going there. He'd vowed after Natali that he'd keep his relationships casual, and he didn't think he'd be able to do casual with Holly. He felt that once he'd stepped over that line from friendship to lovers, he wouldn't be able to step back. And he didn't want to lose her friendship. That was presuming she was interested in him in that way, and he didn't think she was. She'd made it clear that she'd recently got over a heartbreak and didn't intend to start another relationship. So, friends it was. But *Dios,* she was gorgeous.

Holly ran over to the pool and dived straight in. He watched as she swam across the length of the pool and back again.

'I can't wait to be able to do that again,' he said, rolling over and standing up in the chest-deep water. 'I tried this morning but it made my wrist ache. So for now I have to settle for floating.' He turned on his back again and floated away across the pool.

Holly followed suit and they floated side by side in peaceful silence until they reached the other end. Then Holly flipped over onto her stomach and swam back while Matias scrambled onto an airbed and lay back to enjoy the sun – and to watch Holly swimming so gracefully in that tempting bikini.

'I'm feeling thirsty now,' Holly said after a while, standing alongside the airbed which had now floated to the shallow end of the pool. 'Is it okay if I get a cold drink?'

'Of course.' Matias rolled off and waded out of the pool. Holly followed in such haste she slipped and stumbled on the step.

'Careful!' Matias held out his left hand.

'Thank you.' She grabbed it and pulled herself up in front of him, so close that their bodies were mere centimetres apart; he could see the water glistening on her skin, the rise of her breasts peeping out from the yellow bikini top, the widening of her eyes, the parting of her full lips. He heard her gasp, felt his heart thudding in his chest. Then as if it had a mind of its own, his head lowered so their noses were practically touching and his lips were reaching for hers—

'*¡Hola!*' It was Fiona and Pablo.

They both jerked apart, so suddenly that Holly almost fell back into the pool. Matias grabbed her and looked around to their two friends, dressed in swimwear and carrying a bag.

'*Hola*, come and join us!' he shouted.

Holly let go of his hand, slipped on her flip-flops and padded over to Fiona and Pablo. 'Be careful of those steps when you go in, they're a bit slippy,' she warned them.

As he watched her go, Matias felt a mixture of regret and relief. If they hadn't been disturbed, they would have kissed, he was sure – and by the look on Holly's face, she wanted it too.

He grabbed a towel with his good arm and wrapped it around himself as he called, 'Would you both like a drink?'

❋

'You two looked very cosy when we came along,' Fiona said when they returned home later that evening. 'We didn't interrupt anything, did we?'

'Not at all. I stumbled on the steps and Mati just gave me a hand up,' Holly told her. She stopped at the door of her apartment. 'I'm off to bed now, I'll see you both in the morning.'

'Are you sure you don't want to join us for a nightcap?' Fiona told her. 'It's only ten o'clock, still quite early.'

Holly shook her head. 'Thanks, but I've got a couple of things I want to do before I go to bed. I'll see you tomorrow.'

As soon as she got inside she sank down in her armchair and gave way to the thoughts she had tried to ignore all evening. How fantastic Mati had looked in those swimming trunks, how she had longed to trace her hands over his body, how he had almost kissed her and how much she had wanted him to.

Face it, Holly, you're attracted to him and you think he's attracted to you too.

For a fleeting moment she wondered what harm it would do to give into that attraction, to have a 'just for the summer' fling, but she knew that would be a bad idea. They had both got badly burnt in love, but she felt that Matias had been hurt more than her. She had thought she loved Scott but, as time was passing, she was realising that it was more that she had been in love with the *idea* of loving Scott, of getting married and having a family. Meanwhile, Matias had been dumped by the woman he was going to marry just because he had been injured in a road accident. That must have hurt. A lot. And he'd admitted that since then he'd only had casual relationships. Well, maybe he'd like a casual relationship with her but she wasn't up for it. This was her year of doing what she wanted, and she wasn't going to mess that up by getting involved with Matias. She needed a friend, not a lover. And friends were what they were going to stay. Her body might respond to Matias, and she might enjoy going to bed with him – make that *would* enjoy because she was quite certain that he would be a fantastic lover – but it would be a big mistake. One that she had no intention of making.

She logged onto her computer and opened a file. She wanted to put all her time and effort into making her business a success, not falling in love.

Chapter Twenty-Eight

June

'I can't believe that we'll have our first guests in only three weeks,' Fiona said.

'We're nearly ready though, aren't we?' Holly asked.

They'd spent all the hours they could working on the refurbishments and now the rooms in both the *finca* and the *casita* were ready, so all they had to do was tidy up the grounds and prepare their courses. They'd uploaded an outline of the sessions to the website, which had generated a lot of interest, and now they were fully booked up from the last week in June through to the first week of September. Fiona wasn't teaching English through the summer and Pablo had reduced his bar work to the occasional evening so they had time to run the courses.

'Let's have a pool party and barbecue this weekend to celebrate,' Pablo suggested. 'It'd be good to chill out after all the hard work we've been doing the past few months.'

'Fab idea! We can invite all our friends over to see what we've done to the place,' Fiona agreed. She turned to Holly. 'You can invite Matias.'

Holly hadn't been in the pool with Mati since that incident a few weeks ago when they had almost kissed, although they'd still spent a lot of time in each other's company – when they weren't working, that was.

'I will. It sounds fun,' she agreed. She looked over at the gate as she heard the sound of a motorbike. Was that Matias going out on another ride? His wrist was completely healed now and he was back working at the gym three days a week.

The bike stopped, and a couple of minutes later the gates opened and Matias walked in, clad in a T-shirt and jeans and holding a crash helmet under his arm. '*Hola*, Holly!' He waved. 'Want to come for a spin?'

'What! Now?' She bit her lip, her pulse racing. This was something she had always wanted to do but she hadn't had time to prepare herself. Even though she now managed to drive up and down the track quite confidently, she was scared of riding down it on the back of a motorbike.

'*Sí*, now. But there is no need to look so worried, we won't go down the track, not today. We'll just ride to my house and around the grounds,' he said, reassuringly. 'Then if you're okay with that we'll go for a proper spin at the weekend. Maybe have a ride to the coast.'

She could do this. She wanted to do this. 'Okay.' She nodded. 'Do you have a spare crash helmet?'

'Of course, in the box on the back of the bike. And I promise I'll go slow and steady. You'll be safe with me.'

Fiona grinned. 'That'll be another thing off your list.'

It would. Even if she didn't feel brave enough to go for a long ride at the weekend, she'd have done it: ridden on the back of a motorbike.

'Okay.'

His face broke into a delighted smile. They both walked out of the gate, then Matias put on his helmet and took another one out of the saddle box. 'Let me fix it on you to make sure it is safe,' he said, putting the helmet on Holly's head then fastening the strap under her chin, his fingers grazing her skin, sending a familiar little tingle through her body.

Stop reacting to his every little touch! she scolded herself.

Matias swung his leg over the bike. 'Now climb on behind me and hold tight,' he said. 'I will go slowly, I promise.'

Fiona had come to watch and got out her phone as Holly climbed on the back of the bike. 'Hang on! Let me take a photo for your book!'

She clicked away as Holly and Matias smiled and posed. 'I'll send them over to you and you can choose the best,' she said.

'Thanks. *Hasta luego*,' Holly shouted as Matias revved the engine. She wrapped her arms around his waist, just about resisting the urge to bury her face into his back and drink in his male essence, then away they went. Her heart flipped as the bike chugged along the track to Matias's house, through the open gates and around the grounds. It was a bit nerve-wracking at first but, true to his promise, Matias went slowly and carefully and she felt exhilarated as they made their way back to Las Mariposas. It was a fantastic feeling.

Fiona and Pablo clapped as the bike came to a halt and she dismounted. She grinned and bowed.

'There you are, another thing to tick off your list,' Matias said.

'Thank you.' She felt like hugging him but instead she stood on her tiptoes and kissed him briefly on the cheek.

'Would you like to come for a longer ride with me on Sunday?' he asked. 'We can go to the beach.'

'I'd love to. Thank you.'

'My pleasure.' He revved up the engine. 'Sunday after lunch? About two?'

She nodded and waved as he roared off.

'There's definitely something going on with you two,' Fiona said.

'What?' Holly turned to her in indignation. 'Why do you say that? I've told you we're friends, that's all.' She clapped her hand to her head. 'I forgot to mention the pool party to him – will it be on Saturday or Sunday? I'm sure we can change our ride to the beach to another day to fit it in.'

'Sunday would be best actually – a lot of our friends work Saturdays,' Fiona told her.

Holly immediately messaged Matias and a swift reply came back that he'd love to come to the pool party and it was no problem to change the beach day to Saturday.

Holly read his reply happily. Life was good.

They spent the rest of the afternoon talking about the courses they were going to run and sorting out a shift system. Fiona would teach art courses, and Pablo pottery; they also both planned on doing a few creative writing courses, using story starters or the garden for inspiration, while Holly would teach creative design, showing the students how to transfer their designs onto things they could use. By the end of the afternoon they had an interesting schedule, with the courses being run in the morning, leaving the afternoons for 'free work' time – where the students could continue with their writing or painting – and the evenings for socialising. Time off for Fiona, Pablo and Holly had been scheduled into the timetable and also a couple of excursions – Pablo had a friend who worked at a taxi firm and could give him a good discount on a six-seater taxi or minibus for the excursions and airport pick-ups and drop-offs. Meals were included in the price so Fiona and Pablo were busy stocking up on supplies.

'I can't believe we've actually got everything ready in time,' Fiona said.

'Our first-ever retreat.' Pablo wrapped his arm around Fiona's shoulder, pulled her to him and kissed her forehead tenderly. 'This is our dream come true.'

'I know.' Fiona looked at Holly. 'Thank you so much for coming over and helping us.'

'It's a pleasure,' Holly told her, delighted to see her friends look so happy.

'I hope it's a success,' Fiona said, suddenly looking worried.

Pablo kissed her again. 'It will be.'

Making an excuse that she had some things to sort out, Holly said goodnight and went over to her apartment, wanting to give them some couple-time together.

They looked so happy and loved-up. It made her hope that maybe one day she might find love like that.

Not yet though. She had too many things she wanted to do first.

Chapter Twenty-Nine

As promised, Matias arrived after lunch on Saturday to take Holly for a motorbike ride. She was more than a little nervous about going down the track on the back of a motorbike but managed to keep her nerves in check until they turned the bend then stupidly took a glance at the drop below. Panic snaked around her chest so tightly she could barely breathe. She clung tightly to Matias, closed her eyes and concentrated on the feel of the wind blowing across her skin. It was invigorating and she understood why Matias enjoyed riding the motorbike so much.

'You can open your eyes now!' Matias shouted.

'How did you know?' she asked as she gingerly opened her eyes and saw that they were almost at the main road below, the danger had passed. She took a deep breath as a gap in the traffic allowed them to smoothly join the road.

He chuckled. 'I guessed! Are you okay?'

Holly buried her head in his back, enjoying the warm breeze on her skin. 'Yes!'

It was an amazing ride. Matias took the coastal road, whizzing past the ribbon of brilliant blue ocean visible behind mountains covered in trees, then more sparsely vegetated with white, yellow and pastel-coloured houses dotted about here and there, past small Spanish villages built high in the hills then mountains again until finally they were riding alongside the beach road itself. A few people were walking barefoot on the sand, paddling in the sea, but as it was only the beginning of June it wasn't jam-packed yet.

Matias slowed down, turned into a parking space and turned off the engine. 'Fancy a walk along the beach?' he asked.

'Sure.' Holly swung her leg over the bike to dismount, took off her crash helmet and shook her hair, brushing it away from her eyes with her hands. 'That was fantastic,' she told him. '*Muchas gracias.*'

'*De nada.*' Matias's eyes were shining with excitement, his face flushed. He looked so alive, and as he leant forward and kissed her on the cheek Holly felt an intense longing to reach out and touch the stubble on his chin, to run her fingers lightly over his face. That would be a really stupid thing to do. Yes, she was attracted to Matias, who wouldn't be? But they had both agreed that neither of them wanted a relationship.

He took her helmet, put it with his own in the back box and locked his bike. Then he held out his hand. 'Shall we go?'

Holly slipped her hand in his and they walked over to the seafront, took off their shoes and padded over the soft, golden sand, dangling their shoes from their fingers.

Although it was still quite early, the sun was beaming down on Holly's back and she looked longingly at the sparkling blue sea. 'Shall we paddle?'

Matias grinned. 'How about I sit here and keep an eye on your stuff while you paddle. ¿*Vale?*'

'*Vale,*' she agreed, handing him her shoes and bag then running barefoot across the warm sand to where the ocean started trickling in. She ran straight in the aquamarine sea until she was knee-deep in the water, then held her arms out wide and her head up to the sun. It was a wonderful day – suddenly a splash! A huge wave swept over her, covering her from head to toe with water. She burst out laughing and turned to Matias to show him what had happened. He'd already seen and had his phone camera poised, taking shots, a big grin on his face.

She waved, her wet shorts clinging to her legs. 'I'm guessing you got that shot?'

'I sure did! I've got some fabulous shots,' he said. 'I'll send them over to you. You can add them to your memory book.'

Holly's memory book was already half full, a wonderful record of her year of fulfilling her dreams. As she stood there, knee-deep in the Mediterranean Sea, the sun shining brightly, Matias laughing in front of her, she thought that she'd never felt happier. Four months ago, she'd felt like her heart was broken: Pops and Nanna were both gone, her life was in pieces and she and Scott were finished. But now she could see that those events were the catalyst for a new path for her, a new life.

'Thank you, Pops,' she whispered up to the cobalt sky.

She paddled out of the sea and joined Matias. 'Shall we have an ice cream now?'

There were several *heladerías* along the seafront. They went to the nearest one and were confronted by the usual wide variety of ice creams and frozen yoghurts. Holly studied them all carefully.

'What's your favourite?' Matias asked. 'Mine's mint chocolate chip.'

She wrinkled her nose as she peered through the glass at the selection in front of her. 'Mint chocolate chip too. But I'm not having my favourite. I'm trying to decide between banana fudge whirl or raspberry cheesecake.'

'Of course, I forgot, you want to try fifty flavours, don't you? How many flavours do you have left to try?'

'Twenty-one, and I'm having fun going through them all,' she told him. 'I'll have raspberry cheesecake today. *Esto*,' she told the assistant. She pointed to the ice cream. '*Pequeño, por favor*,' she said, remembering the word for 'small'.

She took the small cup off the assistant and counted out the money.

Matias grinned, looped his arm around her neck, pulled her to him and kissed her on the forehead. 'You and your dream list.'

Matias plumped for his usual mint chocolate chip – a small cup like Holly – and they both walked over to an empty bench facing the sea then sat down to eat them.

'Are you always a creature of habit?' she teased.

'I like to try new things.' His eyes held hers and she felt a frisson of something – anticipation? promise? – shiver through her, then he added, 'But if I like something then I don't see the need for change.' He dipped his spoon into the green ice cream peppered with chocolate chips. 'And I definitely like this.'

The thought flashed across Holly's mind that he'd make a sensuous lover but she swiped it away. She didn't want to think that way about Matias: they were friends. Good friends. She felt so at ease with him, she could just be herself, not worry about how she looked or acted, what she wore. He was kind, fun, made her laugh… someone she could talk to about anything.

But if he were to get a girlfriend – and she had to face it, he could take his pick if he wanted – then that friendship would probably stop. The thought of not having Matias to hang out with, laugh with, share special moments with made her feel sad. Why was she even thinking about that? She was only here for the summer. She'd be back home in a few months.

That thought made her feel sad too.

She didn't want to leave Spain. And she didn't want to leave Matias.

*

He couldn't remember when he'd enjoyed a day so much, Matias thought as he and Holly walked along the seafront, hand in hand, over to the harbour. Holly had wanted to see the big yachts. 'I've always longed to go on a motor yacht, that's on my list too,' she said, eyes sparkling. 'I wonder if any of them do excursions.'

'You can hire one,' Matias told her.

'I guess you can, but do the owners hire themselves out too? I need someone to captain it for me.'

Matias thought of his family's motor yacht moored at Puerto Banús. He'd taken it out many a time and could borrow that, but it would mean crawling back to his father, and agreeing to work in the family firm again, which he had no intention of doing. Not even to allow Holly to tick off one of the items on her dream list. He'd turned his back on so much but he didn't regret it. His accident, not being able to walk for such a long time, had made him reassess his values. He wanted his life to be worth something, to help other people realise that they were worth something, not to help line the pockets of big organisations. And if that meant giving up his income as a lawyer, the family holiday homes in Florida, Paris and Venice, and the family motor yacht... well, that's a price he was willing to pay.

He watched Holly's face light up as she looked at the yachts. Her family had been pretty poor, he knew that from what she'd told him, but they'd been happy. His family were rich by comparison, but there was no closeness between them. His father only cared about appearance, winning the next big case; his mother only cared about keeping his father happy; and his sister Camila only cared about herself.

He didn't think he'd ever been with anyone so natural, so genuine as Holly. He cast his mind back to his previous girlfriends: not one of them would have laughed like that at being splashed – make that drenched. Her wet shorts had clung seductively to her legs and gained her a few admiring glances, which she seemed oblivious to. They would have been furious that they'd wrecked their clothes, messed up their hair and make-up, whereas Holly had thrown back her head and laughed, looking so alive, free – and sexy. And her dream list, it was such a simple one. There was nothing on there about wanting a big house, to win the lottery, to go to exotic places. She wanted simple things like a pet, to try out fifty different flavours of ice cream, ride on the back of a motorbike, go on a yacht.

And he wanted to help her achieve those things. He knew she was going back home after the summer, so they only had a couple more months together. He would swallow his pride and ask his mother if he could use the family yacht for a couple of hours. It was worth it to make Holly's dream come true.

'Take a photo of me by this one!' Holly called, her voice filled with laughter.

He looked up and saw her standing by a huge blue and white yacht with the words *Vida Amorosa* – Love Life – written across the front. That just about summed Holly up, he thought. She loved life.

He was going to miss her after this summer.

Chapter Thirty

Being out all day in the fresh air had exhausted Holly and she didn't wake until gone ten the next morning. Remembering that they had a crowd of people coming to a pool party that afternoon, she got straight out of bed, poured herself a glass of fresh orange juice, had a quick shower, applied some sun cream and lip gloss then went outside to see if Fiona and Pablo were up and needed any help with the preparations.

Pablo was outside, using the big net to clear insects and leaves out of the pool, but there was no sign of Fiona yet.

'*Hola*, Holly!' He waved to her. 'Fiona is in the kitchen, go on in.'

She waved back and made her way over to the kitchen, where Fiona was chopping up tomatoes, cucumber and peppers then tossing them into a bowl of already-washed lettuce.

'Morning, hun,' she said cheerily, then she frowned. 'You look tired.'

'Thanks. I didn't sleep very well,' Holly confessed. She watched as Fiona picked up a salad server spoon off the table and mixed the salad around. 'Can I give you a hand with anything?'

'You can pass me the salad dressing out of the fridge, please.' Fiona glanced over as Holly opened the fridge door. 'Did you have a good day out with Matias yesterday?'

'It was wonderful. I'm almost tempted to get myself a motorbike,' Holly told her. 'Now how about I make some sandwiches? How many people are you expecting?'

'About thirty. Pablo has invited some friends from the bar, and some of my students are coming too. Then there's Matias, and us three,' Fiona replied.

That many? It sounded like it was going to be a fun afternoon. 'We'd better get cracking then.' Holly took the bread out of the bread bin and started slicing it.

The strains of a familiar pop song drifted in from outside. 'Pablo is in a party mood already,' Fiona said. She took a jug of sangria out of the fridge. 'Do you think it's too early for a glass of this?'

'Not on a Sunday,' Holly replied. 'Shall I get the glasses?'

She took a glass out to Pablo, who was now inflating a big airbed. A couple of rubber rings were already floating in the pool. Holly felt her spirits lift. The sun was shining, the music was playing, the sangria was delicious. It was going to be a great day, and when Matias arrived she was going to smile and act perfectly normal. She'd soon get over this silly holiday crush she had on him.

Felipe arrived with a bunch of students then Matias, looking drag-to-bed-able in black swimming shorts and a black vest. He waved to Holly and started walking over to her when two of the female students homed in and started talking to him. She didn't blame them – he was by far the most attractive guy there.

She stamped down the little jealous voice inside her telling her to walk over and join in, and went over to Felipe and the rest of the students instead. It was a party; she should mingle, and she certainly wasn't going to be jealous of other women talking to Matias. He was a free agent.

More people arrived from the bar, immediately stripped down to their swimwear and dived into the pool amidst much laughing and splashing. Then Pablo suggested a swimming challenge and threw ten plastic hoops into the pool. 'The person who collects the most is the winner and chooses the next challenge,' he said.

Fiona suggested half a dozen players at a time so the pool wouldn't be too crowded, and Felipe was the first to volunteer. They stood on the side of the pool until the count of three and dived in. Holly watched in amusement: Felipe and Pablo were so competitive they actually pushed each other out of the way to get a hoop then Fiona dived under them and scooped it up.

'Best out of three!' Pablo insisted.

'Hey, the rest of us want a go,' one of the students shouted. 'Don't be a poor loser!'

There was much laughter as groups of six were formed and took their turn at collecting the hoops. Holly joined up with a group of Pablo's friends from the bar and managed to get the most hoops out of her group, then watched as Matias and his group, which included the two girls who were hanging on to his every word, dived in. Matias was down to the bottom of the water and swiftly scooping up hoops before Holly had time to blink. He emerged from the pool, water glistening on the dark hairs of his chest, his wet shorts clinging seductively to his hips, seven hoops dangling from his arm. Everyone clapped and cheered, and the two students flung their arms around his neck and planted kisses on his cheek.

'Hmm, well he's a fitness instructor so he's got an unfair advantage,' Felipe grumbled.

'It's only a bit of fun,' Pablo said good-naturedly. 'Come on, let's get the barbecue started. All that exercise has made me hungry.'

It's made me thirsty, Holly thought. She went over to the ice box and took out a cold beer.

'I think we have the same idea,' Matias said, joining her.

'Be my guest.' She held out a can. 'You were good, you scooped those hoops up in no time. I don't think Felipe was too pleased. He's still diving in, trying to beat your record.'

'*Gracias.*' He took the can off her. 'He is too competitive.'

Holly opened her can and took a swig of the ice-cold, refreshing drink. 'Thank you for yesterday. It was very kind of you to take me on your motorbike,' she said.

'It was a pleasure, I enjoyed it. Would you like another day out next Sunday? I have a surprise for you.'

'That sounds intriguing. I'd love to,' she told him. Then she noticed the two Spanish students watching them. 'I think you've got a couple of fans there.'

Matias shrugged. 'They are nice girls but not for me.'

He didn't fancy either of them, then. That made her feel ridiculously happy.

'What about you and Felipe? He is obviously keen on you.'

She followed his gaze and shook her head. 'Felipe doesn't have a motorbike,' she said mischievously.

'Ah, so it's the bike that attracts you, not me?' Matias asked softly

Something about his tone made her glance at him then wish she hadn't because the way he was looking at her made her think that maybe he wanted her to be attracted to him… maybe he was even attracted to her.

He reached out and touched her face lightly with his hand. 'Holly…'

'Ah, there you are.' One the women suddenly appeared at their side and slid her arm through Matias's. 'Juan wants to talk to you about joining your gym.'

He shot Holly an apologetic look and walked off, leaving her wondering what he'd been about to say.

And what she would have replied.

'Ah, alone at last.' She turned to see Felipe behind her. 'I've been wanting to ask you if you'd like to go out for the day? On a date?'

Damn, she had seen this coming and had done her best to avoid it. She liked Felipe, really liked him, but he felt more like the brother she had never had than a potential boyfriend. She didn't want to hurt him so she wracked her brains trying to think of a way to let him down gently.

'Holly, I forgot to give you a time for next Sunday. Okay if I pick you up about ten?'

She turned to Matias, who had suddenly appeared at her side.

'That'll be great, thanks, Matias,' she said, trying to pretend that she hadn't noticed the awkward atmosphere between the two men.

'*Bien.* Bring your swimwear,' he said. Then with a nod at Felipe he turned and walked off.

'I wish you'd told me you were going out with Matias. It would have stopped me making a fool of myself,' Felipe said, obviously hurt.

'I'm not. We're just friends. Like I am with you,' she protested.

'You don't look at me how you look at him,' Felipe said sadly.

What does he mean? Holly stared at him, wordlessly.

He touched her cheek. 'Don't look so worried, my heart will survive.' He smiled at her. 'Now excuse me, there's someone I need to talk to.'

As she watched him walk away, his words 'you don't look at me how you look at him' swirled through her mind. Fiona had said something similar. Why did everyone think she was in love with Matias? She hoped he didn't think so too. How embarrassing.

Then she remembered that Matias had been going to tell her something when he'd been called away. Perhaps it was something to do with Sunday. Where was he planning on taking her? Wherever it was, she couldn't wait to spend another day with him.

Chapter Thirty-One

'Where are you off to?' Fiona asked as Holly came out of her apartment the next Sunday morning wearing a pair of white shorts and a yellow T-shirt, and carrying a tote bag containing a bikini and towel.

'I've got no idea. Mati said it's a surprise.' She ignored the knowing looks Fiona and Pablo gave each other and pulled her sunglasses down from the top of her head. 'See you later!'

They'd decided to go in Holly's car so they could take a picnic basket. Matias had insisted on making it up and refused to let her peek inside. 'It's part of the surprise,' he said as he came out of the gate, clad in white shorts and a rust-brown vest top.

'Well, you're going to have to tell me where we're going or I won't know where to drive to,' she pointed out as she opened the boot and Matias put the basket inside.

'I was hoping you'd let me drive – that will keep the surprise a bit longer,' he said.

Now she was really intrigued. 'Okay,' she agreed, handing over the keys.

It felt a bit strange getting into the passenger seat of her own car, but she didn't mind being driven around. She looked out of the window as they set off, trying to pick up a sign of where they might be going.

It was about forty minutes later when she saw the sign for Puerto Banús. 'Is that where we're going?' she asked, turning to look at Matias.

He glanced briefly at her and smiled. 'Yes. Have you been here before?'

'No, but I've always wanted to. Fiona and Pablo said we'd go once the courses finish.'

Matias drove into an underground car park a few minutes' walk from the harbour and got a ticket for three hours. 'Where are we having the picnic?' Holly asked as Matias took the picnic basket out of the boot. Matias smiled at her. 'Wait and see. I told you it is a surprise.'

He took hold of Holly's hand and they walked together towards the harbour, where the yachts were moored.

'Some of these are amazing,' Holly said. 'Imagine owning a yacht.' Suddenly she had an idea why he had brought her here: hadn't she told him that one thing on her dream list was to go on a motor yacht? Some of these yachts were probably commercial and took tourists for a short trip around the bay.

'Are we going on a yacht?' she asked.

'Ah, you guessed,' Matias said with a smile. He stopped outside a white and steel-blue motor yacht called *Helena*. 'This is the yacht we are going on.'

'Wow! It's fantastic. *Helena*. It must be named after someone's wife or girlfriend. How romantic.'

'It's named after my mother,' Matias told her.

'This is your father's yacht?' Holly looked stunned. Matias's father must be very rich to own a yacht like this. She suddenly felt a bit awkward with him. He'd said his father was a lawyer but she hadn't realised he was such a successful one.

'He's had it some years now.' Matias climbed on board and held out his hand to help Holly on. 'Let me show you around then we'll go for a spin.'

It was a lovely yacht: six berths, light-oak finish, cream leather upholstery, marble floors, fully tiled bathrooms, luxurious bedrooms, compact but fully equipped kitchen. Holly hadn't dreamt that Matias's family could be this rich.

It doesn't matter how rich he is, he's just a friend, she told herself.

After he'd shown her around, Matias set off. Holly stood on the deck, gazing out at the vast expanse of sea ahead. She was glad that the sea was calm. She might not enjoy it so much on a choppy day.

'Just around the bay. We'll stop and have a picnic before we come back,' Matias said. 'We'll only be a couple of hours. I thought that was enough for your first time on a yacht. How does that sound?'

She nodded. 'That's perfect.'

*

He loved her enthusiasm for everything, Matias thought as he watched Holly taking photos.

'Do you mind if I share these on social media?' she asked.

He shrugged. 'Be my guest.'

They were almost at the end of the bay now, so he dropped anchor, put the picnic basket down on the deck and started laying out its contents.

'Your father must love your mother very much to name this yacht after her,' Holly said as they tucked into the picnic. 'That's such a romantic thing to do.'

Matias thought about this. His father was so formal, he hardly ever showed any emotion yet he was tender with his mother. He always kissed her before he went out and when he came back in, and, yes, they still looked at each other with love in their eyes. He hated how his mother always tried to keep the peace but that was because she loved his father, not because she was afraid of him, he realised. 'When they were teenagers they ran away so they could be together,' he told her. 'My mother's family disowned her, and so did my father's.'

Holly's eyes widened. 'Really? Why?'

'Because Mamá is English. She came over here for a holiday with her parents, met my father and they fell in love. She refused to go home and they ran away.'

'So that's why your English is so good, your mother is English. How old was your mother when they met?' she asked.

'Eighteen and my father was nineteen. About to go to university to be a lawyer. They got married, Mamá worked while Padre studied, and eventually the families forgave them, especially when my sister and then I came along.'

'Was your grandfather a lawyer too?' she asked.

'Yes, my family have been lawyers for generations.'

'Is that why your father is upset – because you aren't following the family tradition anymore?' she asked.

'Yes. My father is successful because he deals with a lot of corporate cases and doesn't always care if they're right or wrong.' Even as he said the words, Matias realised that they sounded petulant and unfair. His father had explained why he did this. 'He said he does it for the employees, so they don't lose their jobs,' he added.

Holly chewed her sandwich. 'I guess someone has to represent companies, and it's true, if they go under they take a lot of people with them. Was that the area of law you worked in too?'

'Yes, until my accident. I don't want to any more. I want to do something that means something, to help people.'

'Do you like being a fitness instructor?' she asked. 'Is it something you've always wanted to do?'

He gazed out at the sea as if considering this. 'I never thought about it until I had my accident,' he admitted. 'But exercise, getting fit, changed my life. And it can change other people's lives too.'

Holly reached over and placed her hand gently on his. 'I hope you and your parents sort things out. They sound like nice people and family is so important.'

He turned to her and for a moment their eyes locked. He felt an almost overwhelming urge to take her in his arms and kiss her. Instead he lightly touched her cheek with his finger. 'Yes, it is. Now I need to turn the boat around and steer back to the harbour. Would you like to have a go?'

'I'd love to,' she said. 'You'll have to tell me what to do though.'

'It is easy, come to the cabin.' He got to his feet.

He showed her how to use the throttle and shift control then stepped back and left her to steer the yacht back across the bay.

'This is fantastic!' she exclaimed, her face animated, the wind blowing her hair.

As Matias watched her, he was pleased he'd persuaded his mother to let him take the boat out, and not tell his father about it. He knew his mother hated this dispute between them, and the price he'd agreed for borrowing the yacht had been to keep in touch. It was a price he was happy to pay. He had no quarrel with Mamá. It was Padre who was so stubborn and opinionated, who wouldn't listen.

'I think you'd better take over now and steer it into the harbour,' Holly said.

Matias stepped forward and took over the controls. 'You did well. Maybe next time you can steer it into the harbour too.'

That was assuming there was a next time. He hoped very much that there would be.

Chapter Thirty-Two

Fiona and Pablo were sitting on the terrace sharing a bottle of wine when Holly returned home. 'Help yourself to wine,' Fiona said, indicating the bottle. 'Where did you go? What was the big surprise?'

'Would you believe going around Puerto Banús on Mati's dad's yacht?' Holly said as she put her bag down on the table and flopped down in one of the garden chairs. She reached for a spare glass, filled it with wine and took a swig.

'What? You're kidding me, right?' Fiona looked astonished.

Holly shook her head. 'Nope. Mati's dad is a rich lawyer. And the yacht is named after his mum.'

Fiona leant forward. 'Wow!'

'Yes. Wow just about describes it. The yacht's a six-berth, very posh, and Mati steered it like an expert. I had a go at steering too, it was brilliant. And we had a picnic on board.' She took another swig of wine. 'Turns out Mati is seriously rich but right now he's at loggerheads with his dad because he's chosen to work at the gym instead of at his dad's law firm.'

'Well, I can sort of understand his dad's point,' Fiona said. 'But it's up to Matias how he lives his life, isn't it?'

'Yes, and he has good reasons for being a fitness instructor. Since his accident he's specialised in training people with disabilities, to help them get as fit as they can so they can get the most out of their lives,' she explained.

'In that case I think his dad should be proud of him,' Fiona replied and Pablo agreed.

'So do I. Hopefully they'll make up soon.' Holly wiped her hand across her forehead. 'I feel all hot and sticky. I need a shower. See you in a bit.'

'Come back out and share this wine with us when you've finished. It's our last week before we're all rushed off our feet,' Fiona told her.

'I will,' she promised.

As she stepped into the cool water and lathered shower lotion over herself, Holly thought how much her life had changed in just four months. Who would have thought she'd settle in Spain so well, be comfortable – even if still a little nervous – driving up the track, learn Spanish, and not only print her own designs onto fabric to make soft furnishing but also teach others how to do it. Yes, she was a little apprehensive about that, but Fiona, who had taught art at college for years, and Pablo who'd run courses on sculpture back in the UK, had both assured her that she would be fine.

She loved her life now, she thought happily as she dried herself and got dressed. She pulled open a drawer to get her perfume and her gaze fell on her memory book on the dressing table. She took it out and flicked through the photos she'd taken in the last four months, starting with one of arriving at Las Mariposas, her, Fiona and Pablo decorating the rooms, the views from the mountain, the flowers – bougainvillea, hibiscus and sunflowers – that had inspired her designs, fresh oranges to make juice, having coffee with Felipe and some of the students, photos of Reino with its quaint pebbled streets and beautifully tiled houses. Turning to the back, she looked at the photos of the things she had achieved on the list.

Stroking Luna – her shared pet
Standing outside the *finca* – living in another country
Several photos of her eating different flavours of ice cream
A photo of her in the Spanish class
Unveiling the first roll of fabric with her very own design on it
Riding on the back of Matias's bike
The drop from the narrow road – getting over her fear of heights

She'd have another one to add soon: Matias had taken a photo of her steering the yacht.

She only had three to achieve now:

Go snorkelling
Learn the steps to a dance
Visit an underground cave

And, of course, the final one: being herself. And she was well on the way to doing that.

Her phone buzzed.

There will be no wine left if you don't hurry up. xx Fi

Holly replied she was coming, jumped off the bed and headed for the door. As she went over to the pool to join them, her face widened into a smile when she saw Matias there too.

'I printed out a photo from today – thought you might like it for your memory book. I can send the rest later.'

She looked at the photo he passed her, one of her at the helm, laughing as she steered the yacht towards the harbour.

'It's great, thank you. For everything. Fancy a glass of wine?'

'Actually,' he picked up a bottle from the table, 'I brought one with me.'

As Holly joined the friends that had made her new life possible, she thought that she had never felt more utterly content.

Chapter Thirty-Three

The following Friday

'They're here!' Fiona called as they heard the minibus pull up in the drive.

Pablo had gone with his friend to meet their first lot of guests at the airport – a group of three women and a man. Two other guests were arriving tomorrow.

Holly and Fiona both hurried out to greet the guests as they stepped out of the car. Two of the women looked in their late thirties, the other woman and the man were older, about fifty.

Fiona hurried over to welcome them. 'Welcome to Las Mariposas. I'm Fiona, and this is our artist-in-residence, Holly.' She air-kissed them all on both cheeks.

Holly followed suit and the guests awkwardly tried to do the same. It always took visitors a while to get used to the both-cheeks air kiss instead of just the one cheek.

'Would you like to put your bags in your rooms then sit on the terrace and have a cool drink?' Fiona asked when the introductions were over. 'Today is a "getting to know us and the place" day. The course sessions will start tomorrow.'

Fiona showed the older couple, Sally and Dennis, to their respective rooms while Holly guided the two younger women, Sadie and May.

They were friends and were sharing a double room, which meant all the guests could stay in the *finca* itself. Fiona had put them in the twin-bedded purple bougainvillea room, and their gasps of delight as Holly showed them to it made her feel really proud.

'The designs on these furnishings are gorgeous. Are they yours?' Sadie asked.

'Yes, they're a new line I'm developing. I used to only print my designs on objects such as mugs, phone cases and clocks,' Holly replied. 'Fiona was the one to suggest I print them on fabrics and make furnishings out of them. I'm thinking of printing them onto wallpaper too,' she added, remembering Susie's suggestion.

'Will you be talking about this in your sessions? And telling us how to do it?' May asked.

'We'll be concentrating initially on creating designs suitable for transferring onto items or fabrics, but I'll be answering any queries in the final session so I'll discuss that then,' Holly explained.

'It sounds wonderful,' May said enthusiastically. 'And this is such a pretty setting, perfect for an artist. There's inspiration all around us.'

'That's what we're hoping,' Holly told them. 'I'll leave you to settle in. When you're ready just turn left, go down the stairs, along the hall and out through the kitchen to the terrace. We'll be serving cold drinks and snacks in fifteen minutes.'

Pablo had already prepared the snacks and Fiona had made fresh orange juice that morning so they brought it all outside on the terrace. A few minutes later the guests came down to join them. They chatted for a while, asking about life in Spain, and then were given a tour of the grounds, stopping to admire the statues and gasping in astonishment when Fiona told them Pablo had made them. Pablo looked a little embarrassed at their praise, but Holly could see that he was pleased too.

Sadie and May were soon taking photos of interesting plants, of the mountains, the scenery while Dennis was trying to identify the plants and Sally was scribbling away in a little notebook. They all seemed really pleasant and Holly was looking forward to spending the next week with them. They'd planned a few days out too, so that the guests could take photos and make notes of things they'd seen then come back and sketch them. The aim was for them to have a portfolio of designs to work on when they went back home, and a finished product to take home with them.

Matias sent Holly a short text message after a couple of days to ask how the course was going but she didn't see him all week. She guessed that he was busy working at the gym and doing the renovations; she knew his aunt was eager to put the house on the market. He'd told her that he was planning on finishing it all by September although the weather was so hot at the moment she thought he would be finding it difficult to work.

Fiona and Pablo had scheduled the days so that the taught sessions took place in the mornings, and the afternoons were private work time for the guests to spend writing or creating. Late-afternoon was pool time, then dinner and drinks on the terrace. The week flew by and Holly really enjoyed running her sessions. She loved seeing the students' confidence grow and teaching them how to experiment with different styles and techniques. For the last lesson, she showed them how to upload their designs to a website where they could be printed onto items such as cushions, mugs and phone cases, and talked about how she'd adapted her designs so they could be printed on textiles. The guests were full of praise when they checked out Holly's Dandibug shop and made a note of the link so they could go online and order what they wanted.

The final evening they had a barbecue and pool party, and certificates were given out to all of the guests. They had all made something to take home with them: Dennis had made a small foot sculpture, which he was very proud of, while Sally had made a hand and painted a few palmistry lines on it; Sadie and May had both made small vases and the other two guests had made sugar bowls. Each guest had also created a sketchbook of drawings and written a short story each.

There were lots of cheers as they held up each of the items and collected their certificates, which Pablo had designed and printed out. They all had a fun evening and Holly was quite sad to see them go the next morning, but the next group would be arriving in the afternoon so it was a quick tidy around and then it was time to start again.

Chapter Thirty-Four

July turned into August, every day as busy as the last. The courses were fun but hard work and the guests were thrilled by what they had learnt during the week and the lovely work they had created. Many guests left promising to tell their friends about Las Mariposas, and to come back the following year.

Holly and Matias were both so busy they had hardly seen each other for the past few weeks. They'd kept in touch by text and Matias popped around a couple of evenings to have a quick glass of wine but but there was no chance to spend much time together. Even though Fiona had scheduled them all time off, they invariably spent it with the guests, sitting talking to them, going on trips with them. Whilst Holly enjoyed it all she was longing to go for another day out with Matias.

So when they actually had a free afternoon the second week of August, when one batch of guests had just gone and they were waiting for the next batch to arrive, she sent him a text asking if he wanted to join them for an hour.

'Give me ten minutes,' came the reply.

True to his word, ten minutes later he came walking up the drive. Holly smiled; it was so good to see him again. 'Want an orange juice?' she asked, pointing to the jug standing in a container of ice cubes on the table. 'It's freshly squeezed.'

'I'd love some.' Matias bent down and kissed Fiona then Holly on both cheeks, before pulling out the chair next to Holly and sitting down. 'How is the retreat going? Are you enjoying it?' he asked.

'Yes, I am,' she replied, her eyes sparkling. 'The students have been great and they've created some fantastic work.' She leant forward. 'How about you? Have you almost finished doing up your aunt's house?'

He nodded. 'I will be finished by the end of this month, then she can put it up for sale. September and October are good months to sell property in Spain.'

'Then what will you do?' Fiona asked.

'Rent a flat in Málaga again, near the gym. It will be good to have less travelling.'

Holly's heart sank at this. Even though she hadn't seen Matias much in the last few weeks, it had been good to know he was next door. She would miss him. But then she didn't know if she would be staying here after the summer. She hadn't given much thought to what she would do when the courses finished.

'Do you get a day off?' Matias asked. 'I was thinking that maybe we might go out for a ride one afternoon.'

'We're supposed to – we've made a schedule so we all have time off but it doesn't seem to be working out that way,' Fiona said ruefully. 'I'm sure we could spare Holly for an afternoon though. That is if you want to, Holly?'

'Sure. It'd be good to have a break. Do you have anywhere in mind?' she asked.

Matias folded his arms and leant back a little, his eyes fixed on her face. 'Are you over your fear of heights?' he asked.

'I think so. I'm not freaked out when I drive up and down the track now. Why?' Holly asked curiously.

'How do you fancy doing El Caminito del Rey?'

'Now that will certainly test you!' Fiona exclaimed.

'What is it?' Holly asked, puzzled. She looked from Matias to Fiona. 'It means "The King's Walk", doesn't it? Is it a walk up to a castle on a mountain?'

'I'll show you.' Matias took his phone out of his pocket, swiped the screen, tapped away then passed it to Holly.

Curious, Holly looked at the screen then gasped at the image in front of her. A narrow pathway ran alongside the face of a cliff, high above a gorge. And people were actually walking along it! Yes, there were barriers and the people were wearing hard hats, but it was so narrow and so high. She felt sick at the thought of it.

'I can see it is worrying you so forget it. We'll go somewhere else,' he said.

Holly gulped. Part of her wanted to do it. It would really show that she'd got over her fear of heights. And it must be safe: according to the write-up it was a massive tourist attraction, and the pictures even showed some older children walking along it. But had she got over her fear of heights enough?

'Let me think about it.' Holly turned to Fiona. 'Have you done it?' she asked.

'No, but we have often said we'd like to,' she replied. 'It's definitely one to tick off the list.'

'Come with us, we can wait until your courses are finished,' Matias told her.

'Actually, we do have a bit of a gap between courses next week. These guests leave early Friday morning and the next group doesn't arrive until late Friday evening. We could go then. That is if you want to, Holly. I don't want to push you into anything.'

She did want to. But could she bring herself to? 'How about I go with you but if I panic and think I can't do it, you three go ahead and I'll sit and have a coffee or something while I wait for you? Is that okay?'

'Only if you're sure?' Matias said.

'I am,' she insisted.

'I'll come by on Friday then. I'll book us a slot for midday.' He looked at Fiona. 'We'll be on the bike – are you and Pablo okay to get yourselves there?'

'Sure, we'll use the van,' she told him.

Just then, a minibus drove through the open gates. The guests had arrived.

'I'll leave you to greet your guests. See you Friday, about eleven?' he asked.

Fiona nodded as she got up and walked over to the minibus. 'See you then.'

Matias kissed Holly on the cheek. 'If you change your mind, it isn't a problem,' he assured her.

'I want to do it,' she said. And she really did. She just hoped she was brave enough.

Chapter Thirty-Five

As usual, the next week was hectic and Holly didn't have time to think about El Caminito del Rey until Friday morning. As soon as the guests had gone, they all set off. *You can do this*, Holly told herself as they whizzed along the road on Matias's bike, Pablo and Fiona following behind in their van. *Remember how nervous you were about going on the back of this motorbike? And driving up the track?*

She was going to do it. She was determined she was. No more scaredy-cat Holly.

But when they finally reached their destination and she was standing by the very high cliffs either side of the El Chorro gorge, looking up at the narrow path above them, a wave of panic engulfed her and she felt nauseous.

Matias reached out and squeezed her hand. 'Okay? Want to sit it out?'

She was about to say yes when she saw two young girls – they couldn't be more than eleven years of age – in the queue with their parents. If they could do it, she could.

She squared her shoulders back and held her head up, sticking her chin out defiantly. 'I'm going to do it!' Then she added, 'But you might need to hold my hand.'

'I will.'

And he did.

She loved the feel of his hand around hers: his hands were firm, strong, but not rough. He held her securely but not too tight, so that she could remove her hand if she wanted to. She didn't want to.

Holly had a couple of very panicky moments – as did Pablo, she was relieved to see – so they both walked close to the cliff wall. Holly looked straight ahead until her panic subsided, envious of the braver people who were looking over the barrier and taking photos of the view below.

'Shall I take a photo for you?' Matias asked.

Holly took a deep breath. 'No, thank you. I'll take one.'

She took her phone out of her pocket, walked to the barrier then looked down at the deep-blue water way below them. She gulped, quickly snapped a photo and stepped back. Matias put his thumb up, a big grin on his face. Behind her, Pablo shook his head in disbelief and Fiona held out her camera to show Holly the photo she'd just taken, of Holly standing by the barrier, photographing the gorge below.

I've done it, Holly thought happily. *I've mastered my fear of heights.*

As if reading her mind, Matias put his arm around her shoulders and squeezed her gently as he kissed her cheek. 'Another one off the list,' he said.

Chapter Thirty-Six

'Well, this is our last course,' Fiona said as they sat relaxing by the pool with their guests after the day's sessions had ended.

Holly felt a little sad. Summer was almost over. What would she do now?

As if sensing her thoughts, Fiona turned to her. 'You're welcome to stay on if you want – the apartment is yours for as long as you want it.'

Did she want to stay? Being in Spain these past few months had been like a slice out of real life. It had given her time to relax, to get over Scott, to try new things. But if she remained, what would she do? Fiona would go back to teaching English, Pablo to working in the bar, and what about her? They no longer needed her to help do up Las Mariposas and she didn't want to be in the way. She also needed to work and earn an income again, and that meant concentrating on her business; surely she had more chance of doing that in the UK?

Matias had almost finished renovating his aunt's house too and was moving back to Málaga later this month. It was all changing. It was time for her to move on, but to where and what she wasn't sure yet. She didn't want her Spanish adventure to come to an end, to say goodbye to her friends. Or to Matias.

'That's really kind of you, and I must admit that I don't want to go back, but I think I should. Pops's money won't last forever, and I need to earn a living.'

'Stay in our apartment and build up your soft furnishings business,' Fiona suggested. 'I'm sure that you'll get plenty of work making curtains and bedspreads. Your designs are so unique.'

'Oh gosh, I'm so tempted. I've loved being here.' She paused. 'But I think I should go home.'

"Well if you change your mind you're welcome to come back,' Fiona told her. 'Pablo and I are planning to run the retreat all year round, not just the summer. You could carry on teaching courses alongside your design work and we could rent you the apartment at a cheap rate, and pay you for teaching, of course.'

'That's so lovely of you, thank you. I definitely will think about it,' she promised. She wasn't really looking forward to going back to the UK – although it would be good to see her mum and stepdad again.

She was interrupted by a message from Matias:

The finca is finished. Do you want to come and see?

She texted back:

You bet!! I'll be with you in a few minutes.

'I'm popping around to see Mati for a bit – he's finished all the renovations and wants to show it off to me,' she told Fiona, grabbing her kaftan off the chair.

'Tell him well done. I wouldn't mind taking a look at it myself sometime.'

'I'm sure he'll be happy to show you. I'll mention it to him,' Holly told her.

This is it, the end of an era. Soon Matias's aunt's house will be for sale, Matias will be gone and I will be back in the UK, she thought sadly as she walked out of the gates and along the path. The gate was unlocked and Luna was waiting for her, tail wagging.

'I'll miss you, Luna,' she said, stroking the little dog's head.

'You are going home?'

She turned to face Matias, who was standing behind her. 'Yes, this is the last group of guests and then the retreat will shut down until next Easter.'

Matias looked at her thoughtfully. 'Do you want to go?'

No, I want to stay here with you. 'I don't know. I've loved it here and have made so many friends but I think it's time to go back. Get back to work.'

'Didn't your grandad give you the money to take a year out, to decide what you want to do with your life?' Matias asked. 'You have only taken six months.'

'I know, but my purpose here has finished. I came to get away and to help Fiona and Pablo get the *finca* ready for their retreat. I've done that. Now I need to give them some space and sort out what I'm going to do with my life.'

He nodded solemnly. 'I need to get back to my life too. My aunt's house is ready to be put up for sale, and I need to move back to Málaga, near the gym. Then I can put in more hours building up my business.'

'When are you planning on moving?' she asked him.

'The third week in September.'

So, they had two weeks left together.

'When does your final course end?' Mati asked her.

'Next weekend,' she told him.

'Then how about we spend the day together next Sunday? We can go snorkelling – you still have that to cross off your list, don't you?'

Her eyes brightened. 'Yes I do. That would be fantastic.'

His eyes held hers for a moment. 'There are some boats near the coast that do snorkelling trips; I'll book us a session. Is it okay to pick you up about ten?'

'Yes, please!' she said enthusiastically. That would be another one off her list. 'Thanks so much.'

'It's my pleasure,' he said softly.

She looked at him, her heart skipping a beat. Matias had become such a big part of her life, it was difficult to imagine him not living next door, she thought sadly.

'Perfect. Now let me give you a tour of the newly refurbished *finca*.' He took her hand and led her inside. She gasped in wonder as she looked around at the fitted kitchen with its beech cupboards, black marble worktop and Spanish-tiled walls; the elegant bathroom, again with traditional Spanish tiles; the fitted beech wardrobes in the bedrooms – it all looked so bright and fresh, with its white walls and light-wood furniture, yet he had still kept the Spanish touch.

'You've made a brilliant job of this, it looks lovely,' she said.

'I hope so,' he replied. 'We need it to sell quickly. My aunt needs the money to buy herself an apartment.'

Another pang of sadness swept over her. Matias would be gone soon. She would probably never see him again.

'I'm sure it will. I'm sorry but I've got to get back, the guests will have arrived,' she said. Excusing herself, she left before she did something stupid, like tell him she would miss him.

But she definitely would.

Chapter Thirty-Seven

Sunday

Matias and Holly set off for the coast straight after breakfast. Holly sat on the back of the motorbike, her arms wrapped around Matias, her body leaning against his, and closed her eyes, determined to enjoy every moment of the day. This would probably be their last day out together, she thought sadly. She had decided to return to the UK within the next couple of weeks; she wanted to see her mum and Owen, and needed to sort out her life. And Matias was moving back to Málaga soon. She would miss Spain, Fiona and Pablo, and Las Mariposas. And Matias, far too much.

They whizzed along the road as it cut through mountains, layers of dirt, stone then shrubs lining the high banks, winding up, then down, then up again, a ribbon of blue summer sky visible over the mountain tops. Finally, the sea came into view.

Matias pulled up near the harbour and they both dismounted then took their bags out of the back box. They made their way to the harbour, boarded the tourist boat Matias had booked them on and set off across the sea. Half an hour later they were being fitted with a vest, flippers and snorkel mask and tube, ready to dive into the quiet bay the boat had headed for, so they could snorkel in safety in the shallow waters.

The flippers were a bit awkward to put on, but Holly managed, then the guide ran through the safety procedure and they were off, diving one by one into the sea. Holly couldn't believe how many fish she spotted, although she quickly avoided a jellyfish she saw swimming a few metres away. She pointed it out to Matias, who was swimming beside her, and he nodded, altering his course too.

It was an exhilarating and amazing experience.

'That's another one off my list. Thank you so much!' Holly said when they returned to the harbour. She impulsively kissed him on the cheek. 'It's been a fabulous day.'

Matias smiled. 'I'm glad. Now how about a picnic on the beach? Not this one, we'll need to get back on the bike for a little while.'

'I'd love that. Have you brought a picnic with you?'

'No, but I've ordered one to be made for us.' He indicated a nearby restaurant. 'I hope you don't mind me selecting the food. I wanted it to be a surprise.'

'I don't mind at all,' she assured him. She was beginning to feel rather spoilt.

They collected the food, which the chef had put in a basket for them, then returned to the bike, putting the basket and their bags in the back box when they took out their helmets.

Matias took them along the coast road then turned to the left along a dirt track and pulled into a small car park.

Holly scrambled off and looked around. They seemed to be in the middle of nowhere. All she could see was dirt and shrubby grass. 'Where's the beach?'

'Over there, it's only a few minutes' walk.' Matias retrieved the hamper and together they walked over the shrubby grass until suddenly the ground started to slope down. There, a few feet below them, was a gorgeous expanse of white sand and shimmering, sun-kissed sea.

'It's beautiful. And deserted.' Holly gasped. 'Is it a private beach?'

'No, but not many people know about it.'

Matias held out his free hand and she slipped hers in it. Together they carefully descended the slope. At the bottom they both stood silently for a moment, still holding hands, gazing at the pretty-as-a-painting view: a couple of palm trees, a yacht sailing on the sea in the distance, the calm Mediterranean, the pale sand.

'Do you come here a lot?' Holly asked. What she really wanted to ask was, *Do you always bring your girlfriends here?* but the words sounded petty and she didn't want to know the answer. She wanted to believe that she was the only one he had brought here. That this gorgeous cove was just for them.

'I haven't been here for years,' he told her. He turned to her then, his face solemn. 'I wanted today to be special so this seemed the best place.'

He wanted today to be special too. Was it because, like her, he wanted a memory he could cherish, that he could think about over and over again, that he could remember her by?

It seemed like hours that they stood there gazing at each other, but it was really only seconds. Holly dropped her gaze first, scared that she was going to do or say something to ruin the moment. *You're friends, that's all,* she reminded herself.

'I'm starving, shall we have that picnic now?' she asked.

Matias took a blanket out of his backpack and laid it out on the sand, then they both unpacked the hamper: Iberian ham, fresh salmon, crispy, colourful salads, cold chicken, crusty seeded rolls, and an exotic fruit salad with fresh cream. Plates, cutlery and crockery were in the basket too.

'This looks delicious,' Holly said as they both tucked in.

✻

'How about we have a bit of a sunbathe now, let the meal go down,' Matias suggested when they had finished eating.

'Sounds good to me.' Holly sat up and Matias couldn't take his eyes off her as she started to pull off her top. He slid his gaze down to her exposed stomach then back up again. Then, looking right at her, he started to pull off his vest top, his eyes never moving from hers as they both undid their shorts and slipped out of them in a mutual striptease. The air was heavy with anticipation as they stood facing each other. Holly looked totally gorgeous in her white bikini; he'd hardly been able to take his eyes off her on the boat, and now they were alone together, it was even more difficult.

'Thanks for today,' she said. 'The scuba diving, the picnic, it's been amazing.'

'You're welcome,' he said, his voice sounding husky even to his ears.

'I'm going to have a paddle to cool down first. Race you to the sea!' she said, running off across the sand.

He jumped up and followed her, covering the sand with long strides, giving her a wave as he passed her. She wasn't far behind him, jumping in the clear sea and laughing as she splashed him.

He bent down and scooped her up so her face was level with his. 'You're amazing,' he said softly. Then he kissed her. A slow, deep, lingering, definitely-not-friends kiss, and she kissed him back. The sea lapped gently around them as they kissed, hugged and caressed, their bodies melting into each other. He pulled her closer, one hand at the back of her neck and the other around her waist; she ran her fingers through his hair, her other hand tracing along the waistline of his shorts.

'*Dios*, you are beautiful,' he murmured, his lips moving down to her throat.

She arched her neck back, savouring his kisses, and he had to fight down the urge take his kisses lower.

'I think we should go back to the beach,' he murmured in her ear.

Arms around each other's waists, they raced through the knee-deep sea to the sand, throwing themselves down where they had abandoned their clothes and shoes, and moving into an embrace.

'I'm not sure "friends" should be quite as friendly as this,' Matias murmured as he ran his hands over her body and her fingers trailed down his chest, playing around the top of his trunks, sending shivers of desire coursing through him.

She rolled on top of him, leaning up on her elbows and smiling teasingly. 'We could be friends with benefits...'

'Now, that sounds a very good idea.' He pulled her down on top of him, his hand caressing her bare back, moving up to play with the catch on her bikini top. She wriggled away. 'This beach might be deserted but I don't think it's private enough for that,' she told him.

She was right. What was he thinking? 'Let's go back to my flat,' he said. 'We're not that far away.' He ran his thumb along her bottom lip. 'I want you, *mi amor*.'

. 'I want you too,' she whispered, 'but it's a bit public here.'

His eyes darkened. 'Then let's go.'

They grabbed their clothes and dressed almost as quickly as they had undressed. Holly reached for her bag when suddenly her phone rang. She took it out and glanced at the screen.

'It's my stepdad, Owen!' she said, her eyes widening with alarm. 'He's tried to phone me eight times!'

She swiped the screen. 'Owen. Is everything okay. Mum?'

'I'm sorry, love. I'm afraid your mum's in hospital.' Matias heard the man's voice break. 'She's had a heart attack, Holly.'

Chapter Thirty-Eight

Holly gripped the phone, her mind swirling. Mum, the only close family member she had left, was in hospital. Could die.

She felt Matias's arms around her, supporting her as she asked, her voice breaking, 'Is she… is she going to be okay?'

'I don't know, love. I hope so.' Owen sounded distraught. She could imagine him now, red-eyed, scared that his world was about to collapse. She should be there with him, with her mum.

'I'll get the first flight home that I can,' she promised. 'I'll go online and check the flights now.' Her mind was reeling. Mum couldn't die. She couldn't. She turned to Matias, her hands shaking. 'It's Mum. She's been rushed to hospital. She's had a heart attack.'

'Oh *cariña*, I am so sorry.' Matias wrapped his arms around her in a big hug and tenderly kissed her on the forehead. She lay there for a moment, resting her head on his shoulder, wanting to stay there forever but also wanting to book a flight right now. 'Come, let us find you a flight to England,' he said softly. 'What airport do you want to go to?'

'Manchester,' she gulped.

He gently released her and pulled up flights to Manchester on his phone.

'There is a flight in three hours. Is that too soon?' he asked. 'I can take you straight to the airport now. Are you okay to travel as you are? Do you have your passport on you?' Most tourists carried their passports with them in case they needed to show ID.

'Yes, it's in my bag, so is my bank card, and I have clothes in my bedroom at home in the UK.' Anything else she needed, she could buy. All she wanted to do was get to her mum. Right now.

'Should I book the flight for you?'

'Please.' Holly dug her passport and bank card out of her handbag and handed them to Matias. She was shaking so much she didn't trust herself to key in the details.

'Are you okay to travel alone? Would you like me to come with you?' Matias asked.

Yes! her heart screamed – she really didn't want to travel alone, but *No!* her head said. Matias had his gym, and other stuff to see to here. It wouldn't be fair to drag him over to England, and there was nothing he could do there. She'd be spending all her time at the hospital with her mum.

'I'll be fine. Honestly. I'll get a taxi from the airport to the hospital. I'll message you as soon as I know how Mum is,' she promised.

Matias quickly booked the flight. 'Done, now let's go.'

They were at the airport in no time. Matias stayed with her until she was about to go through security.

'Thank you for… being there,' she said.

'You're welcome.' His eyes were filled with compassion. He drew her into a hug, kissing her forehead. 'You will keep in touch, let me know how you are? Promise?'

'Of course,' she said, her voice catching in her throat as she hugged him goodbye.

✳

Holly phoned Fiona to explain what had happened as soon as she sat in the departure lounge, Her friend was shocked and sympathetic, comforting her that most heart attacks weren't fatal, and asking Holly to let her know as soon as she found out how her mum was.

As she sat on the plane, Holly felt almost numb. The events of the last few hours had shocked her to the core. She and Matias had spent such a special day together: she'd felt so close to him, closer than she had ever felt to Scott. Or any of her other boyfriends. Her body had been so on fire with desire for him that she'd had to hold back from making love to him right there on the sand. If Owen hadn't phoned, they'd be in Matias's apartment, making love right now. But Owen had phoned and her mum was in hospital; she could die. There was no time to think of Matias.

'Holly!' Owen stood up and came to greet her as she rushed into the hospital waiting room. 'I am so sorry to have to drag you over like this.' He looked pale, with dark rims under his eyes. 'Your mum's okay, love. She's in the cardio ward, recovering. She has to stay in for a couple of days to be monitored, and needs to take medication for angina, but she's going to be okay.'

'Oh, thank goodness for that!' Holly finally let the tears flow. 'I thought I was going to lose her.'

'So did I, love.' Owen gave her a big hug. 'I'm sorry, I should have waited to see what the hospital said before I phoned you. I was just scared it might be fatal and…'

Owen's first wife had died from a heart attack, Holly remembered. 'And you wanted to give me chance to say my goodbyes? You were right to call me. I want to be here for Mum.' She eased herself out of

Owen's hug and pulled a tissue out of her pocket, dabbing her eyes with it. 'Excuse my clothes,' she said, suddenly realising she was still wearing shorts and a vest top. 'I was on the beach when you phoned and my friend Mati booked me a flight right away.'

'Living the high life, eh?' Owen teased.

'Mr Swinton?' They both turned at the doctor's words. 'You can go in to see your wife now.'

'I'm her daughter. Can I go too?' Holly asked.

'Of course. But don't stay long. It's best not to tire her. She's in room 4c at the end of the corridor.'

Holly followed Owen down the corridor then paused outside the door. He was bound to want a few words with Mum alone. 'You go in and I'll follow in a few minutes,' she told him. 'Let her know I'm here; we don't want to give her a shock.'

'Thank you.' Owen pushed open the doors to the room and Holly sat on one of the chairs outside and closed her eyes, letting the relief flood through her. *Mum is okay. Thank goodness.* She'd text Matias and Fiona and tell them the good news as soon as she left the hospital.

She gave Owen five minutes then knocked and walked in. Mum was propped up in bed, wearing a light-blue hospital gown, and with various bits of equipment attached to her, holding Owen's hand. She looked older and frailer than Holly had ever seen her before, but her face broke into a smile when she saw Holly. Holly's heart lurched. She was used to seeing her mother as strong, capable, indestructible. She hurried over to the bed.

'It's so good to see you, Holly. I'm sorry to make you dash back on a false errand. Owen shouldn't have messaged you really.'

Holly kissed her gently on the cheek and sat down on the other side of her. 'I'm very glad he did, Mum. I'd much rather come dashing home and find that you're going to be okay than…' She didn't finish that sentence but they all knew what she meant.

*

Holly was in Matias's thoughts all afternoon. She'd looked so distraught at the thought of losing her mother, so desperate to see her and make sure she was okay, that she had dashed over to the UK with only the possessions she had on her. It had made him think of his own parents. How would he feel if anything happened to them? If his father had a heart attack with this rift still between them?

He would go and see his father tomorrow, see if he could patch things up – he still had no intention of returning to the business, but surely they could remain on good terms. His father had to allow him to lead his own life, to respect his decisions. Matias vowed he would stay calm and try to properly explain why his new career as a gym instructor meant so much to him.

It was later that evening when he finally got a text from Holly saying that her mother was recovering well; she had angina and was receiving medication for it but would be home in a few days.

Thank you so much for being there for me and taking me to the airport.

He wanted to say that he would always be there for her but instead he typed:

You're welcome. Take care. Xx

His mind was still trying to take in the fact that Holly had gone back to the UK, that he would no longer see her bright, sunny smile, hear her laughter, see her sun-kissed chestnut hair dancing around her face as she walked, be able to hold her, kiss her, tell her he loved her – as he'd been on the brink of doing when she got that phone call.

It was for the best, he reminded himself. He was getting too close to her, had even been thinking of asking her to stay in Spain, to move to Málaga with him, which would have been a mistake. Getting close to any woman would be a mistake. He needed to get back to his life, his work, and not be distracted.

But first he had to make peace with his father.

✻

Fiona phoned Holly late that evening. 'Are you all right, hun? That must have been such a shock to you. I'm so glad your mum's okay.'

Tears pricked Holly's eyes as she heard her friend's voice. It had been a shock. And now she was sitting on her bed trying to absorb the fact that she was back in the UK, without her car, her laptop, her clothes – although she had plenty in the wardrobe here – and without Matias.

'I'm fine, just a bit shaken up. Mum's always been so full of life, and it's horrible to see her lying in the hospital bed looking so weak. The doctor said she's got to take things more carefully and take medication for the angina.'

'I'm so sorry, but honestly, hun, a lot of people live with angina. It's perfectly manageable.'

'I know.' She kept telling herself that but couldn't help worrying. What if Mum had another, more serious, heart attack? 'I'm sorry that I've left you with all my things, and my car. I'm not sure when I'll be back. I want to make sure Mum is fully recovered first.'

'Don't be silly, it's no problem at all. Your mum needs you right now.'

They chatted for a while longer then Holly phoned Susie. It would be good to meet up with her friend while she was back in the UK.

Susie was delighted to hear from her, and very concerned about Rachel. 'Thank goodness she's okay, Hol. Why don't we meet up for a drink tomorrow night and catch up on the news?' she suggested.

'Sounds good to me,' Holly agreed.

She felt odd being back in this house again, with Mum in hospital. It was Mum and Owen's house, and she felt like a stranger. She missed Spain too. And Matias. She shut her eyes and relived the feel of his arms around her, his lips on hers. She wanted to get back on a plane so she could see him again, but she also wanted to stay here until her mum was stronger, to help out in the shop until she got back on her feet.

Her mum was more important. Matias was a friend – a good friend. They were physically attracted to each other but there was no future in it. And she didn't want there to be. Neither of them wanted a relationship, they'd agreed that.

Chapter Thirty-Nine

'Wow, look at you! All tanned, toned and utterly gorgeous with your sun-streaked nut-brown hair – which really suits you. You look great. I think Spain agrees with you. It's great to see you again. I've really missed you,' Susie gabbled as she enveloped Holly in a big hug.

'I've missed you too but I've had a fantastic time,' Holly said when Susie finally released her. It was so good to see her friend again. She filled Susie in on the events of the summer, casually mentioning Matias as if he was just a friend, which he was, even if her heart was trying to make it more than that.

'Shame you had to come back so quickly. It must have been such a shock about your mum. Thank God she's going to be okay.' Susie poured more Coke from the bottle into her glass of vodka and Coke. 'What are you going to do now? Stay in the UK?'

Holly ran her finger around the edge of her wine glass. 'I'm not sure…'

'Spain was that good, eh?' Susie took a long drink before adding, 'And how much of your dream list have you managed to tick off?'

'Most of it, actually,' Holly said. She opened the Notes app on her phone and showed Susie the list. 'See, there's only a couple of items to go. I haven't been to an underground cave – Mati and I were going to do those later this month – or learnt a dance, I've been so busy. And there's a few more flavours of ice cream to get through.'

'This Matias seems very helpful,' Susie said, a twinkle in her eye. 'Do I detect a romance?'

'Absolutely not. He's going back to live in Málaga anyway.'

'Which is how far from where you were?'

'About half an hour's drive, but he's going to be busy with his gym and I… well, I'm not sure what I'll be doing yet.'

'There's the last item to tick off too. Be yourself.' Susie leant back and surveyed her. 'I reckon you're nearly there. You look a lot happier and stronger than I've ever seen you.'

Yes, because I was always trying to make Scott – and all the other guys I went out with – happy, Holly thought. Now she just did what she thought was best.

'Let's change the subject from me, how are you and Liam getting on? Any sign of wedding bells?'

'We're happy how we are,' Susie told her. Then, suddenly, her face froze. 'Oh my God! Don't turn around but Scott has just walked in.'

Scott. Holly instantly dropped her hand from the glass she was about to pick up and she froze, stunned. Scott was the last person she'd expected – or wanted – to see. 'Is he looking at me?' she whispered.

'Yes – and he's coming over,' Susie replied quietly. 'Quick, pick up your drink and act normal.'

Scott was coming over to their table and she was supposed to act normal?

'So, will Matias pick you up from the airport when you return to Spain?' Susie asked in a very loud voice.

Before Holly could respond, Scott was beside them.

'Holly?'

She turned to face him very slowly. 'Oh, hi, Scott.'

He was staring at her, really staring, as if he liked what he saw. 'You look great, Holly. Really great. I heard you'd gone to Spain. Are you back for good?'

He looked great too, just as handsome as she remembered with his blond, cropped hair, designer stubble and piercing blue eyes. It seemed like he knew it too, that seductive half-smile on his lips, the slight tilt of the head as his eyes held hers, the soft, almost caressing voice. Did he really think his charm would still work on her?

'No, I came because my mum's ill. I'm going back to Spain soon.' She nodded her head. 'Nice to see you again, Scott.' Then she turned her attention back to Susie to let him know he was dismissed. She could *feel* his eyes on her but refused to look around again.

'Bye then,' Scott finally said and walked away.

'Wowie, you handled that well, Miss Cool,' Susie said admiringly. 'I was afraid you were going to melt at his feet. So, you are definitely over him then?'

'Absolutely. I haven't thought about him for months.'

✷

'Matias, it is so good to see you,' his mother gushed, her bright eyes taking in the beige chinos and dark brown shirt he'd worn as a token to smartness. There was no point in antagonising his father before he even began talking to him.

He leant over and kissed her on the cheek. 'Hello, Mamá, is Padre expecting me?'

'No, I wanted it to be a surprise.'

More likely scared he'd have a fit and ban her from allowing me in. 'Is he in his study?'

'Yes, he's on the phone to a client. Can I make you a drink while you wait for him to finish?'

'*Gracias.* A small Scotch, please?' He needed the drink to cope with what was sure to be a difficult conversation. Come what may, he was determined to keep his cool and leave on good terms. He didn't want a rift with his parents.

'You are not driving?' his mother asked.

'I took a cab,' Matias replied as his mother walked over to the drinks cabinet and took out the decanter of Scotch and two small glasses.

'Matias!' As usual his father's voice arrived before his body. 'To what do I owe this pleasure?' He glanced at Matias's smart clothes. 'It looks like this is a business call. Are you hoping to talk me into a loan for your business? You must be missing your wage from the company.'

Count to ten, Matias told himself. He took a deep breath. 'Not at all. I came to see you because I would like us to talk, for you to understand why the gym is so important to me, and to at least accept it even if you don't understand it.' He took a sip from the Scotch his mother handed him after passing a glass to his father. 'I don't like bad feelings between us.'

'That sounds a wonderful idea.' Matias knew without even turning around that his mother would be clasping her hands behind his back, casting a beseeching look at his father.

He saw a muscle twitch in his father's cheek, then he nodded. 'Very well. I too dislike bad feelings. You are my only son. Come into my study and we will talk.'

Well, that was a first. Matias followed his father into his very impressive study, taking a seat on the dark brown leather couch. He wasn't going to let his father talk to him across the desk as if he was a client.

Antonio looked a bit put out but then sat on the opposite end of the couch. 'Where would you like to start?' he asked, in Spanish.

Matias replied in Spanish, 'I want to tell you why being a fitness instructor for the disabled is so important to me, and I would like you to listen without interruption. When I've finished, I'm happy to answer any questions you have, and to listen to what you have to say. Deal?'

Antonio nodded slowly. 'As you wish.'

Matias told him what he had told Holly. How helpless he had felt after the accident, as if his life had finished, how ashamed he felt for his family to see him as he was then, how one day he had decided to fight back, that he wouldn't allow this to happen to him, he wouldn't let the accident define his life, and how he was determined to walk again. How the physiotherapist helped him, and then an instructor at the gym, when he was stronger. That instructor, Ian, had helped Matias believe in himself again, had worked with him to help him get fit. And when the miracle happened and Matias did finally walk again, he had wanted to do the same for others. So he had retrained as a fitness instructor, specialising in working with the disabled. 'Many of them, they come to me lost, without hope, feeling a burden as I once did. But their faces, Padre, as I help them get stronger, when they realise that maybe they won't walk again but they can still be fit and there is still a lot they can do: that makes it worth all the money I have given up from being a lawyer.'

Antonio listened silently, as if he was really interested.

'I know that was a bad time for you, my son, but I got you the best doctors, the best people I could buy.'

'What I needed, Padre, was hope. Something that made me feel better about myself, something that made me feel a man again. Exercising did that for me. It gave me social interaction, goals, a routine; it made me stretch myself, to dare to aim higher. That is what I want to give my clients.'

'I understand and have been giving this a lot of thought.' Antonio nodded. 'I had hoped that you, my one and only son, my pride and joy, would work with me,' he continued, 'but of course I must respect your decision to live your own life. However, I have a proposition that may suit us both.'

His father was willing to compromise? That was another first! Now it was Matias's turn to nod and listen as his father continued in Spanish.

'Your accident was a terrible shock to both me and your mother. We were extremely worried about you. I know that I did my usual "throw money at the problem hoping to find a solution" – that is because I did not know what else to do.' He sighed. 'When the miracle happened and you walked again, I thought – hoped – you would come back to work in the company. I accept now that this is not your wish, but,' he paused and took a sip of his whisky, 'I have been making enquiries for some time about branching out a little in a new direction, and now we are all set to go ahead. I need a lawyer trained to deal with serious negligence claims, to fight pro bono for clients who have been left disabled because of an accident at work, or in the street. This is not a full-time position, so I was wondering if you would consider taking it. You can work a couple of days a week, alongside your fitness instructor job.'

To say Matias was astonished was putting it mildly. He had never expected a proposal like this from his father. He didn't know what to say.

'Promise me that you will at least consider it?' Antonio said. He picked up a folder from his desk and handed it to Matias. 'The details are all here.'

Matias nodded. He owed his father that much. 'I will.' He stood up and held out his hand. '*Gracias*, Padre.'

The two men shook hands, and then as if she had been listening with her ear to the door – which she probably had – his mother came in, carrying a tray containing a bottle of champagne and three glasses, as if Matias had already made his decision.

'We must celebrate,' she said, her face wreathed in smiles. 'To family.'

Chapter Forty

Holly went to see her mum in hospital again that evening and was delighted to see her looking perkier.

'It's lovely to see you, Holly,' Rachel said, as Holly kissed her on the cheek then sat down on the chair beside the bed. 'You look so tanned, confident and happy. Like a different person. Living in Spain has done you good.'

'Thanks, Mum, it's been fantastic. Fiona and Pablo have been great, and I've made so many friends.'

'Anyone special?' Rachel asked.

Matias with his sensuous tawny eyes, thick dark hair, lips that kissed her like no one had ever kissed her before…

'Don't let a man rule your life again, Holly. Promise me that,' Rachel said softly as if she had read her thoughts.

Holly reached out and placed her hand on her mum's. 'I won't, Mum. I like my independence too much, and I realise now that I don't need a man to make me happy.'

Rachel looked relieved. 'I'm pleased to hear it.' Then she smiled. 'That doesn't mean you can't have a man in your life, of course. Just make sure that you're with him because he adds something to your life, because your life is better with him than without him.'

Holly nodded. 'I will. Don't worry.'

Owen arrived then so Holly left to give them some time alone.

She hadn't been back home more than ten minutes when the doorbell rang. She walked out of the kitchen, where she'd been in the process of making a cup of coffee, to open the door and stood staring in shock at Scott, standing on the doorstep with a bunch of red roses.

'What are you doing here?' she asked.

'I haven't been able to stop thinking about you since we split up,' he said. 'Then when I saw you today I knew I had made a big mistake letting you go. Please give me another chance, Holly.' He thrust the bunch of roses in her hand then rummaged in his pocket and got down on one knee. 'I love you, Holly. I want to marry you. Please say yes.'

He held out a red velvet box, opened to reveal a beautiful diamond engagement ring.

Dumbstruck, Holly gaped at Scott, down on one knee in front of her, holding out an engagement ring. He was actually proposing!

'Say something, Holly. Please. I can't stay like this for much longer, my knee is killing me,' Scott said.

Her mind was reeling. Why now? Why, after all the time they were together, when she had been longing to marry him, willing him to propose, was Scott doing it now?

When it was too late, when she was no longer in love with him. She shook her head. 'I'm sorry, Scott, but I can't marry you.'

She saw the disbelief then disappointment register on his face as he scrambled to his feet. 'Why not? I thought that's what you always wanted?' he grumbled.

What a nerve! He obviously expected her to be so grateful she'd shout yes and have the ring out of the box and on her finger before he could change his mind.

'That's when I thought that I loved you and you loved me, Scott. I was wrong.' She folded her arms across her chest. 'We split up months ago, we've both moved on. So why propose now?'

A scowl crossed his face. 'What do you mean you've moved on? Have you got someone else?'

'It's none of your business. We've been over for ages,' she reminded him.

The scowl left his face and was replaced by the cute, pleading look she remembered so well. 'I know but I miss you. I've realised how much I love you. And you love me too, don't you?' His voice was soft, coaxing. The voice that had always made her heart melt. Not any more.

'No, I don't. And I don't believe you love me either.' She shook her head. 'Sorry, Scott, but we are over. Goodbye.' She shut the door then stood with her back against it while she gathered her breath. Scott proposing to her would have been at the top of her dream list at the beginning of the year. Now, all the love she thought she had for him had gone, and marriage was the last thing on her mind.

How her life had changed.

＊

Matias closed the folder and walked outside. He had to admit that his father's proposition was well thought out, and that he was definitely interested in it. Antonio had made it clear that Matias would be in charge of the branch of the firm that dealt with legal cases concerning people with disabilities, and that the costs would be subsidised for people who couldn't afford the full fees. He was also giving him the power to employ more staff if he wanted. So he was accepting that Matias would not be coming back to the company full-time.

His father had finally found a heart.

Or maybe he was doing his father an injustice, Matias thought as he strolled over to the pool and sat down on the bench beside it. His father had always had a heart, but it was ruled by his business sense. His speech that by saving corporate firms from going under he was saving hundreds of jobs had made Matias realise that. Yes, his father had been distant in Matias's childhood, had always been working, but that had been his way of providing for them. Knowing how his grandparents had initially disowned his father and mother, how Antonio had been determined to make his own way, probably to make them proud of him, made Matias understand his father's reasons for working so hard, his determination to make a success of his life. He shouldn't judge him so harshly. He would be a fool not to accept his offer: and he realised that he actually did miss working as a lawyer, even though he had initially resented his father pushing him into the career. Well, he would be working on his own terms now, and as much as he enjoyed his work at the gym, it didn't earn him a good living. This way he could do both jobs, and still be helping the vulnerable people he cared so deeply about.

He picked up the phone and dialled his father's number.

Chapter Forty-One

Holly's mum was discharged in a couple of days, with strict instructions to take it easy. Louise Unsworth-Murphy, a good friend of Rachel's, had offered to help out at the shop while her mum recovered, so Holly, Owen and Louise shared shifts.

'How's Rachel today? Is she up to receiving visitors?' Louise asked as Holly walked in, ready to take over for her shift. 'I've got a couple of books she might enjoy reading, and a box of her favourite chocolates.'

'She'd love that. She's a bit fed up of being stuck indoors and is dying to catch up on all the news,' Holly told her. 'Message her, I'm sure she'll ask you to pop over right now.'

'Will do, and I've got some good news for her too. I sold the walnut butler's cabinet today, and the man's put a deposit on the French walnut settee too. He's coming to pick it up this weekend.'

That was over £2,000 worth of sales. Her mum – and Owen – would be delighted. 'That's brilliant, thanks Louise. That will definitely cheer Mum up.' She paused. 'It's really kind of you to help us out in the shop. Are you sure you won't accept payment for it?'

Louise waved her hand, pooh-poohing the idea. 'Definitely not. Rachel is a good friend and it's a pleasure to help her.' She went into the back of the shop to get her coat and bag. 'Right, I'll give your mum a ring and see if she wants me to pop to the shops for anything before I go to visit her. See you tomorrow, dear.'

'Bye, Louise.' Holly knew her mum would have a spark back in her eyes after an afternoon chatting with Louise. It was just what she needed to cheer her up. And what a good sale. She hoped that meant things were picking up at the shop. Her mum and Owen worked long hours, and Owen had told her that they were only just about breaking even; he was worried it was stress that had caused Rachel's heart attack. Well, she'd stay and help them until Mum got back on her feet again, then she'd think about what she was going to do next.

She missed her life in Spain, and she missed Matias. He'd messaged her a couple of times to check her mother was okay, but she hadn't heard from him for a few days now. *He's busy. He has a job and his aunt's* finca *to sell,* she reminded herself.

Gradually Rachel recovered and returned to working at the shop, just a couple of days a week at first, then full-time. Holly worked in the shop less and less. It was time for her to make a decision about what she was going to do. She'd been back in the UK for nearly six weeks now. She missed Spain, and Matias. Although she hadn't heard from him for a few weeks now. Fiona had told her that his aunt's *finca* had been sold and he'd popped around to say goodbye. She guessed he'd moved to Málaga and was busy settling in his new apartment. She was a bit disappointed as she'd have liked to keep in touch more, even if they were in different countries.

'Thank you for coming back home and looking after me, Holly. And for helping in the shop,' Rachel said over dinner one evening. 'I really appreciate it and if you want to stay you're very welcome.' She cut a slice out of her chicken fillet. 'But I don't want you putting your life on hold for me. I'm fine now and I promise I'll be taking it easier. Owen will see to that.'

She smiled over at Owen, who nodded his head firmly. 'You bet I will.'

'And Louise has offered to cover anytime I want a break, so please don't think you have to be my nursemaid.' She popped the chicken into her mouth and chewed it, her gaze fixed on Holly, obviously waiting for her answer.

They're both wondering if I'm going back to Spain or getting a place of my own, thought Holly. *I wish I knew!* Fiona had asked her the same question last time she'd called her.

Her car and possessions were still in Spain. She'd been using Mum's car and Owen's old computer while she was here but she couldn't keep doing that. All the files she needed for her business were on her laptop and it was difficult to keep it going without it. Fiona had offered to arrange to have her things shipped over if she wanted but she thought she should go back. She had unfinished business with Matias. And she missed her life in Spain.

'I'm not sure what I want to do, Mum. I think I'll go back to Spain for a bit, if only to collect my car and things,' she said. 'And I made quite a few friends there. It'll be nice to say goodbye to them if I do decide to come back. I'll book a flight for early next week.'

Rachel nodded. 'Do what you want to do, Holly. Remember that was Pops's wish. Make a life for yourself wherever you're happiest.'

'I will,' Holly promised. 'Wherever I decide I want to live, I'll rent myself a flat. It's time I got myself a permanent home again.'

'Well, remember that you're welcome here anytime,' Owen told her. 'You don't have to ask, just turn up.'

Holly reached over and touched his hand. 'Thank you.' He was a lovely man and had been like a father to her but she needed to give them both some space, and to sort out her life.

She checked out the flights and booked one for Monday morning, landing around midday, then phoned Fiona to say she was coming back.

'Brilliant! I'll pick you up from the airport. I've only got one teaching session that morning,' Fiona replied.

'Thank you.' She paused. 'Do you ever see Matias?' She'd been wondering whether to text him and let him know that she was coming back to Spain.

'Not since his aunt's *finca* was sold and he moved to Marbella.'

Marbella? She thought he was moving to Málaga to be nearer the gym, but she guessed Marbella wasn't that far away. Very upmarket. Perhaps he was moving his gym there too. Is that why he no longer messaged her, because he'd moved on and she was just a 'holiday romance'? Well, she'd promised herself after Scott that she would live her life for herself, not go chasing after men. It didn't matter whether she saw Matias or not: she had to go back for her car, her laptop and her possessions, and to either say goodbye and give closure to her life in Spain or make the decision to live there permanently.

Chapter Forty-Two

It was good to be back. Holly took off her jacket and stuffed it into her bag. The end of October meant chilly, wintry weather in the UK but here in Spain it was still warm in the daytime. She'd messaged Fiona as soon as she landed – she only had hand luggage – and Fiona had replied that she'd be waiting for her at the short-stay pick-up point, so she headed there as soon as she had gone through customs.

Fiona gave her a big hug. 'I'm so glad you're back. I've really missed you.'

'It's good to be back,' Holly said with a smile as she put her small case in the back of the van. 'How are you and Pablo?'

'We're good. I'm back teaching and he's back working regularly at the bar now the retreat is finished, but we're planning on running courses from Easter next year.'

They both got in the van, clinked their seat belts and Fiona started the engine. 'Are you here to stay or is it just a visit?'

'I'm not sure,' Holly said thoughtfully. 'The biggie is if I stay, how do I earn a living?'

'Well, you can live in our apartment real cheap, and if you can't get enough sewing work you could take a job in a coffee shop or bar in the village to tide you over,' Fiona suggested.

It was an idea. One she would think seriously about. As soon as she'd stepped foot in Spain, she'd felt at home, realised that this was where she wanted to be.

Holly did a lot of thinking over the next few days. As much as she loved living in the apartment in the grounds of Fiona and Pablo's *finca*, she needed to get a place of her own. She had to stand on her own two feet. She still had quite a bit of Pops's money left, enough to put down a deposit and couple of months' rent upfront. The question was, did she want to live out in the *campo*, like Fiona and Pablo, down in the village or in one of the larger towns? She wasn't sure.

It was when she went down into the village to get some shopping that she made her decision. She saw one of the shops empty, with a *Se alquila* sign in the window, advertising it for rent. She peered through the window. It was quite big, big enough to hold some rolls of her materials, to display a few cushions and other things. Should she give it a try? It would be a base for people to contact her, to display her goods, and maybe even a room at the back to work in. She noted down the name of the estate agent – one she'd walked past a few times – and decided to pop in and ask them. She glanced at her watch. It wasn't yet time for the afternoon *siesta* so hopefully they would still be open.

They were and Holly was surprised and delighted to discover that her Spanish was now good enough to explain to the agent what she wanted, and to understand that the agent was offering to take her for a viewing right now. Holly felt a flutter of excitement; she had a good feeling about this.

The shop was bigger than she'd realised, with – hooray! – a room at the back, and as an added bonus a flat upstairs she could live in. *It's ideal,* Holly thought happily. The rent was reasonable and she'd be living in the village so wouldn't have to worry about being lonely; she already knew so many people here, and she'd be a short drive away from Fiona and Pablo. They could meet up for lunch, or a drink in the evening.

'Are you interested? Do you want time to think about it?' the estate agent asked in Spanish.

Holly shook her head. She was going to take a chance. That's what Pops had left her the money for. 'No, I don't need more time. I definitely want it. When can I move in?'

Half an hour later, the papers were signed, the deposit was paid and Holly was told she could move in in two weeks' time.

I've got a shop and a flat, she thought happily as she drove back up to Las Mariposas. *And I've done all the negotiations myself in Spanish. Wait until I tell Fiona and Pablo!*

Fiona squealed with delight. 'That is bloody fabulous!' she said, giving Holly a big hug. 'I missed you so much when you were away and was scared that you'd go back to England for good. Especially now Matias has moved away. And don't deny that you had a thing for him,' she said, wagging her finger. 'I could tell.'

Holly didn't deny it, but it was obvious that the feeling wasn't mutual so she wasn't going to waste her time moping about it. She was going to get on with her life, and make sure it was a great one!

*

It had been the right decision to move to Marbella, closer to his family and the firm, rather than Málaga where the gym was, Matias thought as he looked out at the panoramic sea view. He had been so busy, moving into his new penthouse apartment in Marbella, working at the gym, familiarising himself with negligence laws, employing a secretary, moving back into his office in the Alvarez office block, that although his mind had often drifted to Holly he hadn't had time to contact her. He wondered what she was doing now. The last time he'd messaged her she was helping out in her mum and stepdad's antique shop while her mum recovered from her heart attack. She hadn't mentioned coming back, and he doubted if she would. Yes, her possessions were over here, and so was her car, but she could pay for them to be shipped back to the UK. He had a feeling that coming to Spain had been a break for her, a chance to get over her ex and try new experiences; now she was back home with her family she would probably stay there, which was a shame. He missed her.

He took his phone out of his back pocket and sent her a quick message asking how she was and if her mother was fully recovered yet. It was over an hour later before the reply came zinging back that yes, her mother was well and working in the shop again, and that Holly was back in Spain and had just signed a lease on a flat and shop in Reino.

Matias read the message over again, stunned. Holly was back in Spain and she hadn't told him? That could only mean one thing. She didn't have the same feelings for him as he had for her.

We both toasted to friendship, he reminded himself. *I'm the one who changed the rules, who thought that because my feelings for Holly had changed then her feelings must have too.*

He texted back:

I am pleased to hear that. Let's meet up for a drink sometime.

Her reply came a few minutes later.

That would be good. Fiona tells me you are living in Marbella. We must catch up if I'm ever over that way or you come to Reino.

It sounded so casual and impersonal. They had been so close, he remembered; when she had helped him after he sprained his wrist, they had talked about so many things, shared so much. Almost made love. Memories of that wonderful day on the beach flitted across his mind. What would have happened if Holly hadn't had that call saying her mother was in hospital?

Well, that was in the past. He needed to forget about Holly and get on with his life.

Chapter Forty-Three

November

'You look amazing, both of you,' Felipe said admiringly.

Holly smiled as she looked in the mirror, smoothing down her red and black flamenco dress. It had a black bodice with red short puffed sleeves and a red tiered skirt, adorned with black frills that went up at the front. It looked very dramatic and fitted her perfectly. Fiona was wearing a similar dress but with multicoloured sleeves and skirt. Holly wore red heeled shoes and carried a red fan while Fiona wore black heeled shoes and carried a black fan.

She and Fiona had been taking flamenco lessons for the last few weeks – one of the last things on her list to do – and both Pablo and Felipe had talked them into entering the local festival. Holly had intended to make the dresses herself, but business in the shop was thriving, with people asking her if she could design material especially for them. They wanted a unique touch to their homes. Holly loved it – it meant that she got to design as well as sew – but it kept her very busy. Too busy to dwell on how much she missed Matias and wonder what he was doing.

'I hope we remember all our steps,' Fiona said. 'I'm not quite sure we're ready for this yet.'

'We'll make sure we're in the middle, then the other dancers can camouflage us,' Holly told her. 'Don't stress about it, it's just a bit of fun.'

She couldn't actually believe that she was doing this herself. The old Holly would never have volunteered to take part in a flamenco show for the local festival, but the new Holly was happy to have a go at anything: her life in Spain had given her so much confidence.

They made their way to the village square where the festival was taking place. The other dancers were already there, and as soon as Fiona and Holly took their place, the music started. Holly took a deep breath and started dancing the steps she'd been taught.

✳

Matias wove his way through the street. Reino was heaving with people who had come to watch the festival. He would have to park the car out of town and walk in. He was in a hurry to meet the estate agent and get the spare key for his aunt's old house. The sale had fallen through and it was back on the market again, much to his aunt's distress. She hated renting, and wasn't supposed to have pets so poor Luna had hardly been allowed out and now had gone missing. The little dog hadn't been at all happy in the apartment and had run off almost a week ago.

Tia Isabella thought that Luna might be trying to get back home, to the *finca*. 'She misses you, Matias,' she had said. 'She thinks that you are her owner now.' So Matias had come looking for her. He had thought of contacting Holly and asking her to check if Luna was anywhere in the area but changed his mind. He and Holly were no longer in touch; it wouldn't be right to expect her to run around looking for Luna. So, he'd come himself. He parked the car and hurried through the bustling town. He turned as he heard a guitar playing and saw a group of women in colourful flamenco dresses walking into the square. Immediately the crowd started clapping. It looked like some flamenco dancers were giving a display. He paused – he always loved watching the flamenco dancers, so vibrant and energetic. He walked slowly over as the dancers swept their arms about their heads, swaying as they tapped their feet.

A woman with rich chestnut hair in the middle of the group caught his eyes. She was a vision in a red and black dress, her hips moving seductively as she swirled and twirled, her arms moving in beautiful slow, fluid movements, feet stamping and tapping to the guitar beat. Then she turned towards him and he gasped. Holly. And beside her was Fiona.

He watched enthralled as Holly danced to the music. Her eyes sparkling, her expression passionate and evocative. She was good, and incredibly sexy. Then she gave a flirtatious flip of her head, fingers snapping rhythmically, and suddenly her eyes rested on him. He saw the flash of recognition on her face and she faltered for a moment then got back into step and resumed her dancing.

Well, she's seen me now, it would be rude to go off without speaking to her, he thought. Besides, he was enjoying the dance too much to walk away.

✤

She could hardly believe it when she saw Matias watching in the crowd. He looked just like she remembered him, tight black sweatshirt stretched across his broad chest, stonewashed jeans hugging muscular thighs. What was he doing here? There was nothing to bring him to Reino any more. Surely he hadn't come for the festival? They must have grander festivals in Marbella. She tried not to think of him watching as she continued dancing; she'd hate to slip up now. He clapped loudly when the dance had finished, waved and started weaving through the crowd towards her. She met him halfway.

'*Hola*, Holly. It is so good to see you again.' He kissed her on both cheeks.

'And you. How are you? I didn't expect to see you here.'

She was so pleased to see him that she was sure it was written all over her face. He looked so good, and she wanted to kiss him, really kiss him, snog his face off kind of kiss him, but she held back.

'I'm here to look for Luna. She has been missing for almost a week and my aunt thinks she may have gone back home, to the *finca*.'

'Oh no, poor Luna!' Holly said worriedly. 'But wouldn't the new owners have seen her?'

'The sale fell through so I'm collecting the keys off the estate agent to check,' he explained. 'I really have to go but can we meet up later? It would be good to catch up.'

'I'd like that but, look, let me get changed and I'll come and help you look for her. I live in a flat above my shop in the town now. I could meet you in a quarter of an hour.'

Matias nodded. 'Okay, I'll meet you at the fountain.' And he dashed off.

Fiona had been watching them with interest so Holly quickly explained then hurried back to her flat where she replaced the colourful flamenco dress with jeans and a long-sleeved shirt, grabbed her bag and phone and set off.

Matias was waiting for her, keys in hand. 'It's a bit of a trek to my car – there's no parking in the town because of the festival,' he said.

'That's fine, I've got my walking shoes on.' She pointed to the black leather flats. 'Let's go!'

'Keep close to me.' Matias grabbed Holly's hand and held it in his as they weaved their way through the crowd. The tantalising touch of his fingers woven in hers made her feel a bit giddy. She had missed him so much. And now here they were, hand in hand, as if they had never been apart.

He's here because he's looking for Luna, she reminded herself. *It was only by chance he bumped into me. And he's only holding my hand because he wants my help to find her, not because he fancies me.*

Even so, it felt good.

They were at the car park now, getting into his car – a top-of-the-range SVU rather than his usual motorbike – and then they were off, out of the town, along the main road and weaving their way up the familiar mountain track. She was sure that Matias, like her, was hoping to see Luna sitting outside the *finca* gates. But she wasn't there.

Matias went over to the gates. 'They're locked so I don't see how she can be inside but I'll check in case she's found a hole in the fence somewhere.' He took the keys out of his pocket and unlocked the gate. 'Luna!' he called. 'Luna! *Ven aquí, chica.*'

Holly scanned the grounds, hoping to see the Shih Tzu bounding towards them. But there was no sign of her. 'Shall we split up?' she asked. 'I'll go around the right side of the house, you go around the left?'

'Good idea.' Matias strode off towards the left of the house, shouting, 'Luna!' at the top of his voice. Holly made her way to the right, calling the dog's name too, memories of the evenings she'd spent sitting outside talking to Matias, swimming in the pool, flooding her mind. They had been good times and now they were gone forever.

They both met at the back a few minutes later.

'She is not here. She would come if she heard us calling,' Matias said.

'Let's check Las Mariposas. Fiona and Pablo have been out all day so wouldn't know if Luna had just turned up.'

Matias nodded.

The gates of Las Mariposas were locked but Fiona had insisted that Holly keep a key in case she came to visit and they weren't in. 'Come and use our pool or sit in our garden anytime,' she'd said when Holly had moved into the flat above the shop, although Holly hadn't taken her up on it yet. She fished the key out of her bag and opened the gates. 'Luna!' she called. 'Come on, girl!'

They searched the grounds but again there was no sign of the white and gold dog.

'What should we do? Do you think we should have a walk around? She could be on the mountain somewhere.'

Matias thrust a hand through his hair. 'I'm not sure. I really don't think she'd wander around the mountain. She'd make her way here.'

He looked so worried. Holly's heart went out to him. She hoped Luna wasn't lying injured somewhere. 'Look, I'll ask Fiona and Pablo to keep an eye out for her. I'm sure that she'll make her way over to them when she finds no one at home at your… your aunt's house,' she corrected.

'Thank you, Holly.' He was gazing at her now, as if he wanted to say something. She held her breath as his hand reached out and his fingers lightly touched her face. 'Sometimes I wish it was still my home, and that you still lived next door. I have missed you,' he said softly.

'And I've missed you,' she whispered.

'Yet you didn't tell me you were back. Or even that you were coming back.' Soft, tawny eyes were looking into hers, as if searching for the answer to something.

She had wanted to, so much, but how could she when they were no longer in touch?

She licked her lips. 'We lost touch. You had a new life, moved to Marbella.'

'And you, I thought, might have gone back to your boyfriend. The one you came over here to forget.' His eyes were probing her face now, searching for what? 'When you didn't come back I thought perhaps you still loved him.'

'I would never get back with him. He actually asked me to but I told him no, we are over.'

Matias moved closer, his face mere centimetres away from hers, his lips almost within kissing distance. 'So, you don't love him?'

'No. And as soon as my mum was better I came back to Spain.'

'Because you loved it that much?'

'Yes. I wanted to make my life here. A new start.'

'And would you have contacted me if we didn't bump into each other today?' He sounded hurt. 'We are friends still, aren't we?'

Could she settle for friends when she wanted so much more?

'Holly…' He reached out and touched her face, his thumb lightly tracing her cheek. 'I would like us to still keep in touch,' he paused, his thumb tantalisingly still, 'if you would like that too.'

His eyes held hers, his lips so close that she could barely resist the temptation to kiss them. She really, really wanted to kiss them. *He said 'friends', Holly*, she reminded herself. *Not lovers.* But how she would like to be lovers.

Don't make a fool of yourself by letting him know that.

'I'd like that too.'

'Maybe we—'

'*Woof! Woof!*'

Suddenly a yapping furball was hurtling across to them, jumping excitedly up at first Matias then Holly, running in a frenzy between the two, licking hands, wagging her tail.

Chapter Forty-Four

'Luna!' Matias scooped her up into his arms. 'You're back. We've been so worried about you.'

He adores her, and she adores him, Holly thought. *What a shame he can't keep her.*

Matias gave the little dog a fuss then handed her over to Holly so she could make a fuss of her too.

'You were right, she did come back home. Your aunt will be pleased,' Holly said.

Matias's face clouded over. 'She will, but her apartment is no place for Luna. A dog needs a garden to run in, and Tia Isabella tires easy. She finds it difficult to walk Luna regularly. We need to find her a new home.'

Holly looked down at Luna, who was now lying happily by their feet. 'Can't you have her?'

'I live on the fifteenth floor of an apartment block and am out at work all day either at my father's office or at the gym.'

'You're working with your father again? As a lawyer?' she asked, surprised.

'Yes, but only part-time.' He bent down and stroked Luna again. 'I must take her back to my aunt for now, until we sort out something else for her. I hope she doesn't escape again.'

'I could look after her until you find a new home for her,' Holly said impulsively. 'That is, if you'd like me to.'

'Really?' She saw the relief on Matias's face then he frowned. 'But you are in a flat too. And you work.'

'It's only a first-floor flat. I have a small garden and most of the time I work in the shop below the flat. When I go to visit clients, I could take Luna with me – she's only a small dog and very well-behaved.'

'You would really look after her?'

'I'd love to. Until you get a suitable home for her. She'll be company for me.'

'Then thank you. My aunt and I, we are very grateful. We will pay for her food, and anything else she needs, of course. And would I be able to come and see her now and again?'

'You'd be very welcome,' Holly told him. 'And I'm happy to pay for her food.'

It looked like she had a pet, for a while anyway. How fantastic. She adored Luna. 'Why don't you bring her back to mine now and help me settle her in?' she suggested. 'I can fix us a bite to eat, some pasta or bread and cheese.'

The look on his face said it all. Matias scooped Luna up and put her in the dog cage in the back of the SVU. 'I hope I haven't ruined the day for you. Were you in any more dances at the festival?'

'No, only the one.' She slipped into the passenger seat and fastened her seat belt as he got in beside her and did the same.

'You were very good. How long have you been learning to dance the flamenco?'

'Only a few weeks but we've practised a lot. Another one off my list,' she said with a grin.

He started the engine. 'How many items are left?'

'Three: visiting an underground cave, getting a pet and three more flavours of ice cream.'

'And how long do you have to complete this list?' he asked as he pulled away.

'Three months,' she said.

'Then we have time to visit a cave.'

We have time to visit a cave. Holly repeated the words in her head as Matias drove down the mountain. So that meant he was going to the cave with her. Matias was back in her life.

※

Holly's flat was bigger than Matias had expected and very cosy. There were two largish bedrooms, a kitchen, a good-sized lounge and bathroom, with views over the rooftops of the town to the sea in the distance. Downstairs, there was a roomy shop where she had some of her goods displayed, and a sewing machine in the corner, then a back room with a large table and shelves of material and stock.

She showed him around proudly. 'See, there is plenty of room for Luna: she can sleep in this back room while I work, or she can play in the garden.' She opened the back door to reveal a small garden consisting of a paved area with a table and chairs, some plants in pots, and a small lawn. It looked cosy – and very Holly. He could imagine Luna curled up by her feet while she worked and knew instantly that the little dog would be happy here.

'I like this place, it's a good location,' he told her. 'In the centre of the village so you're near to everything and get the passing trade, but not by any bars so the noise will keep you awake. Are you happy here? Do you miss the peace and quiet of living up the mountain? And the company? And the pool?'

'I miss the grounds and my little studio apartment, and Fiona and Pablo being around, yes. And I guess I'll miss the pool in the summer, although Fiona said I can use theirs anytime I like. But this place is perfect for me. I can work onsite, I have people around me so I'm not lonely and I have my very own business. I'm happy here.'

'Then that's all that matters.'

They left Luna sniffing around the garden and went back upstairs. Holly opened the fridge. 'Fancy a glass of fresh orange juice?' she asked, taking out a jug of it. 'And have you decided, crusty bread and cheese or pasta?'

'Crusty bread and cheese, please – and let me help.'

Ten minutes later they were outside in the garden, eating and chatting.

'Are you happy living in Marbella and working for your father again?' she asked as she took a sip of her drink.

He seemed to consider this. 'I'm renting an apartment. It's modern, clean and convenient, but actually, I preferred my aunt's *finca* up the mountain. And as for working for my father, well I'm only there two and a half days a week – specialising in disability rights. A topic, as you know, close to my heart. For the other two and a half days, I work in the gym in Málaga, just a half-hour drive.'

'That's a good combination. Was that your father's idea?'

He chewed a mouthful of bread and cheese before replying. 'Yes. With a bit of coaxing from my mother, who hates disagreements. He wanted me back in the business so worked out a way we could compromise.'

'And it means you are still helping people with disabilities, as you wanted. I'm so pleased you both managed to sort things out.'

'Me too.' He hated falling out with his father and appreciated him making this compromise. 'What about your mother, how is she now?'

'Much better – back working in the shop again but she's promised to take it easier, and business has picked up so hopefully she isn't so stressed. She'll be on medication for the rest of her life but the surgeon said that, providing she's sensible, there's no reason why she should have another heart attack.'

'That's good.' He cast a swift glance at her then asked as casually as he could the question he'd been dying to ask since she mentioned that her former boyfriend had asked her out again. 'So Scott realised what he was missing, then? You must have been taken by surprise.'

She stared ahead of her, a faraway look in her eyes as if remembering the scene. 'I was. And I was totally stunned when he proposed to me.'

What? She hadn't mentioned that! Matias almost choked on a mouthful of bread and cheese. 'I bet you were.'

She nodded. 'You know, last year all I wanted was to get married and be happy, like Nanna and Pops. I would have been over the moon if Scott had proposed back then.'

'But now?' he prompted.

'Now, living in Spain and taking time to do the things I want has made me realise that I don't love Scott and don't want to get married, not to him or anyone right now. There's so many other things I want to do. I want to concentrate on my business and myself, not compromise to please someone else.'

He knew how she felt. He wanted the same. He wanted to make a success of his new position at his father's firm, to be able to concentrate on his clients at the gym. He didn't want to compromise for anyone else either. But he did want Holly in his life. And not just as a friend.

'Do you think that's awful? Does it sound selfish?' she asked, aware that he had gone quiet.

'Not at all. It's exactly how I feel myself,' he told her. 'Now shall we go and buy Luna a basket and bowl so she feels settled in her new foster home?' he asked.

Her expression changed but then the smile was back. 'Good idea.' She glanced at her watch. 'One of the local shops will still be open. We can get them from there.'

Luna was exhausted after playing in the garden, and her long walk to her old home, so they left her sleeping in the lounge while they popped to the shop.

They found a pretty tartan fleece basket for Luna, a stainless-steel bowl and water dish, and some toys for her to play with, all of which Matias insisted on paying for.

When they returned Luna was still asleep, but she stirred as they came in and trotted over to them happily, first to Matias and then to Holly.

'I hope she doesn't fret when I've gone,' Matias said. 'I'd hate for you to have a disturbed night. Maybe I should stay a bit to keep an eye on her.'

'You'd be very welcome. I'd open a bottle of wine but I know that's not a good idea if you're driving. So, would a non-alcoholic cocktail do?'

'That sounds delicious. But please, don't you go alcohol-free for me.'

She grinned. 'Well, I might have a dash of vodka in my cocktail.'

He would love a dash of vodka in his too. And he didn't want to go. He wanted to stay here with Holly. Spend the night with her, wake up with her.

Chapter Forty-Five

Matias sighed and looked ruefully at his watch. It had been such a pleasant evening but was getting late now. 'I had better go. It'll take me about forty-five minutes to get back home, and if I stay here any later I'll end up falling asleep on your sofa.'

'You can if you want.' The words were out of her mouth before she realised she was going to say them. 'I don't mind. If you don't fancy the drive home.'

'It's tempting,' he admitted. 'Then I could have vodka in my cocktail like you.' He hesitated. 'And I would like to make sure Luna is settled, especially as this is her first night.'

'Then do it. The sofa is comfy and I have a spare duvet. You can drive home in the morning. You don't have anything you need to get up early for, do you?'

He shook his head. 'I have the whole day free.'

'Then shall I mix you a proper cocktail?' she asked mischievously.

His eyes met hers. 'Please.'

They talked for hours. About their childhoods, their hopes, their dreams. Holly felt like she'd known Matias all her life and she didn't want him to go. They let Luna out in the garden to do her business, then she came back up and settled nicely in her basket and was soon snoring softly.

It was Holly who noticed the time first. Almost 1 a.m. The evening had flown by. 'I'm going to turn in,' she said. 'Would you like to use the bathroom first while I fetch you a duvet and pillow? I'd offer you something to sleep in but I don't think my pyjamas will fit you.'

He grinned. 'I don't usually wear pyjamas. I prefer to sleep naked, but I will keep my boxers on so I don't shock you.'

She really wished he hadn't said that because now she had an image of Matias naked fixed in her mind and she couldn't get it out. She forced herself to look away from the twinkle in his eye, to keep her voice steady as she said, 'Thanks, I'd appreciate that.' Then she disappeared into the bedroom to get the spare duvet and change into her pyjamas. Matias was in the bathroom when she took the bedding into the lounge. She put the pillow and duvet on the sofa and tried not to think of him climbing into bed with her. She'd had too many cocktails. She needed to get into her bedroom and keep away from Matias until morning before she did something stupid and ruined their friendship.

She heard the bathroom door click then Matias came out, barechested. Well, at least he'd kept his jeans on!

'The bathroom's all yours,' he said.

'Thanks,' she said and went in. It seemed odd to have someone staying overnight at her flat; she hadn't shared her home since she'd been with Scott.

He's just a friend, you don't need to feel awkward, she told herself. *He doesn't fancy you.*

But she wished he did. She definitely fancied him.

She emerged a few minutes later to find Matias already tucked up on the sofa. 'Night,' he said.

'Goodnight.' She felt a tiny pang of disappointment that he was so disinterested in her he hadn't even looked twice as she passed him clad only in her skimpy red vest top and checked shorts pyjamas.

It took her a while to fall asleep, she was so conscious of Matias lying on the sofa in the other room. It was as if her whole body was on alert. She longed so much to go out and snuggle up beside him that she seriously hoped she didn't sleepwalk and wake up to find herself lying beside him on the sofa in the morning. Or maybe he would sleepwalk into her bed…

'*Woof! Woof!*'

For a moment Holly thought she was dreaming, but then she remembered Luna. She flung back the bedclothes and dashed into the pitch-black lounge, crashing straight into a hard, firm body, bouncing off it and falling back against the wall.

'Holly, are you all right?' Strong arms felt for her in the dark, brushing past her breasts and finally finding her arms, pulling her up, the torch light from a mobile flashing around the room. 'Where's the light switch?'

'On the back wall by the door.'

She reached up for it at the same time as Matias did, his hand placed over hers as they switched on the light together, his body – clad only in tight black boxers – close to hers, his hand over hers, his mouth just centimetres away from hers.

'*Woof!*'

They jumped apart as Luna barked again. She trotted over to them both, wagging her tail.

'It's okay, *chica,* this is your new home now,' Matias whispered, fussing her. Luna licked his hand then moved across to Holly for some fuss too. Then she trotted back into her basket and settled down again.

'I guess she woke up and was wondering where she was,' Matias said. 'Sorry she disturbed you.'

'That's fine, she'll soon settle,' Holly replied, trying not to stare at his broad shoulders, muscular biceps, toned abs and that dark track of chest hair leading down to the waistband of his boxers. Too late, her eyes had drifted there of their own accord and she was sure he knew she was staring at him.

She felt the light touch of his hand on her arm, so light she could hardly feel it yet it seemed to burn her skin. She slowly raised her eyes to his and saw the desire she felt mirrored in them. *We can't do this,* she thought in panic, *it will ruin our friendship…* But his mouth was moving tantalisingly closer and then his lips were on hers and it was as if her body had leapt into life. She was returning kiss for kiss, her hand wrapped around the back of his neck, pulling his head closer, her body melting into his, her hands running down his back, revelling in the feel of his bare skin. Then his hands slipped under her thin vest top and stroked and caressed until her mind was screaming at him to touch her breasts. Finally he did and there was no going back.

*

Matias lay for a moment watching Holly sleeping, her head nestled into his shoulder, one arm across his chest, her long eyelashes fanning her cheeks, her breathing slow and deep.

Last night had been fantastic. They had come together as one, instinctively seeming to know what the other wanted, satisfying each other over and over again. Dawn had been breaking when they had finally fallen asleep, wrapped in each other's arms. It had been wonderful, mind-blowing, a night to remember.

I shouldn't have done it.

How could they go back to being friends after such a night? He should have remained strong but she had looked so deliciously irresistible in those shorts and skimpy vest top, and the way her eyes had widened as they drifted over his body had made him feel so hot.

It was his fault. He had made the first move. It was what he'd been wanting to happen for a long time, why he'd stopped over if he was honest with himself. In his heart he'd been hoping Holly would ask him to share her bed rather than sleep on the sofa.

Well, it had finally happened. They'd... what? It was more than sex. It had felt to him as if their bodies were proclaiming love for each other.

So where did they go from here? Did he apologise, say it should never have happened, that they should forget all about it and go back to being friends?

Or did he follow his heart and tell her that he loved her and wanted them to be more than friends?

Holly had made it clear over and over again that she didn't want another relationship. If he didn't play it cool, he would frighten her away.

But how could he go back to being friends after this?

Chapter Forty-Six

Holly stirred then slowly opened her eyes. Matias was leaning on one elbow, gazing down at her, a small smile playing on his lips.

'Morning,' she said, yawning. 'How long have you been awake?'

'A few minutes.' He kissed her on the forehead. 'How about I put the kettle on and let Luna out?'

'Is she awake?' Holly asked.

'She must be by now. It's almost ten o'clock.' He swung his legs out of bed and padded across the bedroom floor.

'Tea or coffee?' he asked, glancing over his shoulder at her. She was sitting up in bed, rubbing her eyes, looking so gorgeous that it took all his willpower not to get back in bed with her and make love to her again.

'Er… coffee please. I need a caffeine fix this morning.'

'Stay right there, I'll be back as soon as I can.'

Okay, it didn't look as if he regretted it, Holly thought as Matias left the room. She laid her head back on the pillow, thinking about last night. It had been wonderful. So much, much more than sex. They had been like one, and after it was over he had held her close, and stroked her cheek, and told her how gorgeous she was. Did he love her as much as she loved him?

Here she was again, she sighed, looking for love when she'd vowed that she wouldn't, that she'd live her life without looking for a man to be part of it. No, she corrected herself, she hadn't been looking for love. Love had found her.

Matias wanted to do casual, and yes, maybe they could just do casual. It had been a fantastic night but she wasn't going to go all ga-ga and start dreaming of weddings. She had totally got this. She got out of bed and headed for the shower.

When she came back out, Matias was walking in with a tray containing two cups of coffee, a milk jug and a sugar bowl.

He looked disappointed. 'I told you to stay in bed,' he said.

She gave a mock-salute. 'Sorry, sir!'

He grinned. 'Touché. I guess that did sound a bit controlling.' He put the tray down. 'Do you have plans for today?'

She shook her head. It was Sunday so her shop was closed, although there was a pile of work she could be getting on with. 'Not especially.'

'Then come to Marbella with me? I can show you my new apartment and we can take Luna to see my aunt. She would love to see her, and meet you.'

'That sounds great,' she said.

Holly hadn't expected Matias's apartment to be so impressive. When he drove into a sprawling luxury complex built in the mountains with a fantastic sea view, only minutes from Marbella, she was surprised.

'You live here?'

'I moved in a few weeks ago,' he told her. 'It's modern, easy care and convenient for work.'

And so different to his aunt's finca, she thought. The Matias she knew was such an outdoor sort of person, always in the garden, renovating the house, jogging with Luna, swimming in the pool, she couldn't imagine him living in the beautiful, modern – but to her, character-less – apartment block.

He parked the car in the designated car park at the back and then they walked through the sliding doors into the entrance lounge where a concierge came to greet them. 'Good afternoon, Señor Alvarez.' He glanced down at Luna but before he could say anything Matias raised his hand. 'Don't worry, Diego, the dog isn't mine. I just need to get showered and changed then I'll return her to my aunt.'

The concierge nodded. 'Very well, sir.'

Well, this is impressive, Holly thought, as they made their way over to the lift. While Matias had been talking to Diego, she'd seen signs for pools, a health club and restaurants. This complex obviously offered everything for the well-to-do businessman. And his family too, as she had noticed some villas on the far side.

Matias's apartment was sheer luxury: a black leather suite, smoked-glass table, black and smoked-glass units, marble floors, huge glass windows with panoramic views of the Mediterranean Sea.

'Please help yourself to anything,' he said. 'I will get changed very quickly.'

Holly walked into the huge kitchen with Luna, gazing around at the sleek, streamlined units with white marble tops, the matching island in the middle, the top-of-the-range electrical equipment, and realised that Matias and his family were seriously rich.

This was a world she would never fit into. And she didn't want to. She was a homebody, she liked simple comforts. It would never suit her to be cooped up in a high-rise penthouse like this no matter how luxurious it was. She and Matias were oceans apart. The realisation of the huge gap between them, that the Matias she knew and had grown to love wasn't who she thought he was, hit her hard.

'I'm ready,' he said, walking in looking devastatingly handsome in light-grey chinos and a black shirt. 'You haven't had a drink?' he asked, surprised.

'I was scared to touch anything,' she said, half-joking. 'It's all so… immaculate and expensive.'

His face clouded. 'I know. I am renting – it's only temporary until I find somewhere more suitable, somewhere with land.' He clicked his fingers. '*Ven aquí, Luna,*' and the little dog came over to him. 'Now let us take Luna back to my aunt and then would you like to go to lunch?'

'As long as it's nowhere too posh. I'm only dressed casual,' Holly told him, wishing she'd put on something different to her leggings and lacy cream top.

'You look beautiful,' he replied. 'We will go somewhere along the seafront, if you wish?'

'That sounds perfect,' she agreed.

Tia Isabella lived in an apartment in a smaller complex a short drive away. It was very green and cared for, and her flat was on the third floor. It was cosier than the one Matias lived in, with rugs and colourful cushions to brighten up the tiled floors and cream sofa. But not a place for a dog. Luna loved exploring the garden in the *finca*; here she would be inside all day. No wonder she'd run away.

Isabella's face broke into a huge smile when she saw them. She hugged Matias then scooped Luna up onto her lap and stroked her.

'Thank you for looking after Luna,' she said in heavily accented English. 'My poor little *chica* is not happy here.'

'It's a pleasure, she's adorable,' Holly said.

Matias sat down beside his aunt. 'What about you, Tia Isabella, are you happy here?' he asked.

She nodded, her face lighting up. 'I have company, so many friends and so much to do. And no problems with the electric and the water. The *finca*, it is too much for an old lady like me.'

She insisted that Holly and Matias stop for a cup of coffee – served in tiny yellow-and-blue patterned Spanish cups – and some delicious home-made lemon cake, and they chatted for a while. Isabella was delighted that Matias was working for his father again. 'Antonio, he is stubborn, like you.' She pinched Matias's cheek. 'But also like you he has a heart.' She patted Matias's hand. 'There is more than one way to help, remember that.'

She turned to Holly. 'So, you are living in Spain, Holly?' she asked. 'Are you working?'

Holly told Isabella about her designs and her shop. The old lady listened intently. 'An artist and a seamstress. So you are talented, then?'

'Very talented!' Matias picked up his phone, tapped a couple of keys and showed it to his aunt. 'This is the website for Las Mariposas, the house next door to your *finca* where Holly's friends live. They run an artists' retreat and Holly designed and made the furnishings for all the bedrooms. Take a look.'

Isabella was full of praise. 'These designs are excellent, Holly. I would like something like this in my flat, it would brighten it up a bit. And I know some of my friends would too. Do you have other designs?'

'Yes, I sell them on a website called Dandibug,' Holly told her. 'I do bespoke designs too, so if there is any particular pattern or image anyone wants on a mug, cushion, bedspread – anything, really – I can do it.'

'That sounds wonderful. I must come to your shop,' Isabella said. 'I will bring a friend, two friends.'

Luna, who was lying by Isabella's feet, looked up and barked. She patted Luna's head. 'And maybe I can see Luna too. I will miss her so much, but this home is not for her.'

'You're welcome anytime,' Holly told her.

They spent a pleasant hour with Tia Isabella then had a short walk around Marbella before heading off home.

After settling Luna down in the flat, where the little dog curled up happily in her basket, Matias and Holly went for a meal.

'If you're free next Sunday we could go to see the underground caves at Nerja,' Matias suggested. 'That will be another thing ticked off your list.'

'I'd like that,' she told him. 'I saw some underground caves in a documentary once and they looked beautiful with huge stalactites and stalagmites and lots of underground caverns. Is that what these caves are like?'

'Yes, my parents took me when I was young. I thought they were magical. We'll have to leave quite early though, it's a bit of a trek, and the caves are only open for a few hours in the winter. Is eight okay for you?'

'No problem. I'm really looking forward to it.' Should she ask him if he wanted to stay over on Saturday night, save him driving over from Marbella? *Leave it,* she decided, *don't push anything. See what happens.*

Chapter Forty-Seven

Luna settled in really well and loved sitting in the corner of the shop while Holly sewed, or playing out in the garden. When customers came in they petted her, which she loved. She slept in a basket in the lounge and greeted Holly happily every morning.

'You're such a gorgeous little dog. I'm going to miss you when Matias finds you a new owner,' Holly told Luna as she lay beside her on the sofa one evening. She had really grown to love Luna: she was good company and no bother at all. She didn't want to give her up.

Maybe she didn't have to. She could offer to buy her. But Tia Isabella wanted Luna to go to a family in the *campo*, with a big garden, she reminded herself. She wouldn't be happy for Luna to live in Holly's flat permanently.

Matias phoned every day to check how Luna was, apologising that he was too busy to drop in until Saturday afternoon. 'Sorry, Holly, but I won't be there until about two. I've got a gym class in morning,' he said.

'Don't worry, that's fine. I work Saturday mornings too,' she told him. 'Are you still okay to go the caves Sunday?'

'Yes, I've got the day free. In fact, I was wondering…'

'Go on.'

'Well, how do you feel about me staying overnight rather than going back late then coming over again the next morning. I can sleep on the sofa…'

She'd been wondering whether to offer. 'Good idea. And, Mati…'

'Yes?'

'You don't have to sleep on the sofa unless you want to.' There, she'd said it, let him know that she'd like him in her bed again.

'I don't want to. I'd much rather be in bed with you.'

She smiled at his quick reply, and the knowledge that he wanted her as much as she wanted him.

Luna bounded over to greet Matias when he walked in, wagging her tail furiously, but after a few minutes' fuss she trotted off happily to her basket, where she lay chewing a bone.

'I can see that she's happy here. Are you sure she isn't too much trouble for you?'

'Not at all, I love having her company,' Holly told him. 'In fact, I wanted to ask you something.' She hesitated, not wanting him to feel awkward if he didn't think it was a good idea. 'I don't mind if you don't agree. It's only an idea.'

'Tell me,' he encouraged, turning around to face her.

'I was thinking, maybe I could buy Luna and give her a permanent home. She's settled in so well, and you and your aunt could pop in and see her anytime you wanted. I mean, I know I don't live in the country with a big garden, but she's only a little dog, she doesn't need that much space to run around in.' She stopped and looked at Matias's face. 'You don't think it's a good idea, do you?'

'I think it's a perfect idea, if you are sure? I'll have to run it past my aunt first, though.'

She nodded. 'Of course, and I totally understand if she prefers to find somewhere else for Luna.' She hoped she didn't, though. The flat would seem empty without the little Shih Tzu.

It was late when they got to bed and even later when they got to sleep – not that she was complaining – so Holly was exhausted when Matias kissed her awake the next morning.

'We need to get up, *corazón.* The caves open at nine and last entrance is at three.'

Holly smiled at the sweet term of endearment and glanced at the clock: half past seven, and they hadn't crashed out until almost three. It was as if they hadn't been able to get enough of each other.

'You look very sexy and I feel that I would rather stay here in bed with you,' he said, tracing his thumb over her lips, 'but this is one of the last things to tick off your list.'

'I know.' She wrapped her arms around his neck and kissed him soundly on the mouth. He immediately responded, his tongue probing, kiss deepening, arms holding her so close that she could feel that, yes, he definitely would rather stay in bed. She playfully wriggled out of his arms and threw back the duvet. 'Come on, then. I bags the shower first.'

'We could share,' he said, his voice husky, his eyes watching her as she padded across the floor.

She grinned over her shoulder at him. 'Then we'd never get out in time.'

✻

They arrived in Nerja at ten thirty and thankfully there wasn't a large crowd. Matias had bought their tickets online to save time.

'I bet it's packed out in the summer,' Holly said as they took their place in the queue.

'It is, and there is so much more to see then because they do night tours, and also tours around La Torca and La Mina – caves which aren't usually open to the public.' He wrapped his arm around her shoulders and kissed her on the tip of her nose. 'We will come again, when it is warmer, if you wish.'

'I don't mind. It'll be fun anyway. I'm looking forward to it.'

They were at the front of the queue now. They filed into a room for the audio-visual presentation, which told them a few facts about the caves, then they started the tour. As they descended the steps and along a narrow passageway, Holly was glad they had both worn warm jackets and flat shoes; it was chilly in here. They came out into a large chamber and she gasped in wonder at the magical scene in front of her eyes. Strategically placed lights illuminated huge glistening stalagmites rising up from the ground and shimmering tapered stalactites hanging down like giant icicles.

'This is spectacular. It's like something out of a fairy tale,' she whispered – it seemed disrespectful to speak loudly. She rubbed her hands together, wishing she'd thought to bring a pair of gloves, then put them in her pockets. 'I wonder if people actually lived down here thousands of years ago.'

'Some wall paintings have been discovered that are over 40,000 years old, so I'm guessing they did,' Matias said.

They wandered from chamber to chamber, taking their time so that they didn't miss anything. Holly snapped away with her phone camera, wanting to take as many photos as she could of this wonderful place, even though she knew she wouldn't be able to capture the full splendour of it. Matias took photos too, and it was almost two hours before they came out again, blinking at the daylight.

'That was fantastic!' Holly threw her arms around Matias's neck and kissed him.

'It was, wasn't it? I enjoyed seeing them again.'

'How about lunch now, I'm starving,' she said.

'Me too. Do you want fancy food or pie and chips sort of food?'

'Pie and chips and half a pint of shandy would be fantastic,' she said.

So that's what they did.

✣

It has been a wonderful day, Matias thought as he drove to Marbella later. He couldn't remember the last time he'd enjoyed himself so much. Holly was so vibrant and fun, there was no pretence with her, she was simply herself. He wished he didn't have to go back to Marbella right away, that he could spend another night with her, but he had an important court case in the morning.

It had been quite late when they had arrived back at Holly's, and Luna had bounded over to see them as soon as the door unlocked. Matias had suggested leaving her in the garden as it was secure, so she could run around rather than be cooped up all day. They'd placed her basket in the almost empty shed and left the door open so Luna could go in and take shelter if she wanted to.

They'd both fussed the little dog then Matias had taken Holly in his arms. 'I'm sorry, but I have to go. I wish I could stay.'

'I wish you could too,' she'd said simply.

'I'll phone you in the week and see you soon. Maybe next Saturday?' he'd asked, wondering how he was going to go a whole week without seeing her.

'That would be great. I close the shop at two,' she'd replied.

Okay, so it looked like she was fine with only seeing him at weekends. Maybe that's all she wanted, a part-time romance, whereas he wanted to see her every day and every night.

Take it easy, you've been there once with Natali and look how that turned out, he reminded himself.

❋

Tia Isabella popped into Holly's shop with a friend later in the week. They were both full of praise for Holly's designs and ordered some curtains and throws from her existing range, although Tia Isabella said she would like some bespoke designs too and arranged to come back in a couple of weeks to discuss them with Holly. She made a big fuss of Luna, and Holly showed her the garden where Luna played and the basket in the lounge where she slept. Isabella was very impressed and thanked Holly for looking after her.

'Matias said you would like to keep her,' she said. 'This makes me so happy. I can see that Luna is very settled here and that you love her.'

'I will pay for her, of course,' Holly said.

Tia Isabella tapped her hand. 'I wouldn't hear of it. Luna loves you and you love her. That is all I want for her, a loving home.'

'But—' Holly started to protest.

'No arguments,' Tia Isabella said firmly.

'Thank you so much,' Holly said, delighted. She bent down to stroke the little dog. 'Did you hear that, Luna? You can stay with me forever,' Holly said.

Luna barked and licked her hand, as if she understood and approved.

Chapter Forty-Eight

December

'Have you decided whether you're coming home for Christmas, Holly?' her mother asked as they chatted via WhatsApp.

Holly had been wondering what to do about Christmas. Fiona and Pablo were going home to see their folks, and Matias had made no mention of Christmas at all. She knew that many Spanish didn't celebrate Christmas in the same way as the English, but she guessed that maybe they'd have a family meal together and of course would want Matias to be there. Besides, she'd like to go back to the UK, see how her mum was, catch up with Susie again and visit the folks in Sunshine Lodge. She didn't like leaving Luna but Maisie, the dog groomer, had offered to look after the little dog. She lived out in the *campo* and had a massive garden and a couple of dogs, so Luna would be spoilt and have company too.

'I'd love to come. How about I fly over on Christmas Eve and return on New Year's Eve? I'd like to be back in Spain for the New Year.' Fiona and Pablo were returning then and had told her the New Year's Eve celebrations in Reino were not to be missed. A huge crowd gathered in the square in fancy dress and the New Year was welcomed in with lots of singing, dancing and champagne. She wanted to see that and was hoping Matias could come along too; then they could see the New Year in together.

'That's wonderful, love. And if there's anyone you'd like to bring with you, they'd be very welcome.'

'Thanks, Mum, but it'll be just me.' She and Matias didn't live in each other's pocket; they didn't have that kind of relationship. They were friends and lovers but it was still all very casual.

It suits me, and it suits Matias, she told herself firmly. She didn't need a man to make her happy. She was her own person – a much stronger person than she'd been this time last year.

It was a week later before Matias asked her what she was doing for Christmas. He'd nodded when she said she was going home and asked when she'd be back, suggesting they have a meal when she returned.

'I'd like you to meet my family,' he said. 'We are having a family meal on 6 January. Please say you'll come. Tia Isabella has told them all about you and they are eager to meet you. Especially my mother; she is English as you know.' He hesitated. 'I was going to ask you to come for Christmas – Mamá still celebrates it – but I thought you might want to see your family and check that your mother is well.'

So he had wanted to spend Christmas with her!

For a moment she felt a bit nervous. Dinner with the Alvarezes? His dad was a hot-shot lawyer. They were rich, powerful, would probably look down on her.

Why should they? Matias didn't look down on her, and neither did his aunt.

One of Pops's sayings flashed across her mind. 'Never think you aren't good enough, no matter who you meet. It doesn't matter what clothes people wear or jewels they have. They are only human, just like you and me.'

These people were Matias's family, and they wanted to meet her. He wanted them to meet her. All she had to do was be herself.

She smiled. 'I'd love that.'

She visited Fiona and Pablo the day before she flew over to England, taking the Christmas present she had made for them: a set of curtains and a duvet cover in butterfly-adorned fabric she had designed just for them.

They were both delighted and gave her a big hug before handing over their present to her: an exquisite, hand-painted sculpture of Luna. 'Pablo made it and I painted it,' Fiona said. 'We thought it would look nice in your backyard.'

'It's wonderful,' Holly said. 'Thank you both.'

Matias came around that evening and they both exchanged presents. She had designed a Spanish wall clock especially for him, painting the background of a white house on a clifftop overlooking the sea.

'This is beautiful. I will treasure this forever,' he said, embracing her.

Then he handed her his present: a silver photo frame recording Holly achieving every one of her dreams. There were photos of Holly sitting outside at Las Mariposas, on the back of Matias's motorbike, with a group of Spanish students outside the bar Pablo worked at, at the helm of the yacht, snorkelling in the sea, eating a blue bubblegum ice cream, on El Caminito del Rey, serving a customer inside her shop, sitting on the sofa stroking Luna, in the caves at Nerja; he had even taken a photo of her flamenco dancing. And, finally, one of her laughing as she paddled in the sea, drenched with water from the wave – the very first time they had gone to the seaside together. 'That one is for the "be me" goal,' he said. 'Because that is how I see you, Holly: laughing, free, happy.'

'It's a perfect present. Thank you,' she said in delight. 'But how did you get all these photos?'

'I asked the guide to take the one of you snorkelling. I was going to print it out for your book but then you had to go to England so quickly. Fiona gave me some when I told her what I wanted to do for your Christmas present, and others I took secretly,' he explained with a grin.

They spent a wonderful night together, and in the morning Matias took her to the airport. 'I'll miss you,' he said, kissing her tenderly.

'I'll miss you too,' she told him, hugging him tight. 'But I'll be back soon.'

Chapter Forty-Nine

New Year's Eve

Reino's town square was packed with revellers in various fancy-dress costumes, and all in good spirits. Fiona and Pablo had called for Holly, saying they would never find each other in the crowd if they didn't go together. Pablo was dressed as a matador, and Fiona and Holly were both wearing their flamenco dresses. Many people had gone for more unusual costumes: Holly spotted a dragon, parrot, tiger and even a unicorn. There were masked cowboys, superheroes, princesses, cowgirls, even a couple of horses!

It was an amazing scene. The air was buzzing, people were singing; it was a wonderful, festive atmosphere. There was only one thing missing: Matias. Holly had hoped he'd meet her at the airport but he'd messaged apologising and saying he'd meet her in the square for the celebrations tonight. But so far there had been no message, no phone call, no Matias. She shrugged. Well, she'd probably see him tomorrow. Surely to goodness she could enjoy the night without Matias by her side!

A cheer rang out. It was almost midnight. People were coming out on the balconies surrounding the square, eager to join in the countdown.

'*Diez, nueve, ocho…*' The counting had begun.

Pablo put his arm around Fiona's shoulder and hugged her to him as they joined in the count.

For a fleeting second Holly wished Matias was here to do the countdown with her.

'*Siete, seis, cinco…*'

'*Cuatro*,' said a familiar voice as an arm snaked around her waist: Matias!

She turned and smiled at him. He was dressed as Zorro in a black mask, black cape and very tight black trousers and top. He'd come! Her heart soared as she put her arm around his waist.

'*¡Tres, dos, uno!*' they both said together.

'*¡Feliz año nuevo!*' Matias hugged her and kissed her on the lips. Deeply. As if he had been waiting, longing to kiss her. As if he had really missed her.

'Happy New Year!' she said when he finally released her.

The crowd was chanting, people were kissing each other on the cheek, wishing each other Happy New Year in both Spanish and English. Champagne bottles were popping and the sparkling wine was raining all around them.

'*Dios*, I have missed you so much,' Matias said huskily. '*Te amo, mi alma*, Holly. I love you, Holly, my soul. *Te adoro.*'

'*Te amo también*. I love you too,' she said, melting into his arms.

Much later, when they went back to Holly's flat, Matias opened a bottle of champagne. 'Let us have a toast,' he said, pouring it into two glasses and handing one to Holly.

'Happy New Year!'

'Happy New Year!' Holly said as they clinked glasses.

'To us.' Matias paused. 'To love.'

'To us. To love,' Holly repeated as they clinked glasses again.

'Shall we take our drinks into the bedroom?' Matias suggested, his eyes dark with desire.

Holly picked up the bottle. 'Sounds good to me.'

Later, when the bottle was empty and they were lying in each other's arms, Holly traced her finger over the stubble on Matias's chin and said, 'I'm so glad you turned up in time. I really wanted to see the New Year in with you.'

'And me with you. I want to spend the rest of the year with you, as a couple. Not as friends.'

'Me too,' Holly said. Then she frowned.

'What is it?' he asked gently.

'We are so busy and we live miles apart. We hardly see each other.'

'We will work it out, *mi corazón*. All that matters is that we love each other. When we are apart we will be in each other's hearts.'

He was right, they would work it out. 'You will always be in my heart,' she whispered.

'And you mine.'

They kissed again, a kiss full of love and promise.

As she drifted off to sleep with Matias's arms wrapped around her, Holly thought back over this last year: when Pops had died, when she and Scott had split up and how unhappy she had been. What a year she'd had. She'd made a new life for herself and found love without even looking for it. She wasn't sure where she and Matias would go from here but it didn't matter. They loved each other. That was all she needed.

Chapter 50

12 February

This was the day she had made her dream list, Holly remembered when she saw the date on the calendar. The day she had begun to start her life over. She went over to the wardrobe and took the memory book from the top shelf. Taking it over to the bed, she sat cross-legged, the book on her lap, flicking through it. There were so many photos, so many happy memories. She read the list – each item had been ticked off.

1. Get a pet √
2. Live in another country √
3. Be self-employed √
4. Ride on the back of a motorbike √
5. Visit an underground cave √
6. Learn to speak another language fluently √
7. Go on a motor yacht √
8. Go snorkelling √
9. Learn to dance √
10. Get over my fear of heights √
11. Try fifty ice-cream flavours √

All except the last one:

   12. Be ME

Well, she'd achieved that too. She was finally herself. She put a tick by it then paused and wrote:

   13. Fall in love!

A Letter from Karen

I want to say a huge thank you for choosing to read *The Year of Starting Over*. I really enjoyed writing this story. Spain is such a beautiful country and living here has been an adventure. I hope you enjoyed reading it and that maybe it has spurred you to start your own 'dream list'. Remember, it's never too late to start over.

If you would like to keep up-to-date with all my latest releases, just sign up at the following link. Your email address will never be shared and you can unsubscribe at any time.

www.bookouture.com/karen-king

If you enjoyed reading my book, I wonder if you could spare the time to write a review for me. I'd love to hear what you think. It doesn't have to be a long one, and I'd be very grateful as reviews make such a difference in helping new readers discover my books for the first time.

I love hearing from my readers too, so do get in touch on my Facebook page, through Twitter, Goodreads or my website.

Thank you again for choosing my book to read.
Love, Karen xx

KarenKingRomanceAuthor

karen_king

www.karenking.net

Acknowledgments

I've loved writing this book. I moved to Spain with my husband Dave in November last year and it's been a pleasure to set my story in this beautiful country and remember our own year of 'starting over'. We've had some laughs, some disasters, met some fantastic people and I'm so glad we took the plunge to make a new life for ourselves. It's never too late to start over, so if any of you readers are thinking of making a fresh start for yourself, I hope this book encourages you to do it.

Writing a book is mainly a solitary process but there are people who support you along the way, so I'd like to thank some of them here. My husband, Dave, for taking this incredible starting-over journey with me and for bringing so much love and laughter to my life. My artist daughter, Naomi, for answering my questions about creating designs, printing them onto fabric and other research questions. And all four of my amazing daughters, Julie, Michelle, Lucie and Naomi, for all their love and support.

To my fabulous editor Isobel Akenhead for her invaluable advice and guidance, Deandra Lupu for her excellent copy-editing, Alexandra Holmes, Becca Allen and all the Bookouture team. Also to Kim Nash and Noelle Holton for the marvellous promotion they do for us authors.

To my fantastic Facebook author friends who share the ups and downs of a writer's life with me and let me know that I don't walk this path alone.

I would also like to thank Louise Unsworth-Murphy for taking part in the Macmillan Cancer book auction where she won the raffle for her name to be used in one of my books, so has a scene in here.

Finally, a big thank you to my readers for buying my books, taking the time to message me, write reviews and spur me on to write more stories. And to the many reviewers and bloggers who are kind enough to give me space on their blogs, take part in my blog tours and help promote my books: you are all wonderful.

Printed in Great Britain
by Amazon